The Happy Ending

The
Happy
Ending

David Stokes

Matador
9 Priory Business Park,
Wistow Road, Kibworth Beauchamp,
Leicestershire. LE8 0RX
Tel: 0116 279 2299
Email: books@troubador.co.uk
Web: www.troubador.co.uk/matador
Twitter: @matadorbooks

ISBN 978 1788033 268

British Library Cataloguing in Publication Data.
A catalogue record for this book is available from the British Library.

Printed and bound by CPI Group (UK) Ltd, Croydon, CR0 4YY
Typeset in 11pt Minion Pro by Troubador Publishing Ltd, Leicester, UK

Matador is an imprint of Troubador Publishing Ltd

My father, Charlie Stokes who died in 2015 aged 102, was the inspiration for this book together with my mother, Florence who died in 2009. Like Harry, my dad was supported from the grave by my mum, talking to her every day after she died. Although the plot is entirely fictional and my father never had any involvement with anti-trafficking, he was adventurous and joined the RAF in the 1930's. Many of the anecdotes of Harry's earlier life are taken from my father's rich repertoire of stories. He became the full-time carer for my mother during the later years of her life when she suffered badly from arthritis and other illnesses. His persistent search for solutions to the problems that he encountered was an inspiration to all who knew him.

No book can be produced without a considerable team effort and I would like to thank all those who have contributed to this, the final product. In the writing phase, I received much needed encouragement and advice from other writers, especially those involved in the Writers' Workshop including Debi Alper and Susan Davies whose help was invaluable. In the production phase, the editorial staff at Matador and Troubador Publishing all demonstrated considerable expertise and patience. Any errors that persist are my own.

The insidious and wicked practice of modern human trafficking, which is the serious theme of this book, is finally receiving much needed attention and I would like to acknowledge the work of all those involved in fighting it. If you want to know more about the business model behind this terrible trade then read 'Sex Trafficking: Inside the Business of Modern Slavery' by Siddharth Kara (Columbia University Press). You will be shocked at the continued global scale of the slave trade which we 'abolished' in the nineteenth century.

Finally I give thanks to Sue, my mentor and muse who has patiently read every page in several drafts and inspired me to do less, better.

CHAPTER 1

The Morphine

Every day, I look out from my bungalow over the field towards the cemetery. Wedged in amongst all the headstones is one that simply says:

Elizabeth Margaret Pigeon
1922 – 2011
Beloved wife of Harry
for 70 golden years

That's Betty. It's funny how we try to put a whole life into a few words on a piece of marble like that. Still, she's not far away, so first thing each morning, I look in her direction and say:

'Hello. I still love you.' Then I tell her what's been happening – well, not everything; I wouldn't want to upset her with some of the goings-on down here.

One day, I didn't choose my words very carefully and it was nearly the end of me.

'Betty,' I said from the doorstep of my front door. 'I made out the food order, did the washing, just as we always do on a Monday. Didn't see anyone. Couldn't go out because of the rain. Nobody came round, not even the

1

postman. Just sat at home and read the paper until I fell asleep. Days like that make me wish I was with you, over there, in a wooden box.'

Her reply was as bitter as the east wind that tugged at the overcoat I was wearing over my pyjamas.

'That's not what you told me, Harry Pigeon. "We go when our body says its time to go, not before." That's what you told me, even when I begged you to let me go. So just you get on with life. Do some cleaning if you're bored.'

That blast from Betty hit me so hard I had to grip the doorpost to stop my bent old frame from doubling over. It took me straight back to her last days. She would plead with me, tears in her eyes, to give her more morphine. Night and day, that wicked pain tormented her, wearing her down, draining all the fight out of her until it had eaten up every little bit of who she was. I knew she was on the maximum dose and any more would likely kill her. That's what she wanted, of course. Maybe I should have helped her to go.

I shuffled back to the chair by the window, hoping to see a bird on the feeder or a dog chasing a ball in the field. Instead I watched misty rain turn to icy sleet that obscured the view. After breakfast, I took Betty's advice and did some cleaning. Things had slipped since the funeral; I hadn't even cleared out her clothes. I opened the cupboard on her side of the bed and pulled out a stack of romantic short stories that she liked to read before sleep and a pile of fancy handkerchiefs.

That's when I found the morphine, tucked away at the back.

She must have been saving it gradually over the years,

2

hiding it away for the moment when she could no longer bear the pain. So why hadn't she taken it? She asked for it often enough. Maybe she left it for me, knowing that I wouldn't be able to cope on my own. Closing my eyes, I began to think the unthinkable. What if I took it all now? Faded away, nice and quiet; nothing to worry about any more. Maybe the vicar was right: I'd see Betty again, up there in the sky. That would be a happy ending.

The next thing I knew, my head was lolling on my chest. I forced myself to wake up, wondering what I'd done as I scrambled to check the morphine at the back of Betty's cupboard. All still there. I read the doses on the label of one of the bottles. More than enough to finish me off. A framed picture of Betty stood on top of the cupboard and I could feel her green-blue eyes watching me carefully as her words came back to me.

'We go when our body says it's time to go, not before. That's what you told me, so don't even think about it.'

I didn't throw the bottles away, though. I moved them to my side of the bed.

~

Later, the sleet turned to snow and I watched thick flakes swirl around the garden. It was meant to be spring. Anyone who claims that our climate isn't changing fast doesn't go outside very often.

Snowflakes weren't the only thing to fall that day.

Once the storm had eased, I ventured outside to try clearing the path. I couldn't use a shovel any more but I did manage to push the snow aside using a broom. It was

3

so cold I could feel the hairs in my nose crackling when I breathed in and my chest heaved and wheezed with the effort. Looking forward to a quick snooze by a warm fire, I came back in, stamping my feet in the hallway to shake off the snow from my boots. That's when I spotted an odd sock on the floor that must have dropped out of the washing basket earlier. Bending down to pick it up, I felt my body heading down too far. I struggled to keep myself upright, but I lacked the energy somehow and sat down with a bump. Crawling to a chair, I tried to pull myself back up. Do you know, I must have tried a dozen times if I tried once, but each time that I thought I'd made it, my strength drained away at the last minute and I slid back down. I cursed my frail, old body. As a young man, I could do press-ups, pull-ups, sit-ups, twenty or more of each. Now I couldn't do one stand up. I had to press the emergency button around my neck for help; couldn't help myself any more.

A polite young man assured me that it wouldn't take long for the paramedics to come round and pick me up. A few minutes later he called back to say that there was a major incident on the by-pass so the ambulances were a bit busy and there would be a delay.

I sat there on the cold, hard floor and waited. Just sat there, not able to do something as simple as stand up. Like a little baby, except I didn't have a mother to pick me up. I was even wearing a nappy. That's what the doctor had prescribed for me when I went to see her for a check-up. She'd poked and prodded, taken the pressure of this and the pulse of that. Finally she scribbled 'sanitary pads' on a prescription to take to the pharmacy. She said they would stop the dribbling. They looked just like nappies to me. I really had become a baby again.

~

Betty was with me the first time that I fell. Not that she helped much, bless her. I was in the garden pruning the rose bushes outside the window where she looked out. She loved to sit there and watch the flowers come and go according to the season. Even in the depths of winter, she had her eye out for chrysanthemums, primroses or crocuses so she could call me as soon as they began to appear. In her later years she spent most of her time in that chair looking out of the window, so I tried my hardest to give her a really good view all year round. It was spring and I was busy pruning. I took a step back to see if I'd got the shape right. Betty was very particular about the shape of a rose. I reversed a bit too far and backed into the next bush. The shock of those prickles in my backside made me shoot forward and stumble onto my hands and knees. It's a good thing Betty is there because I'm not wearing my panic button, I thought. I hauled myself up on the thick stem of the rosebush to the level of the window to wave to Betty. Her head was drooped onto her chest as it often did after the morphine. I hollered at her but I think her hearing aid was switched off because she didn't react. The rose thorns were biting into my hands so I fell back down. I tried again but she was fast asleep; must have been dreaming of something nice. If she'd seen my head yelling at her through the window, she'd have thought it a nightmare. In the end a neighbour found me and helped

5

me up. When I went in, my hand covered in blood, Betty was awake and looking at the garden.

'That rose has got a bit straggly, Harry,' she said, pointing at the bush I had been hanging onto.

~

I wriggled my bottom to get some of the numbness out. Now I was on my own. Even a helpless wife was better than this. She gave me a purpose, a reason to be here. Had to keep myself fit just to keep her alive. It was my arms and legs that fed her, washed her, dressed her, even went to the toilet with her; my brain that sorted the dozen or so pills she had to take every day; my voice on the phone pestering the doctors and nurses to come when she needed them. Couldn't afford to be ill. Sniffle of a cold and I would think, Harry, you can't be doing with this. You have to shake this off. If you're not up to looking after her, they'll have her in a home before you can blink.

That was her big fear, of course, going into a nursing home; couldn't blame her for that. Who wants to be lifted out of bed and stuck in front of the TV all day, with the occasional tray of food put on your lap until it's time for you to be put back into bed again? That's no sort of life. After Betty had fallen a few times, the woman from social services asked me if I would consider putting Betty into a home.

'She's in a home,' I said. 'Our home. And that's where she'll stay.'

Both of us had decided some time ago we wouldn't be moving out except in a wooden box. But being there alone,

6

sitting on the floor, unable to stand up, wasn't much fun either. No friends that I could phone. Too busy looking after Betty to make any new friends and I'd lived too long to have any from the past. Last man standing; or rather, sitting. Four score years; that's what you're supposed to get and most of my friends got that or less. Can you imagine? All my pals at school, all my mates that I'd be out on the town with on a Saturday night, all gone. The entire generation that I'd known, all dead.

The heating had gone off. I began to shiver with cold. I shuffled my bottom towards the kitchen to switch it back on, but I realised it was too high to reach from the floor. I noticed a fridge magnet that Betty had put up. It was a quote from a famous singer:

'Old age isn't so bad when you consider the alternative'

Got that wrong, didn't he? It should say:

'The alternative isn't so bad when you consider old age'

I remembered the morphine.

I could crawl around to the cupboard and swallow the lot; stop being a burden to others and having to apologise because I couldn't stand up. They'd be taking me to the toilet next, like I did for Betty. No dignity left when it came to that. Best to go before we got to that. No-one would miss me. The doctors would breathe a sigh of relief that I wasn't calling them all the time, like I was for Betty. They would just think I'd had a heart attack or something; ambulance was coming so they'd find me before my body started to rot and smell. Everything was taken care of: insurance for the funeral; instructions in my will for the headstone.

I started to crawl on all fours to Betty's cupboard and

7

had almost made the bedroom, when I heard a rat-tat-tat on the front door. I kept going.

'Mr Pigeon? Can you hear me? It's the paramedics.'

Damn, they'd be through the door in a flash. I'd just have to take the morphine after they'd gone.

The paramedics got me up, put me into some warm clothes, asked me to sign a form and left. They were so busy they didn't even have time for a cup of tea.

~

Later, when I was preparing for my last night on earth, a car crashed into my house.

I was in the bathroom getting ready for bed. I'd decided to take the morphine just before I normally fell asleep. Balanced with one foot on the floor, the other up on the toilet seat, I was taking off my socks. I like to wedge myself against the bathroom sink so I can't topple over backwards when I tug them off. I'm glad I did. The bang made me jump and I could've easily gone down again.

I grabbed my stick and looked out of the front window. I saw the outline of a car wedged into my wrought-iron gates like an animal caught in a net. Its engine was still running, its headlights glaring brightly. No sign of a driver. I just had to go and investigate. When I opened the front door, the cold air made me realise I was still in my underpants. I grabbed an overcoat and my walking frame in case it was slippery and went outside.

The security light flashed on and lit up the snow all around. That and the car's lights made it as bright as midday in the tropics and I wished I'd worn my peak cap to keep the glare from my eyes. Squinting, I made my way carefully towards the car, glad that I'd swept the snow from the path. From the badge on the bonnet and its sleek shape, I realised it was a posh Mercedes; not exactly a common car in my neighbourhood. The smoky windows made it difficult to see inside but I made out the shape of the air bag that must have inflated when the car hit my gates.

It took me a while to see the body. Her face was turned away from me so all I could see was this shiny sheaf of hair lying on the air-bag. Just like a child sleeping on a pillow.

The impact of the car had forced the gates open a little so I could squeeze through. Tapping on the window, I heard a little moan. When I tapped harder, her head shot up and she turned to look at me. Her big, brown eyes stared at me as though I was a ghost.

'Are you alright?' I asked.

'Who're you?'

'I'm the owner of the gates you've crashed into,' I said. I wasn't sure she'd heard me through the glass window because she just closed her eyes and her head sank back onto the air-bag. I fumbled at the door to try to open it.

She sat back up and grabbed at the door. 'No! No come in. I must go.'

'I don't think you'll get very far with that airbag between you and the steering wheel. Besides, I need your insurance details for my gates. Maybe I should call the ambulance in case you're hurt or in shock.' I pressed my mouth close to the window to make sure she could hear me.

'Not hurt. No ambulance.' She sat upright and straightened her dress, wriggling away from the door.

I was getting cold. 'Look Miss, if you won't even open the door, I'll just have to call the police to sort this out.'

'No police. Please, no police.' She fumbled at the controls and the window buzzed down. Now I could see panic in her dusky face.

'Look, I can't stand out here in the cold for much longer. Why don't we go inside, have a nice cup of tea and see what's to be done,' I said.

She looked past me at my bungalow. 'You alone?' she asked.

'Yes. You'll be perfectly safe.' She was looking round at the field opposite and the other houses in the distance. I'm lucky enough to live in a nice, quiet corner surrounded by farmland. Nobody stirred. The air was still and fresh.

She wiped at her eyes with a tissue. 'I'll come.'

'Best turn those headlights off or you'll flatten your battery. Then you would be stuck. I don't suppose you can push-start a car like this.' I tapped the front wheel with my stick to check it hadn't been damaged when it had hit the curb. Tyres that thick would cost a pretty penny to replace. I slowly pushed my walking frame back towards the house, trusting that she would follow.

She paused, uncertain, at the door; maybe waiting to be invited in. I turned and saw her properly for the first time. Jet-black hair framing a round face, high cheek bones, pink lipstick. Blue dress down to her knees, overcoat on one arm, bag on the other. Petite and perfect. She could have been an angel the way she looked. Except that she wasn't white.

Maybe some angels were black. It's just I'd never seen any: they were all white on the windows of our church. I bit my lip and told myself not to be hasty in judging her. What was on the outside had little to do with what was on the inside. She wasn't exactly black anyway; more of a coffee tone, like most of our doctors and nurses.

When she came through the door, she noticed the picture on the wall. 'This your wife?' she asked.

'No, that's the Queen,' I said.

'Oh, sorry,' she said and giggled nervously, just like a little girl. I liked her from that moment.

'This is my wife,' I said pointing to Betty's photograph.

'Oh, she is lovely. Looks like the Queen. Is she here?'

'No she's over there,' I said pointing across the field. 'In the cemetery.'

'Oh, she's dead?'

'I hope so. She's three feet under.' That reminded me of what I was about to do when I'd heard the crash. I hoped I hadn't left the morphine lying around too conspicuously.

I boiled the kettle and she sat on the edge of her chair, anxiously watching me through the door, dabbing at her eyes with a handkerchief and smoothing her hair. When I came in with the tea, she had obviously made up her mind what to say.

'I've run away,' she said.

It was good thing I had just sat down. You don't hear grown women tell you that sort of thing every day.

'Run away from what?' I asked, putting my cup down so my shaky hand didn't spill any tea.

'From very nasty man. He beats me and shuts me in cupboard. So I take his car and run away.'

'Your husband?' I asked.

She giggled that nervous giggle again. 'No, not husband. Son of boss.'

'If they mistreat you, you're right to leave,' I said, although I wasn't so sure about taking the car.

'Thank you,' she said quietly. 'I hope you understand. Can I use your toilet please?'

'Of course,' I said remembering that my clothes were in the bathroom and I was wearing only underpants under my coat. 'I'll just clear up a bit.'

~

Whilst she was in the bathroom, I went into the bedroom to make myself more respectable and check on the morphine. I glanced at Betty's photo by the bed. She had that old–fashioned look in her eyes.

'What? I'm not doing anything wrong, am I?' I muttered. 'What would you do?'

'You silly old fool, of course you're not doing anything wrong. You look after her. She could be your daughter.'

My daughter. I hadn't thought of her for years. The baby I never met. She was born during the war when I was stationed in France and died a few days later. Betty never talked about it much when I got home but I know she never got over it. There was not even a grave to visit. The body was whisked away and buried somewhere, like a bad memory. No-one ever told us where. I probably should have tried harder to find her, but it seemed easier to just forget.

That was nearly seventy years ago, so this one couldn't be my daughter; granddaughter more like. But she's someone's daughter and if mine had lived and turned up in a strange house like this, what would I want them to do? I leant over and kissed the top of the Betty's picture frame, as I do each night before I turn out the light, and her smile seemed to be a little bit bigger.

~

'Now then, young lady,' I said when we were back together in the sitting room. 'We need to get you sorted out. What about if you quietly take yourself off in the morning and I call the police to say someone left their car parked in my gates, but I didn't see anyone? We just need to make sure there's nothing of yours inside, no fingerprints or anything. It could have been stolen by anyone. You can disappear quietly and get yourself another job.'

She was smiling until I said the word 'job'.

'Oh, no job,' she said. 'I can't work for anyone else. Visa only working for him.'

I don't pretend to understand our immigration laws. They are always tinkering with who can and who can't work here, so I wasn't too surprised at this news.

'So you will have to go back home?' I asked.

'Oh, no. Can't go home. No passport. Boss keeps that. Also, I must send money home or family starve.'

I felt I was getting out of my depth.

'Who is this boss?'

'Mr Sharma. Very rich man. He lives in big house in London with family. I come here just to work for him, no-one else.'

'And he doesn't treat you right?'

13

'Not boss, his son. He ask for massage.' She hung her head.

I've had a couple of massages in the past. Looking after Betty stiffened up my back so much that I couldn't sleep. I was recommended to this Oriental lady who pummelled and prodded my back like a baker making dough. It hurt, but when she stopped, boy, didn't that feel better.

'You don't like doing massage?' I asked.

'I massage his back. He turn over and say he want happy ending. He say girls that work for him make lots of money giving special massage and I can do the same.'

I was struggling again. 'Happy ending?'

'You know,' she giggled. 'Massage down there.' She pointed between my legs. I tugged at my coat to make sure my underpants were not on show.

How could anyone ask this princess to do such a thing? I'd give him an ending that wasn't so happy if I met him.

'Well you definitely can't go back there. You can't go back home and you can't get a job anywhere else. Do you have any friends nearby?'

She shook her head and sniffled. 'No. I arrive UK last month. Not allowed out, met no-one.'

'Why did you come to this neck of the woods?'

She looked puzzled, so I repeated my question. 'Why did you come here?'

'Oh, I came here because I was told there are Filipinos like me living nearby. I hoped they could help me. I drove round and round but found no-one. Then I skidded in the snow.' She was wringing her tiny hands.

'So that's where you're from. The Philippines. Snow must have been a bit of a shock.'

'Never driven in snow before. Sorry for gate.' She looked at me, her eyes moist.

I wanted to give her a re-assuring hug but I glanced at the clock instead. It was quite late. I made up my mind, hoping Betty would approve.

'Don't you worry, we'll sort everything out in the morning. You'll just have to stay here. There's a pull-out bed in the dining room. You can sleep on that.'

'Oh, thank you so much.' Her lips parted into a coy smile and I saw her bright white teeth for the first time. 'What your name, please?' she asked.

That made me smile too. Here I was inviting someone to sleep in my house and in the rush of events, we hadn't even introduced ourselves.

'I'm Harry.'

She took my rough old paw with her delicate little hand and gave it a squeeze.

'Thank you, Mr Harry. My name is Bituin.'

'Bituin,' I repeated, trying to commit it to memory.

'Yes. In Tagalog, language of my people, it means a star.'

She was a star alright. I hadn't had so much excitement in the middle of the night since Betty fell out of bed.

When I turned in, Betty had her old-fashioned look back on. She knew I always had a soft spot for the girls.

CHAPTER 2
The Police

I cleared my throat, choosing my words carefully for my early morning chat on the doorstep.

'Betty, you're probably thinking I'm a foolish old man.' I paused, suddenly remembering that Bituin was sleeping nearby.

'Sorry, Betty,' I whispered. 'I'll have to keep my voice down. We have a guest. I know what you're thinking but she won't be staying long. Just enough time to get her life sorted out. I have to help her after that accident. Then it will be just me and you. Together. Forever.'

It was still dark but I could see the white carpet of snow all around. I glanced towards the road. There nestled into the wrought ironwork of the gates was the dark outline of the Mercedes. It hadn't been a dream. I waved my stick towards the car and the motion must have triggered the security light because it flashed on. When I got used to the glare, I saw the footprints. Delicate small footprints, leading towards the house. Evidence of my visitor was there for anyone to see.

'Have to go now, Betty. Talk to you later.' She didn't say anything but I heard her tutting. What could I do? I had to get rid of those footprints.

Having found my shoes, walking frame and overcoat

I carefully stepped onto the slippery path. Ice had formed overnight on the pathway so I didn't feel very secure. I wheeled my frame gingerly onto the thicker snow and carefully put my shoes onto every one of her little prints. It reminded me of 'Good King Wenceslas' where the page puts his feet in the King's footprints. When I was a boy in Sunday school, my friend Jack always used to nudge me and snigger when we sang the bit about 'heat in the very sod'. Now I was planting my big old boots over every one of her dainty little sods, slipping and sliding in the snow and ice.

The last footprint was next to the car door so I squeezed between the garden gates to reach it. Peering through the window, I saw the keys still dangling from the ignition switch. Best leave them there, I thought, wondering if I should give the steering wheel a wipe to take away the fingerprints, like they do in detective stories. I found a handkerchief in my pocket and pulled at the driver's door. It opened so easily and smoothly for a heavy door. You can't beat German engineering. It was quite difficult to wipe the steering wheel because of the airbag, but I managed to give it a bit of a clean. Seeing nothing of hers in the front, I opened the rear door. The back-seat looked as comfortable as an armchair. I'd never seen anything so plush and the leather felt as soft as a baby's bottom. I had to give it a try. Clambering in, I sat back waving my hand slowly up and down like the Queen.

What was that on the floor? My foot had touched something under the seat in front.

Struggling to reach down to get hold of it, I felt something like a brief case, only when I dragged it out, it didn't seem to have a handle. It could have been Bituin's handbag, so I popped it under the seat of my walking frame to look at later.

Very handy my walking frame; when I was out and feeling a bit tired, I could have a rest on the seat. But that was not all: the seat lifted up and there was a storage area underneath, so you could put the odd item or two in there when you were out shopping. Everyone should have a walking frame when you start feeling a bit unsteady on your feet. There's no shame in it and it's better than getting into a wheelchair and being pushed everywhere.

~

I was shaking when I got back into the kitchen. I'm not sure if it was the cold or the thought of ringing the police. There was no sound from the spare room so I assumed Bituin was sleeping soundly. Thinking back, I should have waited until she was up, but I knew I had to get on with the telephone call because I would fret until I did.

I dialed the emergency number and simply said: 'A car has crashed into my front gates.' That got them going. Which emergency services did I need? Did I need an ambulance? I took a few deep breaths when I got off the phone. I'd never lied to the police before.

Still no sign of life from Bituin's room. I'd explained to the nice policewoman that it was only an abandoned car so they needn't rush to get here. I wanted time to get myself dressed and then wake her up.

~

It always took me a while to take my clothes on and off. Dressing and undressing is something I always took for granted, like eating and sleeping. Not anymore. Twisting and turning my arms to fit into my shirtsleeve and bending over double to put my socks on was a major exercise. The hardest bit used to be the buttons. My fingers became so puffed-up and stiff, they couldn't cope. Then I found this gadget to poke the button through the hole. It was a bit like the hook my mother used for mending my woollen shirts; we couldn't afford the cotton ones, and the wool used to itch so I would be forever scratching my back by rubbing against a doorpost. My mother used to holler whenever she heard me scrapping on that post because she knew I was putting holes in my shirt. The thought of a police officer interrogating me made my hand shake that day, so I was glad I had that little gadget to do up my shirt.

I was just doing up my tie – I wanted to look smart for the police – when I heard a car pull up outside. There was no siren but I caught the reflection of a flashing blue light in the bathroom mirror. I yanked the tie from my neck; there was no time for that. I shot towards the dining room and knocked. No reply. I left her sleeping; they wouldn't need to go in there. Breathe deeply, I said to myself.

By the time I'd opened the front door, one police officer was taking a look at the Mercedes and speaking into his walkie-talkie. Another was already through the gates and coming towards me. He had a familiar look about him.

'That's no way to park a car, Uncle Harry,' he said.

'Brian? Is that you? I didn't know you were in the police.' He was my brother's grandson so I was his Great Uncle by rights but he'd always called me Uncle.

'Been in since I left school which is quite a few years ago. I was just up the road when we got the call about this incident and I recognised your address. I'm an inspector now and I don't normally get involved in this sort of thing but I thought I'd come to see what you'd been up to.'

'Well, bless my soul. You were still in short trousers when I last saw you,' I said, keeping my walking frame firmly in the doorway to block the way. He might be family but I didn't want anyone in the house in case she woke up.

He grinned and stretched a long arm across the walking frame to put his hand on mine. I didn't dare loosen my grip on the handle as I was still feeling a bit shaky. But I did want to take his hand and shake it hard; I was that pleased to see him.

He had always been my favourite of Albert's grandsons. Right little tearaways they were, all three of them. I was on my allotment once when Brian came flying along. "Bobby's pushed Billy into the Long Pond," he'd shouted. I wasn't sure he could swim so I dropped my spade and ran to the pond. The two brothers were thrashing about in the mud, tearing at each other's hair and getting themselves filthy and wet. Brian thought they were going to kill each other and they might have done if I hadn't been there to cuff them round their ears and drag them back to their mother. The three B's, we called them. When their parents named them William, Robert and Brian, they probably didn't realise they would all end up with the same initial, but they did. They all had something to do with the law too. Billy trained as a lawyer and Bobby was forever on the wrong side of the law, in and out of prison more times than a Black Maria. And here was their brother, Brian wearing a policeman's uniform. He should have been the one named Robert.

'Time flies when you're busy,' Brian said. That was true. I had been very busy looking after Betty. I'd no time for family. I was at it morning, noon and night. I did get a little break when she nodded off during the day, but usually there was something to get at the shops so I would dash out real quick and race back in case she'd woken up. I never had time to make contact with family, like Brian.

'Tell me about this unexpected visit,' he said indicating the Mercedes and taking out his notepad. 'Did you hear or see anything in the night?'

'I switch my hearing aid off at night, so I won't have heard anything. First I saw was when I woke up at six.'

'And you didn't see anyone?'

I shook my head, not daring to say the word that I knew was untrue.

'Any signs of someone trying to break into your house?'

I hadn't thought of that one so I shrugged, 'Not to my knowledge.'

'Mind if I take a look?' he asked.

My stomach churned. What if she woke up and looked out of the window just as he was looking in? Not much I could do, except go with him.

'I'll show you round. It's still quite dark.' I wheeled myself out of the door and around the house while he flashed his torch at the windows and walls.

He indicated the closed curtains of the dining room where Bituin was sleeping. 'Anyone else here?'

'No. I've lived alone since Betty passed away and I like

to keep this room a bit private. Full of memories.' I was glad it wasn't very light or he might have seen the flush in my face as I told that little white lie. It was somehow easier, fibbing to someone in the family. Just like I used to tell my Dad that it wasn't my shoes that had brought mud into the kitchen. He was a stickler for cleanliness, my Dad, and you had to be economical with the truth with him or you'd be forever taking a whack from his cane.

'It seems your Mercedes is an important car. We checked the number plate and it was reported missing yesterday by an embassy in London. They also reported that one of their staff had gone missing. A Filipino woman, dark hair, slim, quite young. You haven't seen anyone like that I suppose?' His eyes seemed to be boring right into me.

Again, I shook my head.

'Right. I'd better report back to base. They will be sending someone over to take a few measurements and photos. We'll put some warning cones in the road.'

'Can't you move the car? I can't get my scooter through the gates with that in the way and it's pension day.'

It was his turn to shake his head. 'We can't do a thing until all the procedures have been completed. It's classified as a potentially serious crime because of the diplomatic connection. Anyway you shouldn't be going out on your scooter in this weather. You'll be ending up in someone's front garden, like the Merc.' He looked at his watch. 'Tell you what, we'll run you up to the Post Office for your pension and any other shopping you need as you can't get out.'

I felt the relief flood through my whole body when I

realised that this would get them out of the way. Besides, I'd always wanted a ride in a police car, even if it was a Volvo. Why they can't buy British, beats me. British taxpayers buy these cars, so why can't British workers build them? We make plenty of cars in this country even if the companies are owned by the Japanese or the Germans.

~

It was a comfortable enough ride and I felt a bit special as we drove up to the Post Office. It's a convenience shop run by a lovely Indian family and they all looked a bit shocked as this tall policeman helped me up to the counter.

The mother was behind the counter. 'Hello Mr Pigeon,' she said, her head wagging side to side. 'Are you taking out so much cash that you need police escort?'

'This is my great-nephew,' I explained, trying to get my pension card into the machine. The woman's son was arranging the birthday cards next to me and he saw that I was struggling to find the slot for the card. I don't know why they make these card contraptions so small and difficult; with only one eye working properly, I can't for the life of me push my card into the bottom of it.

'Please, let me help you with that,' he said and slipped it in straightaway, as young people can.

I managed to get the numbers right; I can't really read them but I know how they are laid out on the machine.

'You can have up to three weeks' worth, Mr Pigeon,' the mother said, looking at her screen.

'I'll have it all. Never know when I'm going to be able to get here in this weather,' I said.

Brain took my arm and guided me between the aisles, back to the door. 'Why don't you have the money transferred straight into your bank? It would save you all this hassle. I never carry much cash any more,' he said.

'I like to know exactly how much money I've got. If I can't see the cash in my wallet or in my drawer, how do I know what's left? I'm like my father. He put some money aside each week until he had enough for what he wanted. Then, and only then, did he buy it, not before. He always said it was wrong to spend your money twice, once in cash and once on the never-never.'

I'd had the same argument with some foreign-sounding lady on the phone. She rang to tell me that they were doing away with chequebooks so I needed to apply for a credit card. I soon told her what I thought of her bits of plastic.

I asked Brian to drop me off outside the gates so I could get a bit of exercise walking up the path. I didn't want them getting too close to the house again. Brian wrote his telephone number on a card and told me to call him if I needed anything. I shook his hand and thanked him. It was good to see him again.

Even so I was mighty relieved when their car pulled away and I could check on Bituin. I scuttled in as fast as I could and knocked on her door.

No reply.

I knocked harder and called her name. Still nothing. I knocked again and opened the door. The curtains were still drawn shut so I couldn't see clearly for a moment. The bed had been collapsed back into a sofa and the sheets folded.

No-one there.

'Bituin!' I called loudly, checking the bathroom and my bedroom. She had gone.

I sank into my chair and sighed. Where could she be? Not the weather for a slip of a thing like her to be wandering around outside. Hang on; she would have left footprints like she had done the night before.

I wrapped up warm and stepped outside to examine the path. I could see the tracks of my walking frame and the imprint of Brian's size twelve boots, but no new marks in the snow towards the front of the house. That was odd.

As I turned to go back inside, I saw them in the distance. Little marks in the snow led from the rear conservatory to the brick wall. Clever girl; she'd gone out the back of the house so no-one would see her. I shuffled along her trail until it reached the stone wall that marked the boundary of my garden with the farmer's field. Her route was clearly marked, over the wall, down the dip and up towards the stable. They used to have horses in there but it hadn't been used for years. I looked around to make sure no-one was about, and called her name as loud as I could.

'Bituin. It's alright. You can come out now. They've gone. No-one's here now.'

My bones were chilled but I called and waited. I warmed myself up by covering her footprints in my garden. Just in time because the second lot of police arrived, this time on motorbikes. I hurried to the front gates and watched as they took pictures and measured the skid marks in the slush of the road. I offered them a cup of tea and asked why they rode BMW's when they could have bought a good British bike like a Triumph-Norton.

'We used to make more motor bikes in Britain than

25

all the other countries put together when I was young,' I told them. 'Ever heard of a Rudge or an Enfield? They were everywhere until Honda brought out their two stroke. So quiet and efficient that was. All our makes disappeared after that.'

The older of the two policemen took his helmet off. 'Let me show you something,' he said, and took me over to where his machine was propped against the curb. 'I know the old bikes you're talking about because I'm a bit of a fan myself.' He switched on the ignition and a load of lights lit up around the controls. 'But this isn't just a motorbike. This is a mobile computer. I can put your car registration mark in here and I can see immediately if you're taxed, insured or need an MOT.'

'What did you find out about this one?' I asked pointing at the Merc. 'I've never seen a number plate like that one. Six numbers with an X in the middle. Is it foreign?'

'That one had me foxed as well, until I looked it up. It's a British registration plate for diplomatic staff at an embassy, except they normally have a 'D' in the middle. The 'X' means they are non-diplomatic staff attached to an embassy. They must be on some special mission here.'

The plot was thickening. Bituin said she worked for an embassy. Maybe she hadn't told me all she knew about her employers.

~

As soon as the policemen had gone, promising that a truck would come to take away the car, I scurried around the side of the house towards the gate that led into the field. I reckoned that Bituin had to be in the old stable, but it was going to be very cold staying there: half the roof had collapsed and the weather was still bitter. The snow was even deeper away from the pathways so the going was quite difficult. I had to half push, half lift the wheels of my walking frame but it gave me stability and confidence in the icy conditions. When I made it to the gate I had a breather and gave another call. No-one answered but I thought I saw a dark shape flit by a gap in the boards of the stable. I knew then that I just had to cross that field and find her.

The gate was stuck when I tried to open it. Snow clung to its base and the hinges were all iced up. I managed to push it open a foot or so, but not nearly enough to get the walking frame through. Nothing for it; I took the walking cane I kept clamped to the walker and squeezed though the small opening with just the stick for support.

This was new territory for me. I hadn't been into this field since I sneaked in to pick blackberries for Betty's tea when we first moved there. There were horses in the field then and one had looked at me suspiciously and slowly strutted towards me. Great big black stallion it was and I wasn't taking any chances. I bought some berries from the supermarket instead. There were no horses to worry about now, just a very slippery, uneven surface to walk on. I took my time and made slow progress but progress it was, despite the odd slip and stumble.

I probably would have made it to the stable if the pick-up truck hadn't distracted me. I was facing away from the road when I heard the beat of a diesel engine, so I looked over my shoulder to see what it was. When I saw the

27

orange flashing light, I turned towards it but I was leading with my poor eye so I didn't see the icy rock that I put my foot down on. My leg skidded forward and before I knew it, I was down with a bang. That fall onto the icy snow jarred every bone in my old body and a sharp pain shot up my arm as I tried to cushion my fall. It knocked the wind right out of me and all I could do was lay there on my back for a few moments, cursing loudly, rubbing my elbow. I tested my arm, wriggling it around and it seemed to work so I felt better for that.

When I went to press my panic button to call for help, I felt a lot worse. It didn't work: I was too far from its base-station. I turned my head and in the distance, I could just see that the truck had stopped by the Merc and a man was busy preparing to lift it onto his vehicle. I rolled onto my side and began hollering. He had the engine running and his winch was soon whirling to drag the car up onto his truck. My voice just disappeared into the frosty air. When my throat started getting hoarse from shouting, I tried to turn over onto my knees. That was really painful and my bare hands froze on the cold surface. I crawled a few feet and collapsed back onto the freezing ground, puffing and wheezing.

My hands shook and my teeth began to chatter. You're really in trouble this time, I thought. I struggled over onto my back, crossing my arms to keep warm. I must have looked like one of those knights carved in stone in the cathedral and I remembered the inscription I had read on one of the old tombstones:

All you that do this place pass by,
Remember death for you must die.
As you are now even so was I
And as I am so shall you be.

He was right: I'd soon be like him. I felt cold enough to be a corpse already.

The truck was revving its engine, pulling away with the Merc on its back. No-one was going to find me out here now. It wasn't a dignified way to go. I'd always imagined I'd be in a warm, cozy bed, a nurse holding my hand, dabbing at my forehead. Old Jack died in the pub, in his favourite chair by the fire, pint on the table. A few sips and his heart gave out, lucky sod; he hadn't even paid for his pint. It would take me a while to die of cold. Mind you, they died pretty quick when the Titanic sank; they didn't drown but died of cold, my mother said. Took her a long while to die; consumption, according to the doctor. 'I'll die from his consumption,' my father said when he saw the doctor's new Austin 10 outside. 'If I add up all his bills, I've paid for that car.' Betty's medicines must have cost a packet too; luckily we had the NHS by then. They'd save some money on me; wouldn't need to freeze me in the morgue; I'd be stiff when they found me. I thought about taking my teeth out to stop them chattering.

'Mr Harry, you alright?'

A silky voice floated across the snowy grass. I turned my head to the sound. Is that an angel come for me? It was. I clearly saw Bituin peering from the wreck of the stable.

'You alright, Mr Harry?'

'Can't get up.' My voice sounded weak and pathetic so

I cleared my throat to call louder. I didn't need to. Her feet were skipping effortlessly over the slippery ground towards me. She knelt, panting, beside me, and put a slim arm under my head, brushing snow from my hair. You've no idea how good that felt.

'You must be cold. I get you up.'

'Easier said than done,' I croaked. 'You'll need help.'

'I work in hospital. Don't need help.' She was looking round for something. 'Where's your walker?'

'Wrong side of that gate. It won't go through.'

She took off her long coat and laid it over me, tucking it under me where she could.

'Back soon,' she said racing off towards the gate. I watched her pull at the gate, knowing that she wouldn't be able to open it. I was right but she squeezed through as I had done.

I couldn't believe what she did next.

She picked up my walking frame and tossed it over the gate! I never would have believed she had the strength in that slim body. She was soon kneeling next to me again, giving me instructions.

'You roll onto side, please.' She took her coat from the top of my body and laid it beside me, patting it to indicate where she wanted me. If she could throw walkers around, I decided I'd better do what she said.

'Put hands here and bring knees up, please Mr Harry.'

I knew what she was trying to do, and I don't know where I found the strength, but I did it. I got onto all fours. I was kneeling on her coat so my knees didn't feel so bad. She placed the walking frame near my head.

'Hands and arms on here, please Mr Harry.' She patted the cushioned seat in the middle of the walker.

'Best put the brake on first, in case I shoot forward,' I suggested, struggling to lift my hands onto the seat. She put her arms either side of me and gently helped me up. I was soon kneeling with my arms supported on the walking frame.

'Now we stand up.'

I didn't think I could do it, but feeling the force of her tiny hands under my arms somehow gave me more power. My whole body shook like a diesel engine beginning to fire up as I struggled to my feet. I grasped the walking frame handles and straightened my back with a groan.

'That's better,' I said. 'I thought I was down there for good.'

She giggled a little. 'You strong man. Can you walk?'

'I can try,' I said.

It didn't take long to get to the gate, where she made me lean against a post while she lifted the walking frame up, balanced it on the top bar of the gate and dropped it down on the other side. My poor old walker bounced on the hard ground but it didn't do any harm. She looped an arm in mine and I felt like a new man, trundling back to my house. She'd saved me and I knew for sure that I would now have to save her.

When we got to my garden wall, she looked around cautiously.

She pointed at the wall. 'I go this way. You OK on your own?' She wanted to return the way she had come to avoid being seen.

'Yes I'll go the long way round the front. Put the kettle on; the door's unlocked.'

I was soon indoors but my bones had got so cold I still felt a chill. She saw me shudder when she helped me off with my wet jacket.

'Take off clothes and have hot bath. I'll run one for you,' she said.

'You won't,' I replied. 'We only have a shower.'

She giggled at that and I asked her why she had disappeared into the stable and wouldn't come out. When she told me that she thought I had told the police about her, it all became clear.

'They know nothing about you being here and they never will from me, so just you sit tight and get warm by the electric fire. I don't want to have to chase after you again in this weather.'

I did enjoy that shower. It was when I was sitting there in the shower-chair, warm water running down my back, that I thought of what to do. I was wondering how I could keep Bituin hidden in the dining room with the curtains drawn all day. When the answer struck me, I had to congratulate myself. It was a stroke of genius. I knew straightaway that Betty wasn't going to like it, so I would have to choose my words very carefully when I told her of my plan.

CHAPTER 3
The Memorial

If you saw me talking out loud to Betty on my doorstep, you might think I was a bit funny in the head. Maybe I am, but I'm not daft; I know we don't live on in any sort of physical way. That's just a story the priests make up for simple people so they believe there is something more when you die. I saw Betty lying out in the undertakers in her coffin before they put the lid on and, when I kissed her forehead, I knew that was the last time I would touch her in person. But she lived on in my mind. I could still see her and be with her; all I had to do was think of her and she was there in my head, just as real as when she was alive. I loved the way memories of who she was and what she did were always popping in and out of my brain.

But with Betty, it was more than just memories. She didn't just sit quietly in my head, keeping herself to herself. Oh no, she'd got a mind of her own in there. We saw a film once, Betty and I, about zombies that invade people's brains and take over their bodies because they don't have one of their own. Quite scary, it was, and probably near the truth, I thought. Maybe that was where we go when we die – into someone else's body. Betty'd got into mine alright.

She was very busy in my brain that morning as soon as I told her about my idea.

'I'm going to set up a memorial to you in the dining room, somewhere I can put your old photos and a few of your things so I can remember you more clearly,' I told her.

She saw through my scheme straight away. 'It's not for me. It's for her, isn't it?'

I must admit I had come up with the idea so that Bituin would have somewhere to stay undisturbed. No-one blunders into someone else's memorial room, certainly not without knocking. But I did need somewhere to keep Betty's possessions that were still in drawers and cupboards. I couldn't bear to throw them away.

Betty was not convinced. 'I told you to help her, not get carried away by her, you silly old fool. It's because she's a pretty young thing, isn't it? You wouldn't be having a young lad live with you, would you? Just ring Brian and he'll tell you what to do. The police will treat her kindly and may even give her a new visa, once they find out how cruel those people were to her.'

I told her I wasn't so sure. I read in the paper of a teenager who was sent packing by our Immigration Department and he was tortured when he got back home.

Betty came up with more arguments. 'How are you going to look after a young woman without her going out? She'll need feminine things that you won't have a clue how to buy. She'll need exercise and things to do or she'll go barmy.'

'Well, Betty,' I said. 'I'm going to do it anyway and see what happens.'

That was the first time I'd put my foot down with her for years and I felt better for it.

~

When Bituin woke up, I probably didn't explain my idea very well to her either because she frowned at first.

'I live in cemetery?' she asked.

'No, no you live here, in secret. No-one will come in because I'm calling it Betty's Memorial Room. You stay here until all the fuss dies down, then you can decide what to do. And you'd better have a look through Betty's clothes to see if anything fits. You can't keep on what you're wearing forever.' I knew that Betty's old dresses would drown her, but women are clever with these things. She would manage.

It didn't take me long with her help to make a nice display of photos along the sideboard. I found some of Betty's toilet things: a brush and comb, her last toothbrush, hairgrips, shower hat, even the razor she used for her legs. She had to wear these really tight stockings and if she shaved her legs and greased them a little, it helped them to slip on. They all went on a small table that I covered with her nightdress. I draped her dressing gown and a couple of her nice dresses on a chair. I wasn't sure what to do with her underclothes; it didn't look right to display them now there was another woman in the house, so I kept them in my bedroom. I put a notice on the door that read:

IN FOND MEMORY OF BETTY, MY LOVELY WIFE,
BLESS HER. KEEP OUT

We hit our first problem at lunchtime when I went to the fridge to offer Bituin some food. I've never cooked much except for the odd boiled egg, so I buy these ready meals that I pop in the microwave. I asked what she fancied and read out a few of the labels: sausages, mashed potatoes and peas; lamb with boiled potatoes and carrots.

She stopped me there. 'I'm vegetarian,' she said.

I scratched my head and rummaged in the freezer. 'How about chicken and cauliflower?'

She just giggled. 'No, Mr Harry, no meat.'

'Battered cod and chips?'

'No fish.'

I was stumped. I didn't know of any meals without meat or fish.

'Pizza?' she suggested. As it happened, I did have a small cheese and tomato pizza with round rings of ham on it. She took off the ham and put the pizza in the oven. You can solve most problems if you just work at it long enough.

We'd just sat down to eat in the dining room, when there was a knock on the door. I took a quick peep through the drawn curtains. It was the gardener. I had completely forgotten about him. There are times when I think he has forgotten about me because he just doesn't come some weeks. If one of those big fancy houses along the coast call him, he's off up there and my weeds are left to grow. Trust him to have picked today of all days to come round. Before I could get out of my chair, I heard him coming in; I don't usually lock my door during the daytime.

'You in, Harry? It's Tony.' His real name is Antonio but everyone calls him Tony. 'You wanna the snow cleared? Can't do any gardening.'

I knew that was really why he was here and not in one of his posh gardens earning twice as much as I paid him. But I set him to work shovelling away the snow which removed all traces of footprints from the paths. Bituin and I stayed in the memorial room, out of sight.

I felt strangely at ease sitting there in the dining room, reading my paper whilst Bituin sorted through the few things she had brought with her. Betty was with me everywhere in that room, smiling at me from photo frames; one look at her toothbrush and she was gargling in the bathroom; a touch of her night dress and she was tucked up in bed next to me; a glance at her broom and she was sweeping dust out of the door. Betty liked to sweep and she really missed it when she no longer had the strength, forever tutting at the odd crumb left by the cleaner.

The cleaner! Thank you Betty, I had quite forgotten the cleaner. He came on Wednesday mornings and today was Tuesday. I could hardly stop him from coming into Betty's memorial room, and it would need a clean. Bituin would have to go somewhere else while he was here. I closed my eyes to have a think. The garden shed was the first thing that came to mind but since I'd kept my mobility machine in there, you couldn't swing a cat round let alone sit there for a few hours.

I heard the sound of a shovel scraping on the pavements outside the window which reminded me that I hadn't taken Tony his cup of coffee and he would be coming in if I didn't take one out to him. I opened the outside door and as my eyes swept around the garden looking for him, they settled on my old campervan parked over in a corner of the garden, protected by a waterproof cover. I hadn't been out in that for a good few years, but I couldn't bear to sell it. It was too full of memories of all the wonderful holidays that Betty and I had in it.

'Tony,' I shouted. 'I've brought your coffee. Milk and three sugars, isn't it? Can you clear a path over to the campervan when you've finished please?'

Bituin could spend a few hours in there. It would be cold but I could put on the little heater if there was some calor gas left in the bottle.

I didn't expect the reaction I got from Bituin when I showed her the van. We crept over there, once Tony had gone, making sure we were not too visible. I didn't take the cover off fully, just enough to open the door and squeeze in. When I switched on a light, she clapped her hands and I could see her face beaming as though I had shown her the crown jewels.

'Oh Mr Harry!' She seemed lost for words as she looked around, stroking the cushions Betty had run up and fingering the curtains, like a little girl playing with a doll's house.

'This so neat and small, like apartment back home,' she said, lifting the lid on the sink unit. I showed her how the tap swung up into place but when she pushed the button, the water came out a murky brown colour because it had been standing unused for so long. She just laughed.

'Even water the same as home.'

She opened up the fridge and all the little cupboards and drawers, even exploring the driving instruments and waggling the gear lever. You would have thought she was looking to buy the van.

She pointed to the roof-space. 'What's up there?'

'That's the bunk bed,' I explained.

'Can I go?'

When I nodded, she nimbly pulled herself up and snuggled down on the mattress, looking over the edge to give me one of her flashing smiles. I was glad then that I hadn't sold my old camper.

~

Norman arrived bright and early the next day, whistling as he came through the door. I'd never thought of having a man as a cleaner until one of my neighbours recommended him. He turned out every bit as good as a woman and he can reach the cobwebs on the ceiling more easily too. He's a Filipino, like Bituin. I don't suppose his real name is Norman but that is what we all call him. He's a bit of a Norman Wisdom too because he's always playing the fool. I was half toying with the idea of telling him about Bituin to see if his community could spirit her away and into some kind of work. What he told me made me put that right out of my mind.

'Morning Harry. What's this I read about you in the paper?' His grin was even wider than normal.

He got the local newspaper before me in the mornings so he had me at a disadvantage. He held it up for me to see and pointed to a headline on one of the inside pages:

MYSTERY CAR CRASHES INTO GARDEN

'I couldn't believe it when I saw your address. I was just having breakfast when I read it. Almost choked. Where's the car?' he asked.

'They towed that away. What does it say about it?'

'It says it's from a foreign consulate in London. Someone is missing from the embassy so it might have been stolen.'

I tried to look shocked as though this was all news to me. What did surprise me was that it was important enough to get straight into the papers. What he told me next shook me even more.

'Police have been visiting, asking if we have seen anyone.'

'Visiting who?'

'Us. Last night they knocked on our door and ask if we have seen a young woman who has disappeared.'

'They called on you?'

'Yes of course. The missing person is Filipino, so they think other Filipinos hide her. They visited all Filipinos near us too.'

That did take me back. Someone was taking this very seriously. More seriously than I thought it would warrant. Scratching the paint off someone's gates wasn't exactly a major crime. Even someone disappearing without a proper visa wasn't that unusual. They're arriving by the truckload from the continent.

'So have you got her hidden away somewhere?' I tried to make a joke of it.

He didn't find it funny. 'Oh no, Harry. We would never do that. We'd be sent home if they found us doing anything like that.'

That closed the door on that possibility. I put on some music and sat down. Norman liked to work to music. He knows Simon and Garfunkel backwards and I love to hear him singing along to 'Bridge Over Trouble Water', even if he doesn't quite make the top notes.

It had just got to the 'ease your mind' bit of the song when Betty started nagging at me again.

'Don't you think you should call the police now before *you* get into troubled water? I know you are only trying to help but you could get yourself locked up for it.'

She certainly wasn't easing my mind. I hated it when she looked on the black side of things like that. It could be a perfectly ordinary day and she'd say 'Look at that awful weather,' just because it was spitting with rain, and I'd start feeling miserable even though I knew the garden could do with a drop of water. Once she'd mentioned going to prison, I started thinking about it and wondering what it would be like. I'd seen programmes about it on the TV. Beds looked on the small side but there were plenty of people to talk to in there. Younger ones too, and wouldn't they have interesting stories to tell! They'd give me jobs to do I'm sure. Probably better than living here on my own with no-one to talk to all day; feels like a prison here when I can't get out because of the weather.

'Anyway it was you that told me to look after her like a daughter,' I told her. That shut her up for a while.

~

Norman stuck his head round the corner. 'Someone here to see you,' he said. It was another policeman; only this one was a woman.

She was brusque and to the point. 'Could I ask you a few questions, Mr Pigeon?'

41

She wore trousers and a hat like a bowler with a checked ribbon round it. She didn't take it off.

'Have a seat please. I thought I'd answered all your questions,' I was a bit anxious about this unexpected visit, to say the least.

'We're following up a new line of enquiry about a missing young woman who may have been involved in the car accident outside your house.'

She opened a folder and showed me a large photograph. On one side was a tall, elegant man with a moustache wearing a suit buttoned up to his neck like Mr Nehru used to wear. Next to him lounged a younger man who looked just like him except he didn't have a moustache. On the other side was a plump woman with a large, red dot between her eyebrows wearing one of those loose flowing type of dresses. In the middle was a gaggle of children in white clothes sitting on the ground with several Asian-looking women standing behind them.

'Do you recognise anyone?' she asked.

I couldn't bring myself to say no because one of them was Bituin. 'I saw lots of people like this when I was out in Aden before the war. That silly fool Mussolini had just invaded Abyssinia – it's called Ethiopia now – and I was sent out on a ship to strengthen our defenses in the Gulf. There were quite a few people like this running the shops out there in Aden.'

She took a deep breath and let it out loudly. 'This photo was taken in the last year I believe, not the last century. Do you recognise any of these women, or have you seen anyone like them around here recently?' She stubbed her finger right over Bituin.

'They look a bit like the nurses we have at the hospital. You should ask Norman about them. He's a Filipino.'

'Thank you, Mr Pigeon. So you definitely haven't seen a woman like that recently?' She held the photo closer to my face.

'No.' Finally, I had to lie.

'One of your neighbours said she saw someone in the field behind your house who looked like one of them.'

It was a good thing I was sitting down when she said that. The old brain went into overdrive.

'That wouldn't be Doris would it? She's always seeing and hearing things that no-else does. Touch of dementia, they say. She told me she'd seen the horses in the field the other day but they haven't been there for years. I haven't seen anyone.'

That took the wind out of her sails.

'Do you mind if I take a look around outside,' she said standing up and putting the photograph away.

'Not at all. Come through this way. You can check the field yourself. You get a good view from the dining room, or Betty's memorial as I like to call it.' Norman had just finished cleaning it so the light was on and I didn't open the curtains. You should have seen her face when she saw Betty's things displayed all around. She didn't stay there long. We went into the little conservatory I have at the back and I pointed to the field.

'I'm surprised Doris can see the field from her house,' I said. 'Especially as she's short-sighted.'

She was looking at my back wall and the stable beyond. 'How can I get into the field?' she asked.

By the time I watched her trudge through the sludge

and open the gate, it was a bright and sunny day. I was glad the snow had turned to slush so she wouldn't find our tracks out there. I turned the music back on and went outside, trying not to look at the campervan. When the police lady got back, I thought she would want to poke around my garden and she did. She had mud all over her boots so I was glad she didn't come into the house. Just like Brian, she walked all around the outside checking the windows. I sat on my walker outside the back door trying not to tremble too much in the sunshine.

Simon and Garfunkel were singing 'Cecilia'. I didn't catch the policewoman's name when she first came in but it occurred to me she could be a Cecilia. She was big and muscly like I'd always imagined Cecilia to be. She would certainly shake my confidence daily. I winced when they sang the line about 'making love in the afternoon'. I hadn't done that for a long time and I certainly wouldn't want to do it with PC Cecilia. Luckily, Betty wasn't listening or, if she was, she kept quiet. She never did like talking about those things.

'Do you mind if I take a look in your shed?' PC Cecilia asked.

I fetched the keys and opened up the big padlock and then turned another key in the door lock. I like to be secure.

An image popped into my head of PC Cecilia dragging me inside and unbuttoning her uniform. Fortunately I stopped the thought before she could undo them all.

'Very tidy for a shed,' she said.

I don't know why a shed shouldn't be tidy but I nodded and said: 'That way I know where everything is.' I patted

44

the seat of my mobility machine. 'I might be able to take this out today if the weather stays like this.'

I'd hoped she would take the hint that I wanted to get on with things, but she didn't. When she emerged, blinking in the bright light after the dinginess of the shed, she looked around and spotted the campervan. The cover was still on so it wasn't easy to recognise.

'What's that?' she asked.

'That? Oh that's my old campervan rotting away. Haven't used that for years.'

Not to be deterred, she made towards it. I thought about making a distraction, like falling over or fainting. I hummed to myself instead: 'Cecilia I'm down on my knees, I'm begging you please.'

She walked around the van and lifted the cover up to the door handle. She tried to open it. It didn't budge. I had locked it once Bituin was safely in there. I didn't want her running away again and causing problems.

PC Cecilia grunted and let the cover drop. Jubilation! I didn't quite fall on the floor laughing but I felt like it.

~

She left shortly after, asking me to keep an eye out for the missing Filipino woman in the photograph. I made myself a ham sandwich for lunch with a smearing of French mustard. It's the one thing the French have over us. Their mustard has more flavour. You put a dollop of English on and it just about takes your head off; you certainly can't taste the ham with English mustard on it.

Norman finished his cleaning. 'See you next week

Harry – if they haven't taken you away that is!' He laughed and went on his way singing 'So long, Frank Lloyd Wright'. I must ask him who he was; I never did know.

I made a cheese sandwich for Bituin, no mustard but a little mayonnaise, and put it on my plate with a few baby tomatoes. Cautiously, I pushed it on my walker across the lawn to the campervan. I used to have afternoon tea in there with Betty sometimes so there was nothing exceptional in that. I tapped on the door and slowly unlocked it.

'They've gone but you'll have to stay put till its dark,' I said quietly.

It was a job to haul myself up the step into the van but I used the handles on the side and managed on my own. There was no sign of Bituin.

'Where've you got to now?' I said switching on the light.

'I'm up here, Mr Harry.' I saw a pair of big brown eyes looking sadly down at me from the bed in the roof of the van.

'I've brought you some lunch.'

I took the plate from my walker and closed the door. She scrambled down and sat opposite me at the table that clipped onto the wall. We were both hungry and munched away in silence. I ran my tongue around my teeth to make sure I didn't spit any food out when I started talking. It's a bit embarrassing when that happens and Bituin was sitting quite close, as it's a small van.

'Now young lady, I haven't known you for very long but I think it's time, don't you?'

She looked a bit startled. 'Time for what, Mr Harry?'

'You know. It's time you stopped all this Mr Harry nonsense and just called me Harry.'

She giggled. 'Oh, of course Mr Harry.' She giggled even more before she put on a serious face. 'I mean, yes, Harry.'

'Now that's out of the way, we need to have a serious talk. You need to tell me exactly what has been going on. I don't think you've told me everything, have you?'

CHAPTER 4
Bituin's story

It was Betty who had put me up to quizzing Bituin. To tell the truth, I had begun to ask myself some difficult questions about her. How had a slip of a girl like her managed to drive a big Mercedes all the way from London? Why were the police taking such a special interest? Betty convinced me during our morning chat to have it out with her.

'Have you checked your wallet?' she had asked me.

'Why would I do that?' I replied.

Betty tutted impatiently. 'Sometimes you've less brains than you were born with. She's no money, has she, so she'll be after some of yours, won't she?'

I felt my wallet in my back pocket. It could have been a little thinner, but then I didn't check it that regularly. Yes Betty was right; I needed to know more about this girl who had landed on my door-step.

She was now sitting opposite me in the van, trying to find a way into her cheese sandwich. I'd given her a thick wedge but she didn't seem able to get her teeth into it. I'd finished mine but she was still nibbling around the edges of hers. She looked startled when I asked her to tell me exactly what was going on.

'I tell you truth, Mr... I mean Harry. I don't lie,' she said.

'I didn't say you had. I said I didn't think you've told me everything. There's more to this little crash of yours than meets the eye or the police wouldn't be buzzing round here like flies. Tell me all about what happened with this employer of yours. Why did you runaway?'

I could tell from her look that she wasn't very comfortable talking about it. 'I was looking after their children. They had six.'

'Six! That's a big family for these days. Did you look after them all yourself?'

'No there were others; some cooking, some cleaning. I look after two babies and get the big ones up for school, have clothes ready, tell drivers when to take them and look after in evening because Mr Sharma always go out.'

'Where was Mrs Sharma?'

'She was second wife and only interested in her babies. She didn't like Mr Sharma's other children and I never see their mother. Dead, I think. At first, everything OK. I work hard but we get on together. After few weeks, Mr Sharma say he go to UK and take me with him on special visa. Never been outside Manila so I was very happy to go to another country and I could send home money to family.'

I had never heard of Manila so I was itching to ask her where it was. She giggled when I did. 'Manila in Philippines, on coast. Not capital but very big city. I was born there. My father drive taxis so we had a good life, with own apartment. I went to school and university to be a nurse. Then my...'

She paused and I saw her big, brown eyes fill with tears. I offered her a tomato to give her time to compose herself. She shook her head. 'My father have heart attack in taxi and he crash into wall.'

I was going to say like father like daughter but it was I good thing I didn't because there was worse to come.

'He died and man in taxi injured. Owner of wall ask for money to mend it. Then we find my father have no insurance. Maybe he forget or maybe no money to pay but his insurance finish the day before the crash. We have to pay everything ourselves even for taxi which was rented. We had nothing left, not even our apartment. My mother and sister move into slum. I was oldest girl and had to get job straight away. Embassies always pay top wages so I get job there, and work for special envoy, Mr Sharma.'

'Envoy for what?'

'He never talk about what he did. People in suits always coming and going so some kind of business I think. When we arrive in UK, his son join us. That's when trouble start.'

She took a nibble of her sandwich, looking down with that sad expression that sometimes came over her face.

'What sort of trouble?'

'At first he is nice to me. Give me flowers and say I am very pretty. Ask me about Manila and Filipino food. I cook him meal and he pour wine, only for me; he don't drink. Keep pouring wine and take my hand. Look in my eyes and say I am very pretty and he take special care of me. Other hand he put on my knee. I say thank you for taking care of me and my knee but please not to put hand any higher.' She glanced up at me, her eyes stern.

I nodded my approval. I'd met plenty of these arrogant young men in my air force days. Private school types, training to be pilots, and they thought they owned every good-looking girl in town. I had to put them straight on that score more than once.

'Did he take any notice?' I asked, although I was sure he hadn't.

'Oh yes, he laugh. He say his hands can be very gentle like one stroking my leg. Or very rough, like this one. He hold up other hand and smack me hard on face. He ask which one I prefer, gentle one or rough one.'

I flinched at that. Not even the young pilots would have gone that far.

'My foot come up quickly and kick him between legs. I say my feet same; gentle or rough. He grab me by the hair and drag me to a cupboard and lock me in, say he won't let me out until I change my manners. Very small cupboard and I couldn't breathe so I say I will change manner if he leave my knees alone. He laugh and say not my knees I should be worried about. He keep me there till morning.' She dabbed at her eyes with a tissue.

'Did you tell his father?' I asked.

'Mr Sharma gone on trip and son in charge of house. Next day, he call me into office. He sit in Mr Sharma's chair, grinning. He say he cannot trust me with children because of my violence to family member, so he sack me.'

'Sounds as though you were well out of it,' I said.

'Need money for family. I ask him for reference and he laugh and say, yes as kick boxer. I am very sad. No good job without reference.'

'So that's when you ran away?'

She shook her head firmly, creating waves with her fine, black hair.

'No, that evening he come to see me and say sorry he had to sack me. He find me new job. He pour wine again and ask what jobs I have done. I say I work in hospital. He say he can get me job in massage parlour. I say I am trained as nurse not masseuse. He say nurses know about massage. I tell him physiotherapists know about massage, not nurses. He slap me and tell me not to be so clever. I have to practice massage now, on him, or he put me in cupboard. I hate cupboard so I say OK, I try to give massage. I massage his back and he groans and talk about girls who give him happy ending. He say I must do same … or …' She didn't quite finish because she began to cry.

I fished around in my pocket and pulled out my handkerchief. I'd only used it a couple of times so I gave it to her. She seemed to want to get the story off her chest so after she'd wiped her cheeks and eyes, she cleared her throat to continue.

'I tell him I need plenty practice on back before anything more advanced. He fall asleep. I tip toe out to my room. I sleep but he burst in shouting: "You haven't finished massage!" I tell him that finish when he was asleep. He say he wants happy ending or I spend night in cupboard. I say I prefer to spend night in cupboard. He grabs me by the throat and say he will throw me in the Thames. I say he can throw me in the Thames. That will be happy ending for me. He say he has friends in Manila who will throw my mother and sister in river. I say OK, I will give him happy ending next day because now I was too tired.'

I gripped the top of my walking stick. I would teach this boy a lesson or two if I ever caught him.

'Next day, Mr Sharma arrive home early from airport. He ask why children not at school. Son sack me, I tell him. He look angry and call to chauffeur to take girls to school. They look for books, put on clothes and shoes and he shout to hurry as very late. He tell everyone to get into car and get ready while driving. I tell him they can't tie shoes or ties; I always did it for them. He push me into car and tell me to help them. We all in back, dressing while car speed round London, children shoving each other, trying to put on clothes, complaining, shouting. Girls get out at school and chauffeur sigh with relief. I tell him first time I see London. He say he needs to buy cigarettes so we can take long way home. I watch him drive car: power steering, automatic gears, power brakes, sat nav. I knew I could drive that car.' I saw her fists clench as she said that.

'Where did you learn about cars?' I asked.

She smiled, obviously remembering happier times. 'My father teach me. He was taxi driver. Very good taxi driver. He had to be; he drive in Manila. He needed back-up for when he was ill or day off. So he teach me to drive.'

'You drove a taxi in a big city?' That I found hard to believe.

'Why not? He had good car. Mercedes, like Mr Sharma. Except his C class. Mr Sharma's is top-of range S class, but not so different to drive.'

I've never been a Mercedes fan. The gun sight they have on their bonnet reminds me too much of the war. I watched Bituin nibble at her sandwich thinking that there was more to this girl than just a pretty face.

'There are women pilots now,' I said. 'I was reading about one, probably not much bigger than you, who flies one of those great big jumbo jets. There was a picture of her in a smart blue uniform that was no different to the men's.'

'Yes, we drive. We fly. We do many things but stupid son think I am only good to give happy times in massage parlour.' She was getting quite agitated. 'Driver stop at shop and he get out to buy cigarettes. Leave keys in ignition. I don't want job in massage parlour. So I get into driver's seat, start engine and drive away. I didn't plan to; I didn't know where I was going. All I knew was that I not work like prostitute for stupid son, and that I must drive on left.'

'What made you come this way?' I asked.

'I met a nurse in Manila who told me about UK hospital where she work with many other Filipino girls. I put name of hospital in sat nav and follow directions. I want to find some of my people and ask them what to do. Instead I find you.' She gave me half a smile.

'I bet I wasn't in your sat nav. How did you manage to drive over a hundred miles in that big car?'

'Journey out of London easier than Manila rush hour and then motorway no problem. Trouble start when snow on road. I never drive in snow. Sorry for gates,' she said with her little giggle.

'Don't you worry about the gates. It's you I'm concerned about. How anybody can treat someone like you have been I don't know. Would you like some apple pie?'

'Oh, no thanks. You are very kind to me.'

I looked at my watch and saw that time was getting on and I had some washing up to do.

'You'll have to stay put here for a few more hours until it gets dark. The police are looking for you everywhere. We can't risk someone seeing you.'

'I'm making clothes,' she said showing me one of Betty's old blouses that she was taking in to fit her.

In her younger days, Betty would have been as slim as her, but quite a bit taller. She was never a chesty woman but she was as elegant as you like with her brown hair all neat and tidy and a lovely shape to her face. When I saw her laid out in her coffin, she had shrunk back to the sort of size she was when we had first met. I could picture her just as she was then, not the little old lady she had become.

~

I hauled myself up and out of the van, making sure I pulled the cover down again. It was a good thing I did because I spotted Doris coming along the road on her mobility machine.

She waved at me and shouted: 'Wait a second, Harry. I'd like a word.'

Doris always liked to give the orders. Betty never got on with her from the moment she moved in up the road. She spoke with a posh, plumy sort of voice and I think that made Betty feel a bit inferior. "Who does she think she is?" Betty said to me once. "The Queen of Sheba?" Doris had just been round for tea, and I could see Betty's face fall when she turned the saucer of her teacup over to inspect the make on the bottom. She'd bought the cottage up the road when her husband died. Downsizing she called it although she still had three bedrooms. It would have been upsizing for us.

I pushed my walking frame towards the gates to head her off. I didn't want her nosing around the house or garden. She walked perfectly well so I didn't know why she needed that scooter. No wonder she was overweight: too many cream teas with the Women's Institute.

She had a close look at the gates.

'Doesn't seem to be much damage, does there? But I would still claim for some new ones, if I were you. I'm sure the embassy can afford it. Any sign of that girl?' she asked.

She seemed to know more than I had bargained for so I decided to play it a bit dumb.

'What girl?'

'The one who has gone missing. The policewoman must have asked you about her.'

'Oh that one,' I said casually as though there were a lot of girls in my life.

'Did you tell her you'd seen her? I did. I told her I'd seen her in the field. I thought you would've seen her there too.' She was pushing at the gate as though she wanted to come through but she couldn't make it open. I didn't offer to help.

'What makes you think that?'

'Soon after I saw her running across the field, I saw you heading in the same direction.'

'Are you sure it was me? I'm surprised you can see that far from your house.'

She reached into the bag on the side of her mobility machine and produced some spectacles on a stick.

'I use these,' she said. 'I haven't been to the opera since Henry died but they come in useful to watch what is going on around me. Have you seen the geese that are wintering in the fields?'

I shook my head.

'First time I've seen them here,' she went on. 'I was sweeping round the field looking for them with my glasses when I saw this young girl. She looked just like the picture the policewoman showed me,' she said.

'What picture?' I asked.

'The picture of the Filipino who may have driven the car into your gates.' She tapped the ironwork with her stick.

Doris was proving to be more formidable than the forgetful old lady I had taken her for when we last met at Betty's funeral.

'Would you like to come in for a cup of tea?' I asked, opening the gate.

'Sorry can't stop. I've got a Skype call booked with my son in New Zealand. There's only a limited amount of time we can do it with the time change. I just wanted to make sure you were alright.'

Yes and find out how much I know, I thought.

'I didn't see anybody in the field or anywhere else and that's what I told the police. Obviously I had a good look round to see if there were any signs, but I couldn't find any,' I said.

Doris sidled up close to me and dropped her voice. It was normally on the loud side so her whisper was still quite audible. 'The policewoman told me that the girl had stolen something belonging to the embassy.'

I could smell something on her breath and shuffled back a little. 'You mean the car?' I said.

'No, not just the car. She let slip that there was

something else but she wouldn't tell me what it was, but it must be important. She asked me to keep an eye out and call her as soon as I saw anything. If you see anything, you can always tell me and I can relay it on for you, if you don't want to phone the police yourself. We neighbours have to stick together, you know, or we'll have illegal immigrants all over the place.' With that, she turned and stalked back to her scooter.

I watched her disappear back to her cottage. Just what I needed: Doris had turned into a vigilante. With her watching my every move, how could I keep Bituin hidden in the house?

CHAPTER 5
The Seaside

The next morning, when I told Betty about Doris's visit, she started tutting: 'It's got nothing to do with that old busy-body. I can't wait to see her face when she finds out you've had the girl hidden right under her nose.'

I almost laughed out loud at that. Just as I was having my doubts about hiding Bituin with Doris on the prowl, Betty had come round to the idea because it would spite our stuck-up neighbour. Fortunately, Betty went on to make one of her decisions. She didn't make them very often. Although she made plenty of comments on what I decided to do, she rarely suggested ways of doing things herself. When she did, she was usually spot on.

'There's nothing for it Harry. You are just going to have to sort things out yourself with this Mr Sharma. Tell him in no uncertain terms what his son has been up to and make him see sense. He'll take the girl back if you tell him right.'

The more I thought about it, the more I realised she was right. I had to talk to him somehow and sort this out between us, man to man.

~

When we were having breakfast together, I asked Bituin where Mr Sharma lived in London. Funnily enough, she didn't know the address. All she remembered seeing when she was in the car with the children was a big shop called Harrods. I knew a fair bit about London from my time there during the war, so I knew Harrods was in Kensington but that was quite a big area. I didn't want Bituin to find out what I was up to, so I didn't press her too hard for an address, even though it was odd that she didn't know it. I decided to write to Mr Sharma at the Indian Embassy.

If you're thinking that this would give the game away about Bituin, you're wrong. I may be getting on a bit but I've still got some marbles left, and I had Betty to advise me. She was good with words; she didn't speak a lot, but when she wrote things down, you could tell her head was full of some clever words. She insisted that the message had to make him interested without mentioning anyone in particular. My arthritic fingers didn't always go where I wanted them to, which is why I wrote it in capitals.

DEAR MR SHARMA,
I HAVE FOUND SOMETHING IMPORTANT OF
YOURS THAT I WOULD LIKE TO RETURN.
BUT FIRST I HAVE TO KNOW IT WILL BE
SAFE. PLEASE CALL THE NUMBER BELOW

~

That was it; no name, no address, just a telephone number at the bottom. I plugged the mobile in to charge it as I hadn't used it since Betty died. She had wanted me to have one when I left her alone in the house to do a quick errand in case she needed me. It had been intended for emergencies only but she'd ring just as I was at the checkout asking if I could buy a cucumber or some tissues.

I walked to the post box up the road early the next morning, before Bituin was awake. It's on the way to the cemetery so I gave Betty a wave after I had pushed the letter through the slot. I think she was asleep because I heard nothing from her. The weather had changed for the better and spring was appearing everywhere. After that late snow it seemed even more like magic. How those little crocuses, pansies and primroses know that it's time to pop up I don't know, but they do., When I returned from the postbox, I rested in Betty's chair, looking at them through the window, wondering what Mr Sharma would think when he got my letter.

I must have nodded off because the next thing I knew, I heard Bituin calling to me.

'OK to come out now Mr …I mean Harry?'

I went into the hall and saw her standing in the doorway of her room. You could have knocked me down with a feather. She was wearing one of Betty's old green blouses. Betty wore a lot of green; she said it set her eyes off although I never really understood why because her eyes were blue, a very light blue that you don't often see. Betty told me that we could make out more shades of green than any other colour because we used to live in the jungle. Because everything there was green, we had learned over millions of years to recognise all the different shades and hews of green. She always mentioned this when she showed me a new top or skirt and I said it was just like the other green ones she had. "You must be from a different species of human who lived in the deserts not the forests if you can't see the difference," she'd say.

Bituin had turned one of Betty's favourite tops into a nightshirt. It was a willowy green blouse but it came down to her knees and she had taken it in so that it wasn't too loose. I felt the wetness around my eyes as she stood there and I saw Betty on the night we first met. She was seventeen and wore green even then.

'I make you some breakfast, Harry?' she asked.

I was about to tell her I'd already eaten when I realised she was being polite.

'You must be hungry yourself. I've got some cornflakes or I can do you some porridge.'

'I love porridge but can make myself,' she said flitting into the kitchen with nothing on her feet.

'Better be careful you're not seen through the windows,' I said, following her to quickly draw the curtains.

Bituin busied herself in the kitchen whilst I sat quietly enjoying her company. She came in with two bowls of porridge. It was more of a soup than the sticky porridge I make; I like it solid so I can pick it off my trousers or shirt when I miss my mouth. But I was more than content to tuck in. I couldn't remember the last time someone had made me a meal in my own house.

After we'd done the washing up together, Bituin looked out of the window at the clear, blue sky.

'What we do today, Harry?' she asked.

That surprised me. I hadn't had to think about what to do for some time because I'd had my daily routine looking after Betty and trying to fit in all my other jobs.

'Can we go somewhere?' Her eyes were bright at the prospect.

I didn't want to disappoint her but I knew that was next to impossible. 'We could, but you might be seen by somebody.'

'I hide in back of campervan while you drive.'

For some reason my campervan excited her. The last time I had taken the van out was for its MOT last summer. That's all I had done with it for several years, taken it for the MOT. I always hoped that a miracle might happen and Betty would somehow find the strength to get into it again. She used to love our trips in the van. We went all over the country in it when we first retired. Even when we got too old to go touring, we would take it out on day trips up to the coast. Now here was this slip of a girl asking me to take out my campervan once again. I wondered what Betty would think.

'You'll have to put something else on. That blouse won't keep you very warm,' I found myself saying.

She giggled. 'I find something warm, no problem. Where we go?' I'd never seen her so happy.

~

A few hours later, we were on the road. The sun was shining although there was still quite a nip in the air. I glanced over at Doris's cottage as we drove past wondering if she was watching through those funny spectacles of hers, but there was no sign of life behind the lace curtains. I headed away from the town through farmland where the spring corn was beginning to show and the sheep would soon be lambing. I felt a young man again. Bituin sat quietly in the back, trying to see out of the front window as I had the side curtains closed to make sure no one saw her.

'Ever been to the English seaside?' I asked.

'No, never been to any English sides,' she said.

As it was early on a week day, the car park on the north Norfolk coast was empty when I pulled in. I got close to the water's edge so we could get a good view of the birds wading in the black mud and the boats resting in the shallows of the narrow channel. The sandy beach was a mile away across the salt marshes and you had to walk along the coastal path or take a boat to get there. It was low tide so we looked out across a creek that was about a quarter the size it would be when the tide came in.

'Keep your eye on the water level. I may have to pull the van back when it rises,' I said.

Many a time, some unsuspecting newcomer had disappeared off to the beach and come back to find their car up to the axles in salt water. The local garage had a Land Rover ready to tow them out; never warned them of course as it made the village a pretty penny or two every time someone got stuck.

I must have nodded off in the warm sunshine because next thing I knew Bituin was shouting excitedly.

'Look Harry, boat is floating!'

Sure enough the water was racing in and the clinker wherry boat that had lain on its side in the mud, when we arrived, was now righting itself and beginning to float.

'Like a baby standing for first time,' she said.

It did look as though it was staggering to its feet; more like the lads in the pub at closing time, I thought.

She clapped her hands. 'Now it turn round,' she said in disbelief at the boat's antics.

'It's anchored at one end,' I explained. 'So when the tide flows out, it goes down onto the mud one way round and when the tide comes back and floats it off, it turns it back the other way. That's why the boats are not anchored too close, or they would bash into each other as they swing about.'

She watched fascinated as the water levels reached the larger cruising boats along the banks of the creek and they swung around to face the incoming tide. Several were lifted and turned in unison.

'Look, they dance in the water!' She sounded as excited as a child on her first trip to the sea.

I was feeling peckish by now so I eased my way down out of the cabin and found my walking stick.

'I'm going to buy us some food from the shop over there. Make sure you aren't seen too much,' I said.

I had good chat with the old boy who runs the chandlery at one end of the shop about the storms during the winter, and what the floods had done to the marshes and the birds that live there. The sea had come right over the banks into the marshes making fresh water salty overnight. The whole habitat had changed. He told me how the migrating terns and geese had been thoroughly confused when they'd arrived to find that the wetland had gone very brackish.

What you see on the news about people who have had their houses flooded and their furniture ruined is only half the story. They don't tell you much about the wildlife that have had their homes destroyed, do they? Imagine flying all that way from Russia or Canada only to find things aren't quite as you had left them the year before and your normal food had disappeared.

That reminded me that I was meant to be buying some sandwiches so I grabbed a couple of packets and presented them to the lady at the till. She obviously recognised me from previous visits because she asked where my wife was. I told her that I was on my own – I didn't want to tell her all my business, did I?

She looked beyond me, towards the car park. 'I wonder who's moving your van then?'

I whirled round and sure enough the van was jerking backwards. It stalled, then the engine started again and it jerked back some more. I paid up quick and hurried out of the shop.

It's funny what races through your mind during moments like this. First I thought someone was stealing my van; then I remembered that Bituin was in it and I thought maybe she was running away again. I panted up to the door and waved. She was sitting cool as anything in the driver's seat. As soon as she saw me she scrambled into the back as I climbed in.

'I move campervan because water come up fast. Reverse difficult to find; not used gears before.' She smiled, all innocent-like.

The water hadn't quite reached the van so it wasn't really in any danger, but I supposed she wasn't to know that.

'You gave me a bit of a fright. I thought someone was stealing the van.'

I drove out of the village in case the woman from the

shop decided to investigate who the mystery driver of my van was. I got onto a wide, straight road and pulled over. There was no-one about so I called to Bituin.

'Come and sit her in the front and I will show you how to change gear.' She was there in a flash and listened all ears as I took her through the movements of the clutch and the gear lever.

'You're lucky we have synchromesh gears today,' I told her. 'When I learned to drive we had a gate shift so you had to double de-clutch and if you got that a little bit wrong there would be grinding and squealing as if you'd put your foot on a wild pig instead of the clutch.'

'Did your father teach you to drive, Harry?' she asked.

I chuckled. 'He didn't know how to himself. The only thing he could drive was a steam train. That's what he did for a living. He was an express train driver so he wasn't too fond of cars. No, I was taught by a fitter at the garage where I worked as a boy. He would take me out in his car on a Sunday because he liked to go to the pub for lunch. After a few pints, he'd be in no condition to drive himself home, so he'd be belching and passing wind, shouting at me for grinding the gears, all the way back. I learned pretty quick because I didn't want to put up with that for too long.'

She giggled. 'You funny, Harry. Can I drive now?'

I'd never intended for it to be a real driving lesson. But she asked so directly and forcefully that I couldn't say no, could I? I had comprehensive insurance and she told me she had a full driving license back home. The road was empty so I swopped seats with her. Do you know, she drove that van almost as well as I did.

I can always tell a good driver. They plan ahead, trying

to predict what is going to happen next, not just reacting to something when it is already in full swing. That way you can avoid the idiots who overtake on the brow of a hill or drive too close to your rear bumper.

I'd never met a woman who could drive like that, but Bituin could. We drove for miles that day, all around the places I hadn't seen for years. Bituin didn't want to stop and I was happy to be the passenger for a change. Betty would forever be saying: "Look at that and have a look at this," but you can't when you're driving, can you? Now I could see it all; the hedgerows where the rabbits scurried out of our way, the fields and trees with birds overhead, glimpses of the sea when there was a gap in the hedges. It was good to be alive again, even if I did have to buy another tank full of petrol.

~

It was getting dark when we got home, and I was tired. I slept like a log that night and I didn't wake up until sunrise. I was reading the paper and Bituin was washing up the breakfast things when the phone rang. I didn't recognise the tone at first because it didn't sound like my phone. Then I realised it was the mobile which hadn't rung since Betty last called me at Tesco's.

'Yes, who's calling?' I said.

I thought it was one of those salesmen calling about insurance or windows because he had the accent of someone in a foreign call centre.

'Who am I speaking to please?' he said.

'Who am I speaking to?' I said. 'You tell me who you are and I might tell you who I am.'

'I was asked to ring this number in a letter,' he said.

The penny dropped and I lowered my voice so that Bituin could not hear in the kitchen. 'You must be Mr Sharma. Yes I do need to speak to you.'

'I am not Mr Sharma. He is asking me to ring you and find out why you are writing a letter to him and who exactly you are,' he said.

Careful Harry, I heard Betty say. Don't tell him too much.

'I have some information which Mr Sharma needs to know about. I can only tell it to him.'

'Can I tell Mr Sharma what kind of information you are talking about?'

'It's about what his son gets up to.' I may have sounded a bit curt but thinking about what that boy did made me feel angry.

There was a small pause. 'I am sure Mr Sharma would indeed be grateful to have this information. How can he get it?'

That sounded hopeful, but I realised that I was not going to get very far on the telephone.

'I would like to meet him. Just the two of us.'

'Where would this meeting be?' he asked.

With Bituin around, I couldn't have him come to meet me in my house or even my own small town, and I didn't know of anywhere in between.

'I will meet him at King's Cross station in London,' I said.

'How is Mr Sharma recognising you at this station,' he asked.

I thought about that for a moment but Betty suggested

what I should say; she probably got it from one of those detective stories she watched on the TV.

'He won't. I'll find him. Just tell him to wait under the main departures' board at 10am tomorrow. Alone.' I put the phone down. Then I remembered it was a mobile and you don't just put it down; you have to switch it off as well. I picked it up again.

'Hello, hello,' I heard someone saying.

'Did you understand? I will meet Mr Sharma tomorrow at 10am,' I repeated.

'Yes. Bring this phone with you. He can call you at the station if you cannot see him.' He put his telephone down this time or maybe he switched it off. Either way, it went dead.

Bituin came in and must have seen me looking a little pensive.

'Everything alright, Harry?'

'Yes fine. I have to go out tomorrow to sort out a few personal matters. You'll be alright here on your own, won't you?'

CHAPTER 6

London

The next morning, Bituin was up early to say goodbye. When I told her I would be back later that day, she was quite tearful as if I was going away forever. It wasn't until I was relaxing in my seat on the train, watching the countryside speed past the window, that I found time to think of Betty. She had obviously been waiting for me.

'What are going to call yourself when you meet this man?' she asked.

'What do you mean?'

'You can't call yourself Harry Pigeon and let them know all about you, can you? You need to use a different name, a pseudonym like some of the stars use. Remember Tommy Steele? He was Thomas Hicks before he went on the stage and started singing.'

I hadn't thought about this at all, but Betty must have had a sleepless night over it. She had it all worked out.

'How about Norman? It's a nice name and one you'll remember because it's the name of our cleaner, who is of course a Filipino so there's a connection if you forget.'

'Alright, Norman it is. But Norman who?'

'Just tell them Norman. Best to keep it simple and on your terms. Don't let them tell you what to do. Sometimes you give in too easy just for a bit of peace and quiet. No, you've got to dictate terms.'

She sounded as though she had been watching one of those TV dramas, but I doubted she got the signal anymore, up there.

'Remember what those detectives do when they cross-examine people,' she said. 'They're not all polite with please and thank you. They're rude and rough. You'll have to be firm, Harry. I mean, Norman.'

'Yes dear.'

My head was aching so I just listened to her until she calmed down. Her advice turned out to be just right, as usual.

~

My compartment was bursting with passengers by the time we got to King's Cross. It was quite a fight getting out of the carriage; the step down looked steep so I decided to turn round and do it backwards. That didn't go down very well with those behind me. They were so impatient to get out that they nearly pushed me off the train.

There were people everywhere. Most were rushing away from the platforms to the exits but a few were fighting against the flow of bodies to get to their train. A few were standing still, anxiously staring up at the big departures' board. I thought that was a good place to wait so I took my place in the line of people waiting for their platform to be announced. I managed to find a seat and glanced at my watch. 9.45am. I was in plenty of time. I hoped I would recognise Mr Sharma from the photograph the police lady had shown me. The problem would be seeing him in these crowds. If I do this again, I thought, I will do it out of the rush hour.

I must have sat there a good twenty minutes when my mobile phone rang.

'Are you waiting already at King's Cross station?' I recognised the voice from the call yesterday.

'Yes I'm under the departures' board.'

I looked around and saw that there was more than one person on a phone near me. Which one was it?

'What are you wearing?' he asked.

'I didn't want my best suit to get dirty on the train, so I'm in my number twos,' I said.

I always had two suits when I was a boy, and I still do. My number one suit – the newest one – I had to keep for Sundays only. Every day for school I wore my number two's. Until the day that wore out and my number one's became my number two's and I got a new number one suit.

'What colour would your number twos be please?' the voice asked.

'The jacket used to be dark blue but it's faded in places so it's more medium blue now.'

I had spotted a swarthy-looking individual on a phone who was looking hard in my direction.

'Are you sitting down?'

I struggled to my feet, trying to see through the crowds.

'I was, but I'm standing now.'

The swarthy man had taken off his sunglasses and was walking straight towards me.

'It is you I think I am looking for,' he said with a big smile, stretching out his hand.

He wore one of those thin, shiny suits that look cheap but are actually quite expensive. His sleek, black hair gave him the streamlined look of a city-slicker who was always in a hurry.

'Mr Sharma?'

I knew it wasn't because he didn't have a moustache, but I couldn't think what else to say.

'Mr Sharma is waiting for you outside. He doesn't like railway stations. I am Kumar, his personal assistant,' he explained.

His hand was in mine now and he looked me in the eye, waiting for my name. I remembered Betty's instructions.

'Good morning. I'm Norman.'

It felt very strange when he replied: 'Good morning, Norman. That is a fine English name.'

I suppose it originated from the Normans who came from France but I didn't correct him.

'Please follow me and I will take you to meet Mr Sharma,' he said, looking at his gold watch.

'Wait a minute. Where exactly is Mr Sharma?'

'He will be waiting just outside, in his car. You can talk in private there.'

He turned and strode towards the exit. I wasn't happy with this car business; I had seen too many films where people got up to mischief in the back seat of a car. Reluctantly, I followed him to the archway out of the station where he pointed at a black Mercedes with smoked glass windows. It was just like the one that had crashed into my gates.

'This way, Norman,' he said.

I pointed in the other direction. 'Tell Mr Sharma, I prefer my own transport so I will take a taxi. You can follow that.'

He frowned. 'Where will your taxi be going?' he asked.

'To the Fitzroy Tavern, Windmill Street.'

I joined the queue for taxis and watched Kumar talking excitedly to the driver of the Merc. I thought they would just follow me but they didn't. The car sped off and Kumar ran over just as I was getting into my taxi.

'Mr Sharma is joining you at the Fitzroy Tavern. May I accompany you?'

I didn't think it would do any harm and he might even pay the fare, so I nodded. When he sat down next to me. I noticed that his pointed shoes hadn't been cleaned for sometime. I wouldn't be trusting this one.

'Have you had a long journey today, Norman?'

I chose to ignore his question by giving the cab driver instructions.

'How are you knowing this Fitzroy Tavern, Norman? You don't live around here, do you?' Kumar persisted.

I couldn't resist telling him the story. 'I was stationed here during the war for a while, in the Air Ministry just around the corner from the Fitzroy. One of my airmen was the landlord there. He took us in a few times for a drink.'

'Which war was happening at this time, Norman?'

He was younger than I thought, or maybe just ignorant.

'Second World War. I was here when Hitler was bombing London. Terrible it was.'

We were just passing a sign to the underground and

I pointed. 'Families had to shelter down there. Can you imagine sleeping on the platform with hundreds of other people? I used to go down into the tube first thing in the morning and meet the mothers coming up carrying dirty blankets and children with bottles hanging from their lips. The smell was terrible down there.'

'Sounds like my home city,' he said in a quiet voice.

'Where's that?' I asked.

'I am from Bangalore in India,' he said, his eyes brightening up.

'I get a lot of phone calls from there. Whenever someone comes on about insurance with an accent like yours, I always ask them where they are calling from. They usually tell me the name of the company and I say, no I want to know which town you are calling from. It's often Bangalore and we have a nice chat about what time it is there, the weather and things like that and they forget about this insurance rubbish. There are some very nice people in Bangalore but they don't seem to sleep much. They're always calling when it's the middle of the night over there.'

He was looking anxiously round as we pulled into a side street.

'Have you been to this Fitzroy Tavern since the war, Norman?'

'No, I haven't been there for years. I don't really go into pubs anymore.'

'It is still here, it seems.' He sounded relieved as the taxi pulled up.

Do you know, it hadn't changed that much in all those years. When we went in I could see that they had knocked down a few walls and the bar was a bit bigger, but it had that old feeling to it. All sorts of pictures and memorabilia hung from the walls and I wandered around looking at them while Kumar waited anxiously at the door. I had just found a photograph of the bar in the 1940's with one of my old friends in it, when Kumar tapped me on the shoulder.

'Mr Sharma is here now, Norman,' he said.

He was standing by the entrance and I instantly recognised the handsome, bronze face from the photo. He had the poise and self-assured look of an aristocrat, and the charm too with an accent that sounded as though he'd spent time at an English private school.

'Norman, thank you so much for coming all this way to see me. Did you have a good journey?'

He shook my hand and didn't let it go until he had put his other hand on top of mine as though I was his brother. We sat down in a quiet corner away from the bar and Kumar was dispatched to fetch us a pot of tea.

'I am sorry that you did not want to travel in my car. Does it have some bad memories for you?' His teeth almost glowed from beneath his neatly trimmed moustache.

'Not exactly a bad memory, just a bit of a shock,' I said.

'You mean when it was crashing into your house?' he said.

I nodded. 'These things happen.'

That's all I said and it was only later that I realised that this was where I gave the game away. He'd asked the question so smoothly and naturally, I didn't see the trap.

Kumar returned with the tea and he hovered as though waiting for instructions.

'I would like to talk to Mr Sharma alone if you don't mind.'

'Of course,' said Mr Sharma, looking intently at Kumar. 'You can go and make that call now.' We watched him hurry from the pub towards the Mercedes that was still outside.

'You were here in the war, I understand. Has it changed very much?' he asked.

'It was a bit more crowded in those days,' I said looking around at the empty bar. 'There was a big grand piano over there by the window and they had this pianorist.' Mr Sharma's smile got even bigger at this point. 'He had black hair and a thin, greasy moustache which stuck out six inches either side of his face, but, boy, couldn't he half play. He would work himself up into a frenzy, his fingers flying everywhere until the crescendo at the end. Then we would all applaud and he would twist and twiddle his moustache.'

'You paint a wonderful picture of the past. You must have many memories from that time,' he said sipping his tea.

I felt it was time to get down to business.

'Yes and some from the present which are not so pleasant. Which is what I want to talk to you about.'

'Indeed? I think you may have found something which you wish to give to me?'

'Yes, it's about your son. He is treating young women very badly. I want you to talk to him and stop him.'

He took another sip of tea and thought about that. 'Have you a son, Norman?' I shook my head. 'Then maybe you can remember how much notice you took of your father when you were young?'

78

'I respected my father and did what I was told,' I said.

'Everything you were told? Even when you were nineteen or twenty years old?'

He had me thinking there. 'He wanted me to join the railways, like him, but I joined the RAF. That upset him a bit.'

'This is exactly the problem I am having now with my own son, Norman. He is a good boy but he has his own ideas of what he does, what sort of business he runs and I can't really stop him.'

'You have to try. I have information which could really get him into trouble.' I tried to sound a bit threatening.

'Can you show me this information, Norman?'

He must have taken me as a fool if he thought I was going to tell him about Bituin.

'The source of my information is somewhere safe but ready to return if you agree to my terms.'

He leant forward in his chair. 'And what exactly are your terms?'

'Your son has to stop being cruel and disrespectful to young girls. His behaviour towards them is nothing short of disgusting. He has to change his ways or I will have to take the matter further.' That was being firm; Betty would be quite pleased with that.

He looked at me long and hard until it began to feel a little uncomfortable. Suddenly he flashed his white teeth beneath his black moustache.

'I am indeed grateful that you have brought my son's actions to my attention. I will ensure he changes his ways. When you return the information to me, I will happily compensate you for any inconvenience it has caused you.'

'Thank you. It would be nice if you paid my train fare because I had to come in the rush hour and that wasn't cheap. Kumar paid for the taxi,' I said.

He looked at me blankly and then chuckled loudly. 'Norman, you are a very clever man. I trust £10,000 will cover the cost of your train fare?'

'I could buy the train for that. I am more interested to know that the girls you employ are not subject to abuse from your son. Once I am assured of that, you will have back what is yours.'

'I can assure you I am talking to my son as soon as I leave you today,' he said, glancing at his watch.

'That won't be quite enough I'm afraid. I will need you and your son to sign an agreement, a sort of contract guaranteeing that everything can go back to how it was and he won't misbehave again.'

I could tell by his face that he wasn't expecting this.

'A written contract?'

I nodded.

'What exactly does this contract say?'

'Once we are agreed in principle, I will have my lawyers draw up the necessary paperwork.' Betty had told me to say that. 'Oh and I will need your address, unless you want me to send it to the embassy?'

He was looking less than calm and assured now.

'No, no. Don't send anything to the Embassy.' He fumbled in his jacket pocket and handed me a card. 'This is my address please. Send it by special courier marked for my attention. When will you do this, Norman?'

'I'm seeing my lawyer this afternoon,' I said, reaching for the teapot.

'Here let me pour that for you. Shall we order something to eat? I would love to hear more about your career in the RAF.' He looked at his watch again.

I didn't need a second invitation to talk about my RAF days, and I had a bit of time on my hands. Not that I was a fighter pilot or anything glamorous like that. I probably wouldn't be here today if I was. As I told Mr Sharma, I was part of the ground crew that kept the planes flying. You don't hear much about us when they talk about the Battle of Britain. They'll tell you all about Squadron Leader Bader and his pilots in 242 squadron who kept knocking the Messerschmitts out of the sky, but if me and my mates hadn't worked day and night to repair their planes when they landed full of holes, they wouldn't have been up there in the first place.

'You knew Douglas Bader?' Mr Sharma asked.

'Oh I knew him alright,' I said. 'He swore at me terribly when I told him once that we'd run out of a particular spare part for one of his Hurricanes. "Just tell the b... Air Ministry that the Luftwaffe will be sightseeing over London tomorrow if they don't get me those parts," he said, only a bit richer than that. It was me who had to tone his message down a bit and tell the sergeant on the line to get the parts to us or there would be hell to pay.'

I had ordered a pork pie as I was feeling a bit peckish and Mr Sharma was eating some fruit.

'You mentioned that your father was not wanting you to join the RAF, but he must have been proud of you in the end,' he said.

I could see my Dad, just then, when I told him I was

joining up. He just gave me one of his cold stares and wiped his hands on his cloth.

'There was no war on when I enlisted,' I told Mr Sharma. 'I wanted to see the world. I was young and had only seen our backyard and the garage where I worked.'

'Did you travel very much?' he asked, looking at his watch again.

'As a matter of fact, my first real posting was only seven miles from where I lived.'

He chuckled. 'You must have been disappointed.'

'Not really. I used to come home at weekends and that's when I met my wife. She was right there on my doorstep. I didn't need to see foreign parts after that. She was my world.'

He was about to ask me another question when I noticed how late it was getting. 'Is that the time? I'd had better be going or I won't get that contract done,' I said struggling to my feet.

'This time I am sure you will enjoy a ride in my car to wherever you want to go.' Mr Sharma waved to Kumar who was still waiting patiently outside.

That made it a bit tricky. I had actually arranged to meet someone in this very pub, but I didn't want them to know that.

'That's very kind but I can manage. I will just use the facilities and then I will be on my way.'

We said our goodbyes and I shuffled as fast as I could to the toilet. My legs had been crossed for some time.

~

It always takes me a while in the toilet these days. It's more difficult getting everything up and down and back together when your fingers are stiff and your joints don't bend. When I finally emerged, there was Billy, my great nephew, standing at the bar looking towards the door. I hadn't seen him for years but I'd recognise him anywhere. There was quite a lot of Chinese about Billy. His father, Ron had been a naughty boy with an immigrant farmworker called Li Wan and Billy was the result. To Ron's credit, he looked after the boy when his mother turned to prostitution in London and Billy grew up as a member of his family. You'd think he was one of us to hear him speak, except he had narrow eyes and a round face that looked as though someone has pushed it in, a bit like an owl's.

'Hello young man,' I said, coming up behind him.

'Uncle Harry!' he wheeled round.

I'd got so used to being Norman, I'd almost forgotten my real name. I looked round anxiously in case Kumar was still lurking in the corners. I put my finger to my lips.

'I'm Norman when I'm in London,' I said quietly. 'In any case, I'm your Great Uncle.'

He glanced around the pub too but it was empty except for the barman and he was reading a book.

'What's this all about then?'

We sat in the corner where I'd sat with Mr Sharma only a few minutes before and I told him everything.

I didn't know why I trusted him, especially as his brother was a policeman on the case, but I did. Betty always had a soft spot for Billy. She said he had a respect for older people that some of the young ones in our town never had. She had a soft spot for his mother too, even after she had gone on the game in London.

Billy was the only person I had told the whole story to and it was a great relief to get it off my chest. He listened carefully, nodding and asking the odd question or two. He asked me to describe Mr Sharma in some detail and scribbled some notes in a little book. I showed him the address card.

'Julius Sharma, Special Envoy,' he read. 'Sounds a bit of a mystery man. I'll run a check on him.'

'I was going to ask you about that. What exactly is it that you do?' Brian had told me that he was involved in legal work but that was as much as I knew.

'I find missing people, or at least I try to. These days it's getting more and more difficult. The streets are so full that it's difficult to tell the legit newcomers from those hiding from something or someone.'

'You mean you're after the illegal immigrants?'

'No, I leave that to the Home Office. I'm looking for young people that run away from home, for good reason or bad, and their parents ask me to find them.'

'How'd you get into that line of work? I thought you trained as a lawyer.'

'I did go to law school, but I discovered my face didn't fit into conventional legal circles so I never did finish my training. I dropped out and lived rough for a while. That's when I met other young people who had left home.'

'So you're a poacher turned gamekeeper?'

'I try not to be. People don't just leave home for no reason. Some have been abused or worse by their own parents. Others just fall in with the wrong crowd, get into drugs and it's downhill from there. They're the ones I go after.'

'Talking of missing people, do you ever hear anything from your mother?'

'No,' he said abruptly.

'I just thought you may have bumped into her when you were living on the streets.'

I felt myself go red as I said that. Maybe he never knew what his mother did for a living. I quickly changed the subject.

'Anyway never mind that, who pays you for finding these people?'

'Relatives, friends. Not always the parents because often as not they are part of the problem. Often it's the grandparents.' He stirred his tea and smiled. 'But I've never been commissioned by a Great Uncle before. What do you want in this agreement with Mr Sharma?'

'Nothing too complicated. I want him to give Bituin back her job and to drop any charges against her for taking his car. Most of all, I want his son to stop pestering and abusing her. Then I'll send her back to them.'

'I'm happy to draw up a contract, Uncle Harry...' He stopped and looked around guiltily. 'I mean Norman. But it might not carry much weight. What's to stop them tearing it up once she's back in their house and carrying on like before?'

I hadn't thought of that.

'I always thought a man's word was his bond especially if he signed something. Mr Sharma seems a respectable sort of man and now I've told him what his son gets up to, I would have though he would want to stop it.'

'Let's hope so. You certainly can't hang onto this girl forever without someone finding out.'

I didn't want to be home after dark, so I asked Billy if he could get a taxi for me. We shared it as far as the station.

'I forgot to ask,' he said folding down the seat opposite me. 'What's the name of Mr Sharma's son so I can put it in the agreement?'

That stumped me. 'I'll ask Bituin when I get home and give you a ring,' I said.

~

I fell asleep for most of the train ride home, and I was still drowsy when the taxi dropped me off at the gates of my house. They had been pushed open which was a bit odd as I had left them closed. I found something even more strange when I reached the front door. It was swinging open and splinters of glass lay on the floor.

CHAPTER 7

The Break-In

I stood there for a few moments, taking in the mess. The drawer of the cabinet by the wall had been thrown on the floor, its contents scattered everywhere. I pushed past the debris into the sitting room which had received the same treatment: everything – paper, books, cutlery, you name it – all over the carpet; drawers thrown out of the sideboard, bookshelves emptied; ornaments from the mantelpiece smashed in the hearth.

'Bituin!' I shouted. 'Where are you?'

The dining room door was open; the no-entry sign to Betty's memorial that I had carefully written lay trampled on the floor. I wheeled in with my walking frame, pushing past the clothes and blankets strewn all round.

'Bituin!' I called again.

Tears blurred my vision as I surveyed the mess. I sat down on the sofa-bed, unable to take in any more. When I was younger, I probably would have taken a setback like this on the chin, worked out what to do and got on with life. Not any more. That's another thing that's changed since I've got older. I cry more. When I saw Betty's winceyette nightie and hairbrush thrown onto the floor, her handbag emptied and dressing-table overturned,

I sat on the sofa and sobbed. It was as if someone had desecrated her grave.

I must have sat there for a good ten minutes, blubbering and sniffing, before I could pull myself together. A picture of Betty lay broken, face up on the floor. She was looking at me through the cracked glass, her lovely face smiling under the wide-brimmed, floppy hat she kept for weddings.

'You wouldn't be grinning like that if you could see what's been going on here,' I told her, wiping my eyes on a handkerchief.

'What exactly has been stolen?' she asked.

She was always one for the practicalities when things went wrong. That made me stop wailing and start thinking. The TV and the fridge were still there. I looked into our bedroom; the bottom drawer where I kept my spare cash had been turned out but the money had been thrown on the floor with all my socks. Not a penny had gone.

'They weren't thieves,' Betty said. 'They were looking for something – or someone. Found her too, didn't they? I told you that girl would cause you nothing but trouble if you hung onto her.'

She was right. They must have come for Bituin. But why did they wreck the place before they took her away? That ruled out the police.

Whoever it was, must have known she was here. It was odd that they'd come when I was out of the house because I hadn't told anyone where I was going, not even Bituin. The only person who knew I was in London was...

I suddenly saw a picture in my mind of Mr Sharma looking at his watch.

You silly old fool! He was keeping you talking while he had the house searched. It was all a ploy to snatch Bituin away and I'd fallen for it. All those questions he and Kumar had asked about my journey to London came flooding back to me. Mr Sharma knew exactly where I lived once I'd told him that it was my house that the Mercedes had crashed into. It took two to three hours in a fast car from London, but that still gave them plenty of time to get here and do their nasty work before I got home.

Betty was livid. 'Don't just sit there, Harry. Call the police.' She was right, I should call the police, but what could I tell them? That I had been harbouring a young girl who had been seized and taken back to her rightful household?

I couldn't face the clearing up. I needed some fresh air. It was dark outside and I could feel the breeze through the open door. I stood there, taking in deep breaths on the doorstep, looking out at my drive and the gates that the Merc had hit. What had happened since that night didn't seem real any more. It must have been a dream. I'd felt alive for a few days, caught up in the excitement of it all. Now I was back where I was before, miserable and alone, too old to do anything about it.

I just hoped they hadn't smashed the bottles of morphine.

A movement in the garden caught my eye. The cover on the campervan was lifting, flapping in the breeze. Maybe they'd broken into the campervan too. I was about to shuffle back inside and put the kettle on, when I heard a low call from the garden.

'Harry? Mr Harry? Is that you?'

I peered into the dark.

'Who's there?'

I waved my hands at the security light and once it had flashed on, I could see her slight frame, half hidden behind the van.

'Bituin? It's OK. It's me.'

She ran across the lawn and fell into my arms with such force that I staggered back to keep my balance.

'I thought they'd taken you,' I said, feeling her silky hair tickle my chin.

'Oh no, Harry. I was in campervan when I hear someone breaking front door. I lock myself in there until they go.' Her eyes were wide like saucers and she was trembling.

'Don't you worry. They've gone. You're safe now,' I said, wondering what she was doing in the campervan. 'Did you see them?'

'Heard glass smashing so I hide until I hear car start outside. I look and see black van drive off. I see front door is broken so I stay in campervan in case they come back.'

'You did well to keep out of their way. I don't think they're very smart the way they wrecked the house.'

She seemed to notice the mess for the first time. 'Oh Harry, so sorry to cause you trouble. Don't worry. I clear up.'

With that she jumped up and started to put the house back together. I didn't stop her, even though she put the spoons where the knives should go and my books in the CD cabinet. I was too tired to help. I did make her a cheese sandwich which she munched very gratefully. I don't think she'd eaten all day, cooped up in the campervan.

She saw me nodding off in my chair. 'Time for bed, Harry. I finish cleaning your room.'

'Thanks. I think I will lie down for a bit. It's been quite a day.'

I read the paper in bed listening to her scurrying around the house, wondering where she was putting everything. It went quiet and I was dozing off when I heard a tap on the door.

'Harry, you awake? Can I come in please?'

I sat up and switched on the bedside light as she perched on the end of my bed, holding her pillow.

'Can I sleep on floor please? I'm frightened on my own with broken door.' Tears rolled down her pretty little face.

'Bless you,' I said. 'Of course you can sleep in here. We'll lock the bedroom door to make sure we are both safe.'

I looked down at the threadbare carpet on the floor. I'd spent several hours sitting on that floor waiting for the paramedics to pick me up, so I knew how hard it was. Bituin was looking for somewhere to put her pillow.

'You can't sleep down there. There's plenty of room in this big bed.' I glanced at the picture of Betty on my bedside table. I turned it round to face the wall. 'You can sleep on Betty's side. She doesn't need it any more.'

Bituin looked relieved. 'Oh thank you. I sleep on floor but prefer bed.' She turned down the sheet but stopped before she got in, putting her hand on her mouth, giggling. 'I run away from man in bed.'

It took a while for the penny to drop, then I chuckled. 'Don't you worry about that! I won't be asking for any happy ending.'

91

~

It had been many years since Betty had told me that she could no longer cope with my urges; not with her arthritis. Which was just as well, because by then I wasn't really having urges any more. I must confess, though, I did take in the sweet smell of Bituin's hair on the pillow beside me. I would have to choose my words very carefully when I told Betty about this. She had never let me forget about the Woman's Institute affair. Not that I had done anything naughty. It was just the way it looked. I was doing these demonstrations of the latest Calor Gas cooking equipment to the ladies of the WI just after the war. 'My old ladies' I used to call them when I came home late. They were using paraffin stoves out in the villages which made a terrible smell and were forever blowing out. So they were very impressed when I showed them the latest gas technology. There was a waiting list for the new ovens and they couldn't do enough for me to get themselves higher up the delivery schedule. I used to bring home all types of farm produce: strawberries, apples, cauliflowers, legs of pork, even whole chickens. Betty was happy at first because it helped the housekeeping money go further. That is, until she met one of the 'old ladies'. We were at the Saturday market and Betty was over at a stall picking some potatoes when this WI lady spies me and sidles over. I don't think she'd seen Betty because she got in quite close and said: "That was a wonderful talk you gave last week, Harry. I do hope we will see you again soon," and other nice, smarmy words.

She was very presentable and knew how to use her assets to the full, if you know my meaning. I knew what she was up to; she just wanted to make sure I had her on the top of my list.

Betty didn't see it that way. "I thought you said they were old ladies. She wasn't old. Bold maybe, but not old," she said. She never let me forget that. Whenever I got chatting to a younger woman, she'd always say: "Another one of your old ladies, Harry?" She knew that I never really looked at anyone else but she always liked to have something up her sleeve to keep me in line. So I knew I'd never hear the last about this young woman in my bed, slim brown shoulders peeping out of the sheets.

~

I woke before Bituin and crept out of the bedroom. There was something I had to do so I got dressed and had my breakfast. As soon as the clock said it was 8am I was on the phone.

'Morning Billy. I hope it isn't too early. There's been a few developments my end and I need your advice.'

He whistled when I told him what I had found on my return home.

'I did some checks on Mr Sharma after you left,' he said. 'It seems he is not quite as respectable as he makes out. He's from a family that owns a company that the City would say has a certain reputation.'

'What sort of reputation?'

'Some business owners spend more on bribery than they do on advertising and their employment practices are dubious, to give it a polite word. Mr Sharma's connections seem to fall into this category. They have a reputation for not doing things strictly by the rules.'

'I see. Have they ever been caught for anything?'

'Nothing's ever been proven but they have been accused of using child labour,' he said.

'Blimey. No wonder his son is free and easy with the women.'

'It means your agreement isn't going to be worth the paper it's written on.'

'So what do you suggest I do instead?'

Billy made a sucking noise on the phone. 'Something's not right here. I don't understand why they would ransack your home looking for a girl who, on the evidence we have, means nothing to them. There has to be more to this than just a dispute between a lecherous son and an immigrant servant.'

'I did wonder why they searched for her in tiny drawers and small cupboards,' I said.

'Exactly. They were looking for something else. I'd advise you to call the police, Harry. Let the processes of law deal with it. You're too old to be mixed up in something as sinister as this.'

Too old! That did it. I could have told Billy that being old meant I was exactly right to be mixed up in this. I wasn't bothered what happened to me. They could come and finish me off for all I cared. Anything but go back to how I was. All I knew was that a poor girl had been treated badly, and I'd promised her I wouldn't call the police. If talking to Mr Sharma face to face hadn't sorted it out, I would just have to find another way.

'I can't do that Billy. They'd have her on the next flight home,' I said.

'That might be the best thing for her.'

I doubted that. And I knew it would not be the best thing for me.

'I'll think about it Billy. In the meantime, why don't we play Mr Sharma along a bit? Send him the agreement as we arranged and pretend nothing's happened. You never know, he might come round to my way of thinking. Perhaps it wasn't even him that trashed the house.'

Billy sighed and I could tell he was not happy. 'I'm worried about your safety. You're not dealing with ordinary people, Harry. I'm not even sure that Bituin has been straight with you. It seems odd that they should go to such extremes to get her back.'

I had been thinking about that too but I'd learned to trust my stomach more than my head about people. If my gut told me someone is a wrong-un, I was usually right. And my gut was telling me that Bituin was an innocent young girl who deserved better than what she was getting, although I was having more and more doubts.

'Let's give it one more go, Billy, before we call in the police. Just for me.'

'It's for you I would like to call in the law. But if that's what you want, I will continue to act on your instructions. Did you get the first name of Mr Sharma's son?'

'Vishal; he's called Vishal Sharma.' That was a name I would not forget in a hurry.

~

When I put the phone down, I thought about what Billy had said. Betty had said the same thing too: call the police. I stared at the receiver. One call and I wouldn't have to worry about this any more. Brian and his friends would take over and I could relax. And do what? Watch TV? In a home? Not likely.

'Morning, Harry. Would you like tea?'

She stood there in the doorway in bare feet and Betty's green shirt. My heart skipped a beat. She took me right back to my courting days when Betty would flit about the house in her nightie. Lovely it was. I wasn't going to hand her over whatever the consequences.

'I'd love a cuppa,' I said. 'I was just thinking we ought to go on a trip.'

Bituin looked puzzled. 'You mean shopping trip?'

'No, a proper trip. Away from here. Take a few days over it. Go somewhere nice in the campervan.' I even surprised myself when I said that. I hadn't stayed a night away from my bungalow for over ten years or more.

Bituin clapped her hands and giggled. 'Oh yes, Harry! Can I drive?'

'Once we are away from here and no-one knows who you are, you can drive as much and as far as you like,' I said.

CHAPTER 8

The Journey

Betty surprised me when I announced the next morning that I was going away in the campervan. She didn't argue about the trip, nor why I was taking an attractive, young lady with me. She just worried about the house. She always liked to have things ship-shape before we went away. It sounds daft I know but our home was always more tidy when we weren't there than when we were. Before we left for a holiday, the garden had to be up to date: lawns mowed, hedges cut, roses pruned, not a weed in sight. Inside, everything had to be pristine.

'I hope you're going to clean up all the mess before you go and get the front door fixed.' That was all she said when I told her that Bituin and I had to move out for a while. That was her way. When she knew I had made up my mind up about something she disagreed with, she didn't argue for long. She just became morose and brooded on it. If this trip went wrong, she would remind me for years that she had told me so, but in the meantime she prompted about all the little jobs that needed doing before we left.

'Don't forget to cancel the milk and tell the neighbours to keep an eye on things,' was her final instruction.

I had no intention of telling Doris of my plans, but, to

my surprise, she telephoned me early that day and asked me to call round. I'm glad I did because she had some very interesting news.

'Come in Harry,' she said, after I had cautiously rung her bell. 'I need to talk to you about this.' She pointed at a sticker on her door window that said: 'Neighbourhood Watch'.

'Oh yes. What's that?'

'It's designed for people like you and me. Vulnerable, older members of the community who can watch out for each other and report anything suspicious,' she said, marching along the corridor, expecting me to follow.

I always hesitated at Doris's threshold wondering what to do about her thick, white carpet. Should I keep my shoes on and risk soiling the pristine pile, or take them off with the possible embarrassment of a hole in one of my socks? I put one foot on her carpet and lifted it up quickly to see if it had left a mark. It hadn't; I kept my shoes on. She bustled into her sitting room – or lounge as she likes to call it – and stood expectantly by the window.

'Something suspicious like that,' she said, pointing her walking stick into the distance.

I shuffled closer to the window and peered out. A man was standing by his dog, plastic bag at the ready, as it did its business underneath a tree.

'You mean Fred Alvey's dog?' I asked.

'No, no, not the dog. The van.' She thrust her stick against the window pane under my nose. 'Over there.'

My eyesight is none too good, but I could make out a dark blob that merged into the bushes and trees of the little lane. It had the same shape as one of those white vans that you see all over the place, except it was black.

'Perhaps the farmer has got himself a new truck,' I suggested. The lane did lead to a farm after all.

'Farmers don't drive around in shiny black vans,' she said, flopping down into an arm chair.

'How long has it been parked there?'

She reached for a notebook on the low table, or coffee table as she calls it although she never drinks coffee. Licking her fingers, she flicked through the pages. 'First sighting 15.00 hours, Tuesday 31st March. VW Transporter van, black with no markings, parked in Burley Way. Two male occupants of van walked to number 4.'

I was all ears now. 'What did they do next?' I asked.

She looked at me blankly. 'I thought you could tell me. That's your address, Harry.'

I nearly told her that I did know my own address but I held my tongue. 'I must have been out. I didn't see them,' I said.

She looked at her little book again. '15.28 hours van departed. 19.32 hours resident of number 4 Burley Way returned home in taxi.' She peered at me over the top of her glasses. 'Was anything stolen?'

'No, nothing I've noticed,' I was relieved I didn't have to lie about that. 'Did you get a good view of these two men?'

'Unfortunately not. I didn't have my field glasses with me when I first saw them, and they must have returned to the van when I was out of the room. I only just caught sight of the van as it departed. I didn't really think it was important until I saw you come home and realised that you had been out and they had been in the vicinity of your house for thirty minutes when no-one was in occupation. That's the sort of thing they train you to notice.' She must have noticed the puzzled look on my face. 'Neighbourhood Watch. You really should sign up.'

My brain was working overtime now. Whoever had wrecked my house was back and watching my every move.

'Perhaps they did take something and I just didn't notice. I'll go home and check.'

I turned to leave but a sudden thought struck me. I could hardly drive off in my van and have these villains following me. I had to shake them off somehow.

'Look Doris, I was going to tell you that I'm hoping to be away for a few days—'

'Exactly what you should do. Ask a trustworthy neighbour to watch your premises during any prolonged absences. That's what the manual says.'

'I see. What does it tell the neighbour to do if they see anything suspicious?'

'Make written notes of every detail, however trivial it may seem as it can provide a vital clue.' She waved her notebook at me. 'Which is what I have done.'

'Anything else?'

She looked quizzical.

'Does the manual say you should do anything other than just take notes?' I asked.

'Of course it does. If the circumstances warrant it, you should call the relevant emergency services.'

'Do you think the circumstances warrant us calling the police?' She wasn't the type to take orders from the likes of me so I had to be a bit careful how I said things.

'I thought of that of course, but I decided to wait and see if anything was missing from your house. As there isn't, we don't have anything substantial to report. They are doing nothing illegal. They could even be undercover police watching out for that missing Filipino girl.'

She had a point there. Whoever they were, I needed a diversion so I could get away without being followed.

'Perhaps we should go over there and ask them what they are doing?'

She looked horrified. 'Direct intervention is to be avoided at all costs in order to minimise the risk of personal injury.'

I was beginning to get tired of her manual. I would have to sort this out for myself.

'Right. I'll be going then. I'll let you know if anything's missing.'

'How long are you away for?' she called after me as I shuffled off.

'A few days. Depends on the weather,' I said. Maybe forever, I thought.

'Where are you going?'

I shut the door pretending not to hear.

~

The next day, I was ready. I found a blanket and draped it over my walking frame so that Bituin could scuttle along doubled over beside me and not be seen from the lane. We quickly crossed the lawn and she scampered into the van.

'Hide yourself on the top bunk,' I said and returned to

the house to do a final check. I was just securing the front door when I heard a familiar voice.

'Morning, Harry. It's your lucky day. You've got some post.'

I whirled round to see Ashleigh the postman fiddling with the gates.

'Wait there. I'm on my way out so I'll come to you.'

I didn't want him coming in too far so I almost ran towards him. My shoe must have hit a bump in the paving stones because the next thing I knew, I was falling headlong, my stick flying from my hand. Ashleigh, bless him, caught me in his big arms, my head banging into his chest.

'Steady on, Harry. There's no rush.'

I rested there, winded, for a few moments, glad of the comfort of his strong grip.

'Sorry Ashleigh, I'll have to get this pavement fixed,' I said, trying to stand.

'Are you alright? Let me take you in and make you a cuppa.'

'No I'm fine. Best be getting along. I'm going away for a while.'

'In that?' he asked, nodding towards the campervan. He must have noticed that I had taken the cover off.

'Yes, I thought I would have a little trip out now that spring is here.'

'Are you sure it is safe to drive a heavy van like that at your age?'

A thought struck me. 'Oh I'll be alright once I get going. Though you could give me a little test run if you've got time when you've finished delivering?'

He grinned. 'Love to. Always wanted a drive one of those. I'll be back in ten minutes.' He whistled merrily as he hopped back in his little red van.

I told Bituin to stay well-hidden during what I described to her as 'a test run'. She grimaced and wanted to leave immediately, but then she didn't know about the black van. I didn't have to look for it any more; I could feel it watching me, like a black slug eyeing up the cabbages.

'Why don't you drive it first?' I said to Ashleigh when he returned.

'I've always preferred these old machines,' he said beaming, jumping into the driver's seat, checking the controls.

Once we had pulled on to the road, I directed him towards the lane and asked him to drive slowly past the entrance. As we did, I could see the van facing us, ready to leave. I turned to see if it would follow.

It did.

'Give it some right foot, Ashleigh. Let's see how much power is left under the bonnet,' I said. He responded by revving so hard through the gears that I thought the bottom would drop out of the engine. The black van still loomed large in the rear-view mirror.

'Do you deliver to the estate, Ashleigh?' I asked.

'I wish I didn't. It takes up most of my time. Hundreds of houses in there. You can easily get lost if you don't know where you're going.'

'I haven't been there for a while. Can you give me a tour?'

Ashleigh gave me a tour alright. The estate was a giant maze of twists and turns and dead ends. London overspill they called it when it was first built after the war and Cockneys came by the thousand to get away from the dirt and smoke in London. They just kept adding more houses until we ended up with this giant puzzle of a housing estate. I asked Ashleigh to give my old campervan a good workout to make sure the steering and brakes were all in good order. He was soon throwing it around corners and tearing along streets with cars parked on both sides so you had to turn your wing mirrors in just to get through. Postmen certainly know their way round and when we had made one sharp corner, I asked him to turn immediately left again into a dead end. As we turned around in the circle at the end, I saw the black van race by at the top of the road. It hadn't seen us.

'Blimey, I've just seen the time. Best be getting back. I'd like to get away before the rush hour,' I said.

'Right you are,' said Ashleigh. He was obviously enjoying himself and had quite forgotten he was meant to be testing my driving. Once we had re-united him with his van, I climbed into the driver's seat and took the fastest route away from any built-up areas. I checked my rear-view mirror. The black van was nowhere in sight.

'You can come down now. We're on our way,' I shouted to Bituin, slipping the van neatly into third to accelerate up a hill.

'Where we go, Harry?' she asked, stretching herself in the back seat after her confinement in the roof space.

Whenever I went away with Betty, I would spend hours planning the route and wrote all the roads and mileages on a piece of paper so she could read it out for me as we went along. She was a good navigator, although we did occasionally have an unexpected tour of an industrial estate or a car park not on my list. Betty would blame my poor writing for that. I hadn't had time to give this journey that much thought.

'I thought we would head west where it's a bit more hilly.'

'I like to see all your country. Except London. Bad memories there.'

I fumbled beside my seat and pulled out a road atlas. 'Why don't you navigate? It's safe enough to sit in the front now.'

She looked intently through the pages, frowning. 'No satnav? Never use book like this.'

'Why do I need satnav when I've got a map? Anyway it can lead you astray. I read about this woman who drove off the side of the river when she arrived at the ferry because the satnav didn't tell her to stop.'

She had a good giggle at that. 'Perhaps I drive and you read map, Harry.'

Dusk was falling. I knew my old eyes wouldn't be able to read a map in this light.

'I'll just follow my nose. I know most of the roads round here. It's only when we get further away that I'll be struggling with all the new motorways they've built.'

Looking back, I should have told her about the black van that was still trying to find us. She seemed so happy to be on the road that it seemed a shame to ruin her mood. So I kept my worries to myself, constantly searching my rear-view mirror and the road ahead.

Every other vehicle on the road that evening seemed to be a van. I've never really noticed them before but they are everywhere; mainly white but plenty of blue, yellow, green, red, even brown ones. Have a look next time you're out for a drive and you'll be surprised how many there are when you are looking for them. I had tried to get a good look at the one that had followed me around the estate earlier, but what with my poor eyes and Ashleigh throwing us around the corners like Stirling Moss, all I saw was a shiny silver VW symbol on a black front grill.

It wasn't until I got onto a long straight stretch of road that I saw it again. It was two-way traffic and I am not the fastest of drivers so there was a queue of traffic waiting to overtake me. I tried to help them by slowing down and indicating left when the road ahead was clear. That was until that van filled my mirror. The setting sun caught the chrome on its grill. A silver VW sign on a black van. I gripped the steering wheel hard.

'Lay low for a bit would you, Bituin?'

'What's problem Harry?'

'Not sure. Just keep your head down.'

I accelerated, trying to leave it behind but my old vehicle could never out-run a modern van. Instead, I jammed on my brakes to see what it would do. Tyres squealed and the van behind lurched. I probably overdid the braking because I thought they were coming straight into the back of me. They were close enough for me to see anxious, angry faces in my mirror, a man with a peak cap at the wheel, a young lad beside him. The next thing I knew they were overtaking, lights flashing, a fist waving as they tore past.

'Sorry mate, wrong van,' I mouthed silently.

Poor Bituin looked terrified but she didn't complain;

she just sat very still and said nothing. Unlike Betty who was in my ear straight away.

'I told you. You're not up to this, Harry. Call the police and admit you've bitten off more than you can chew this time,' she said.

'I've got new dentures. I have to try.'

I felt shaky and we needed some fuel so I pulled into a service station. While I worked the pump, Bituin went to the toilet, or washroom as she liked to call it. I was at the till paying when she came up to me all excited.

'Look Harry. Satnav on special offer,' she pointed to a shelf. 'Very cheap.'

It was a lot more expensive than a road atlas, but I bought one for her. As Betty said, I always did have soft spot for the girls. She couldn't wait to tear the cardboard box open and get that gizmo working.

'Where we go Harry? I tell satnav.'

I thought of somewhere far away that Betty really liked. 'How about Wales?'

She tapped away at the machine. 'Any street name or postcode?'

'Can it take us to a campsite?'

She fiddled some more. 'Big list. Which one?'

'Try one near Bangor.'

She peered into the machine, and pressed a button. 'The route has been calculated. Please drive onto a digitised highway,' a voice said in a stern tone, like a headmistress.

Bituin clapped her hands, delighted and jumped up into the driver's seat.

'All working, Harry. We arrive in two hours, thirteen minutes.'

CHAPTER 9

The Business Plan

With Bituin driving, all I had to do was sit there and look about while the satnav said, "continue to follow the road," and "at the roundabout take the second exit." It didn't sound at all like Betty but it took me back to some of the journeys we had made together. When I used to deliver Calor Gas out to the villages, I did take her with me sometimes when she had a day off work. She got bored sitting in the cab while I made my visits.

'You would be round a lot quicker if you didn't spend so much time talking,' she'd say.

I had a reply for that. 'Good service starts with understanding your customer.'

'Doesn't mean you have to know all their business,' she'd muttered, but of course it did. It was lonely living on a farm and I didn't mind hearing how the rain had ruined the rhubarb or what the wind had done to their washing. By listening to their little tit-bits of news, I was keeping out the competition. Trouble was, of course, it was mainly the wives I met because the farmer was off on the land somewhere. Betty knew that. There was one in particular who would invite me in with more than a cup of tea on her mind. Whenever she got close, I could smell the cigarettes and alcohol on her breath and I had to make my excuses to get out of there quick.

I must have nodded off because the next thing I knew Bituin had stopped at a service station.

'Need rest and some food,' she explained.

I needed the toilet too so I took out the walking frame and went into the café with her. It was well past dinner time and the cooked food on display was congealed with old fat, making me feel sick at the thought of eating that. I lifted the seat of the walking frame to look in the compartment where I often kept the odd apple or packet of biscuits for a moment like this.

That's when I found the case. Or rather re-discovered it as I had originally found it in the Merc, but completely forgot about it. I pulled it out and sat down next to Bituin.

'This yours?' I asked, laying it on the table of the café. It was made of a tough-looking fabric, flat and quite small, the sort you had to tuck under your arm as it had no handle.

She stared at it, horrified. 'Where you get that Harry?'

'From that big car you parked in my front gates. You recognise it?'

'This belong, Mr Sharma. He always carry it himself. Staff always carry his bags but never this.'

'Well he lost it under the seat of his car. I found it when I checked to see if you had left anything in it before they towed it away. What does he keep in it?'

'Never see inside.'

We both stared at it, wondering what to do. I have always believed in returning anything you find to its rightful owner, but this seemed different. There was something about this whole business that I did not rightly understand. Maybe the case could tell us something. Besides, you have to open things up to find out where the owner lives if you want to return them.

I picked the bag up and examined the zip. There was a small lock on it so it could not be opened.

Bituin watched me poking at it. 'You want it open?'

'It's locked.'

She pulled a grip from her hair and took the case from me. A few tweaks with the hair grip and the lock was open. She pushed the case back towards me.

'Now open,' she smiled, waiting to see what I would do.

'Shame to waste that clever trick of yours,' I said, tugging at the zip.

I was expecting some paperwork or letters in the case, so what fell out onto the table surprised me. It was like a very small television set, a flat screen with white edges. It lay there looking at us, as we stared at it.

'Tablet,' announced Bituin.

'Wouldn't want to swallow that,' I said. She did her little girl giggle and gave me an explanation that I didn't really understand except that it was some kind of computer.

'Can you work it?'

She gingerly turned the thing towards her and pressed a button. The screen lit up and a box appeared.

'Locked. Need password,' she said.

Feeling disappointed, I had a rummage in the case to see if there was anything else inside. It was empty. I put the gizmo back, zipped up the case and returned it to the compartment in my walking frame.

'How many more miles does that machine of yours reckon we have to go?' I asked, when we were back in the van. She switched it on.

'62 mile. We arrive 22.05,' she announced.

'Quite late to find somewhere to park up. Best get going.'

~

The run around the bay in North Wales would have been lovely but it was pitch black outside with no moon to light up the water. Just like the time when I first visited this part of the world. War was looming and we had a joint exercise with the navy to give them practice at dealing with air attacks. We had orders to surprise our ships by coming in low over the hills as they anchored in the bay. It was us that got the surprise. We hit thick mist over the sea and couldn't even see the navy. One of our planes went into the briny and never came up, the crew of three with it. We didn't have satnav in those days.

I must have nodded off because the next thing I knew we had stopped and there was a buzzing in my ears.

'Satnav say we arrive at our destination.' Bituin announced.

When I wound down the window to see what was going on, the buzz became a blast of noise that hit me like a slap in the face. We were parked by a field outside a pub and a crowd of young people were chatting, laughing, dancing and falling about. The thump, thump of pop music came from a band in a barn with the doors wide open. Not my idea of fun but they were all enjoying themselves. Some of the girls must have been too hot because their skirts were nearly up to their waists.

'Can I help you, sir?' a polite voice said. I whirled round to see a burley young man watching me. He was dressed smarter than the others in a jacket and white shirt, his wavy hair greased up and gleaming in the bright lights from the pub.

'Do you work here?' I asked.

'I'm supposed to stop any trouble,' he said, grinning. 'So I'm hoping you are not going to start any.'

'The only trouble I'm likely to cause you is if I fall out of this van,' I said, opening the door and stretching my stiff old legs towards the ground.

'Let me help you down,' he said moving quickly towards me. 'It's an end-of-term student party here tonight which always tempts a few of the lads from town to try and crash the fun. That's when the trouble can start so it's my job to keep them out.'

'On your own?' I asked.

'I'm trained in the martial arts and if that's not enough I call the police.' He held up a phone in his hand.

I didn't hear the Welsh accent in his voice so I asked him if he was local.

'No, I hail from Bristol originally. I'm here at the university and when I need some money, which is most of the time, I work as a bouncer,' he said.

'A bouncer?' I'd never heard the term.

'Security guard for entertainment venues. We check everyone in and throw out anyone causing trouble.'

'I see. So what are you studying at university?' I asked.

'I.T.'

'I what?' I asked, reaching into the rear door of the van for my walker.

'Information Technology. Computers,' he said.

That was too big a coincidence to ignore. I probably shouldn't have trusted a complete stranger as I did at that moment but when you get as old as me, you want to get things done there and then. You never know if you will be around the next day to finish a job.

'I've got a little computer with me that we can't get to work.' I lifted the seat of my walking frame and pulled out the case. 'Could you have a look at it for me?'

'As a matter of fact I have a side line in repairing computers,' he said opening up the case and taking out the tablet. He turned it around and looked underneath before he pressed the start button.

'What's the password?'

'That's the problem. I don't know it.'

'And you can't ask anyone for it?' He was looking at me curiously.

'No, she's forgotten it.' Well, I couldn't tell him the truth now could I?

'Your friend in there?' he asked, indicating Bituin who was trying to remain inconspicuous in the cab.

I didn't want her drawn into this. 'No. My wife. She's back home and I need to use her… her tablet as you call it. I can pay you for it.'

That seemed to get his interest.

'Some places will charge you £100 or more to unlock this but I can do it for £40. I can't do it tonight though. Where are you staying?'

'I don't rightly know. Our satnav says this is a campsite.'

He laughed at that. 'That's the problem with satnav. It can't tell you when a campsite is being used for a birthday party. I don't think you'll find it very restful here.'

I looked around more carefully and saw the tents and the toilet block. We had found the campsite but he was right; we wouldn't be staying with this lot as neighbours.

'I tell you what. There's a caravan park near my flat. It's pretty empty at this time of year, so I am sure you can get in,' he said.

'How far away is that?'

'Not too far at all. In fact if you can hang on here for a while longer, you can give me a lift home and I will show you. I can sort out your computer in the morning and as you would be saving me a taxi fare, I'll do it for £35.'

We shook hands on that and he told me his name was Dan. I stood there, alone, listening to the music and the excited voices of the crowd shouting to each other, straining to make themselves heard above the noise of the band. I could make out some Welsh accents. I do like to hear that lovely lilt.

Soon after Betty died, I was introduced to a lady at a church tea party for bereaved people and she had that beautiful sing-song in her voice. I could have listened to her for hours.

When I asked her where she was from, she said: 'I'm from Wales.'

'Really!' I said, excited to meet someone from those parts.

She frowned. 'I think so,' she said. 'Yes, I'm sure I'm from Wales.'

'Whereabouts in Wales?' I asked.

She thought for a while and then smiled. 'I'm from Bangor,' she said.

'You're not!' I exclaimed. That was a coincidence; it was Betty's favourite town. Well, she nearly started crying.

'I thought I was,' she said. 'Are you sure I'm not?'

'No, no. You are, if you say so,' I said. 'It's just I've been there a few times and know what a nice town it is.'

When I went to the next tea party to hear her lovely voice again, she wasn't there. I was told she took a bus all the way to the coast one day and was lost for hours. Probably looking for Bangor. They put her into a home and I never saw her again. That put me off the vicar's tea parties.

'Harry, you alright?' Bituin was leaning out of the cab window.

'Yes, fine. I was just admiring these girls,' I said, noticing the goose-bumps on their arms and legs. 'They've such lovely voices.'

For some reason, she found that very funny and started giggling.

It was gone midnight when Dan showed us the way into the campsite. It was fairly deserted so we found a sheltered site close to the toilet block. My head was still buzzing from the noise and excitement of the party so I made a cup of hot chocolate before bed. We sat outside, Bituin and I, mulling over the events of the day.

'You have children, Harry?' she asked, suddenly.

'No,' I said, giving the reply I'd automatically used over

the years whenever this topic came up. 'Betty couldn't have any.'

I felt a pressure at the back of my eyes. I couldn't hide the truth anymore.

'That is, she had a baby when I was away in the war, but she didn't live long.'

It was out. I'd never told anyone before.

'Oh, Harry.' Bituin slipped her little arm in mine and put her head on my shoulder. I don't know why but I started crying, quietly at first then great big sobs. I put my head in my hands, I was shaking that much. I just couldn't stop, wondering about that poor little baby, all alone in a cold grave somewhere. Never went to see her, did I? Never told her I loved her even though we never met. I was so looking forward to seeing her when I got back. But she was gone, whisked away and put in the ground. I'd never find out where she was now, would I? Truth was I should have looked for her when it first happened. So sorry, little girl.

'I didn't mean to make you cry, Harry.' Bituin put her arm around me and gave me a squeeze.

I took a deep breath and dabbed at my eyes. 'Not your fault. I should have done that a long time ago.' I looked at the damp patch on my handkerchief. 'Seventy years these tears have been waiting to come out.'

'Your wife couldn't have any more children?' asked Bituin.

'I didn't get home for nearly a year after it – she –died. Heard about it in a letter sometime after D-day when I was in northern France.'

I could still see that crumpled piece of paper.

Dear Harry,

Sorry to tell you our baby died yesterday. The Doctor said she was born with malfunctioning kidneys. I didn't want to tell you bad news when you are so far away but no-one knows when you will be back. Love Betty

That's all she said; she never did write long letters.

Bituin took my handkerchief and wiped at some dampness still on my cheeks as I mumbled on. 'By the time I came home, Betty had put it to the back of her mind and we never did talk about it properly. I don't really know what went on even to this day. I did say once that maybe we should try for another child as everyone seemed to be having babies after the war. She just shook her head and said: "I can't go through that again." For a long time I thought she meant we couldn't have any more children, physically couldn't give birth to another one, so I didn't argue.'

I didn't know why this was all coming out but I couldn't stop myself. 'A lot later, Betty had just finished watching a television programme about babies when, out of the blue, she said to me: "Harry, why didn't you make me have another child?" Well you could have knocked me down with a feather when she said that. I realised for the very first time that when she'd said she couldn't have any more, she'd meant mentally, not physically. She couldn't face the thought of losing another one. It was too late of course. She was in her sixties by then. Pity, I would have loved a few children. Would have had grandchildren or great grandchildren about your age by now.'

Bituin's big eyes filled with tears and she wrapped both her arms around me to hug me tightly. I could feel her chest heaving as she had a good old cry too. We sat there for a few minutes holding on to each other until she pulled back and held me by the shoulders, looking into my eyes.

'There are plenty children for you to look after, Harry. My father dead, grandfather too. I need father like you.'

I felt better after that.

~

The campsite was quiet the next morning and we both slept late. We were still having breakfast around a foldaway table outside the van when I saw Dan striding towards us clutching the case.

'Morning, Dan. What have you found out for us?'

He unzipped the bag and put the computer on the table.

'I found out that your wife is a very cautious person,' he said. 'She fitted this with a number of security devices.'

I think he'd guessed that this was someone else's computer as he put a special emphasis on the word "wife".

'What does that mean?' I asked.

'It means I should have charged you more. It's taken me several hours to open it.'

Bituin was staring expectantly at the screen. 'What's on it?' she asked

'Actually not much,' he said, pressing a button and stroking the screen with his fingers. 'The biggest file was this presentation.'

A page with fancy edges opened up with a heading in large letters:

Investment Opportunity In The Human Asset Business

I can't remember much of the detail of what followed when Dan scrolled through the pages. What stuck in my mind was one slide that talked of:

> *Three Stages: the Acquisition,*
> *Movement and Exploitation of Assets*

Then there were lots of figures that talked about the profits in each stage. Finally, a heading claimed that:

> *Integration of the Three Stages*
> *Maximises Profits for Investors*
> *Return of $10 million for $1 million invested*

It was gobbledygook to me back then although I have since found out to my cost what it was all about.

'What do you think it means?' I asked, looking at Dan.

'It's a business plan presentation. Our management students do them all the time,' he said.

'What are these "human assets" it talks about? What sort of business is that?' I asked.

Bituin was glowering at the screen. 'Bad business. They buy and sell people.'

'Not here, they can't. William Wilberforce had the slave trade abolished in 1833,' Dan said.

'Not legal in Philippines either, but they do it. What does this say?' she asked pointing at a heading that said:

Appendix: Target Locations

Dan flicked the screen and a list of letters and numbers came up.

'Postcodes, like in satnav,' said Bituin.

'Yes,' Dan agreed. 'I recognise this one. It's my city.'

'I look up in satnav,' said Bituin, scrambling into the van.

A few moments later she handed Dan her little machine. He peered at it and smiled. 'It's the club district. I've worked in quite a few of these places. Tacky joints where the boys grope and the girls puke. Meat-markets all of them. Just don't go into the toilets unless you've had a tetanus jab.'

'What have they got to do with this… this business plan as you call it? It doesn't make any sense.' I put my mug down on the table with a bang. I never did like riddles.

Dan shrugged. 'To be fair, I'm not a business student. I just opened the computer for you. I didn't say I could do a full appraisal of what was in it.'

'I try another postcode,' said Bituin. She handed Dan the machine again. 'This one in same city. The Bollywood Bar.'

He chuckled. 'Interesting one this. It's for men in overcoats not students. It's run by a shady character they call the 'Mumbai Woman'. I've never managed to get any shifts there because they have their own team of bouncers from India that guard the place very carefully.'

The Indian connection grabbed me immediately. 'Perhaps we should visit the place and find out what this is all about.'

'If you're a fan of exotic dancing, you definitely should,' Dan said. 'But you had better take me for protection – and in case you have a heart attack.'

'Don't you need to be here, at university?' I asked.

'No, your timing is perfect. Term has just ended and I would not refuse a lift home in return for a tour of my local clubs, if that's what you want?'

Bituin looked worried but I was too old to hesitate.

'That's just what I want,' I said.

CHAPTER 10
The Club

Before we left the next day, I found a quiet spot in the campsite to talk to Betty. There was something else I needed to know about my daughter.

'Betty, why on earth did you give our little girl a boy's name?'

There was a long silence before she replied. 'It can be a girl's name as well, you know. My friend Ethel told me I was having a boy, and she was always right about these things. I only thought of boys' names, not girls'. When they asked me for a name for the birth certificate, the baby was already dead so I picked the one on my list that sounded most like a girl. They said Sam would do.'

That strange time was all coming back to me. 'I'm sorry Betty. I tried very hard to come home to help but we were fighting a war, no question of any leave. I suppose the name didn't really matter.'

'Remember what you used to say when we had an argument? "Let's sit down and talk about it together, before we go to bed." That's what you always said. But you hardly mentioned the baby, did you?'

I saw myself in that bleak airfield in France where I lived in a tent and worked every waking hour. 'I couldn't think of what to say. With the war on, it was hard to find somewhere quiet where I could write you a nice letter. My mind was full of keeping the aircraft flying.'

'And now it's full of someone else's problems.'

'Yes and I'm going to do something about them. I can't help you any more Betty and this is the next best thing.'

With that, I returned to the van and made ready to leave.

~

I would have liked to explore the mountains of Wales, just like Betty and I used to do. Instead, Dan guided us down the motorways to his home city so that we could reconnoitre the nightlife. I'd never had much time for clubs and bars; give me a cosy pub and a game of darts any day. Nightclubs spell trouble. Like the time, a few days after the end of the war, I was driving a Bedford truck around the old cobbled streets of Brussels. The lads in the back were getting a bit thirsty, so I stopped at this club. As soon as we went through the door, I knew there would be trouble. The place was packed with soldiers who were meant to be on the same side, but there was only a handful of girls. We were soon fighting each other. When I finally got my young lads out of there, all battered and bruised, I swore never to go near a nightclub again. And here I was following Dan to what he had described as a seedy joint with a walking stick in my hand – we had decided that a walking frame wouldn't make the right impression. We'd also decided it was safer to investigate the nightlife in the daylight so I'd taken a taxi from our new campsite just outside the city to meet up with Dan again in the morning.

I felt quite disappointed when we found the Bollywood Bar. No big signs, no neon flashing lights, just a solid door and two muscly blokes outside. Dan spoke quietly to them while they looked me up and down, smiling. He must have said the right thing because one of them opened the door and the other waved us through.

The step down into the darkness nearly caught me out but Dan grabbed my arm as I stumbled.

'You'll have to act more sober than that. They weren't going to let you in but I persuaded them that you would behave yourself,' he said, as he led me along a corridor towards a dusky lady in a bright, flowing dress who looked as though she could do with a good night's sleep. Another muscle man in a suit and dark glasses was next to her.

'That will be £20 please,' she said, almost smiling.

'What do we get for that?' I asked.

'One of you is getting to come in,' she said, the half-smile disappearing. 'It's £40 for two.'

'Any deductions for senior citizens?' I asked. The man with dark glasses took a step towards us and Dan nudged me, so I reached for my wallet and paid.

Another bouncer ushered us through some curtains and finally we were in. A sweet spicy smell hit my nostrils and jangling, eastern music filled my ears as I took in the view. I'd never seen anything like it. Rotating balls in the ceiling flashed multi-coloured lighting into different parts of the room. Behind a curved bar glowing with blue lights and chrome fittings, a handsome lad in a white frock was mixing drinks and wagging his head at two men perched on stools. Dan was tugging me in a different direction and I soon saw why. My mouth fell open when I saw the dancers. Lovely girls twirled and twisted lengths of brightly coloured cloth around themselves, giving brief glimpses of what was underneath, which seemed to be mainly naked skin. Quick as a flash, they spun the cloth back around themselves so you wondered if you had really seen anything as they gyrated about to the hypnotic music.

Dan found two chairs at a table near the dancers. A waiter hurried across as soon as we sat down. Dan ordered a beer and I asked for water.

'Is that still or sparkling water you will be drinking, sir?' the waiter asked.

'As it comes, from the tap,' I replied.

'I am sorry it is not coming from a tap sir. It is coming from a bottle. Still or sparkling water in a bottle.'

Why they have to put water in bottles these days when it comes out of the tap perfectly clean, I'll never know, but I ordered a bottle of sparkling.

'That will be £10 sir,' he said.

'I asked for a bottle, not a barrel,' I said.

Dan sputtered so I paid up and we settled back to watch the dancing. When I looked at the girls a bit more closely I saw they were not as Indian as I'd first thought. All six of them had fair hair and blue eyes. They had finished their wrapping and unwrapping routine and were using the lengths of cloth to wipe themselves, around their backs, over their chests, down to the waist and finally between the legs. It looked quite painful the way they pulled the material right up into their pants and slid it back and forth.

One girl in particular caught my eye. She had cropped

blonde hair and a snub nose, slim with not much of a figure, a sort of pixie look about her. I couldn't take my eyes off her to be honest, not because she had next-to-no clothes on but because she looked so out of place. She should have been in school not writhing about a length of cloth. Next thing I knew she was walking slowly towards me, one finger lightly touching her lips, an enticing look in her eyes that a youngster like her should never give to an old man like me. She wrapped an arm around my neck and slowly sat on my knees. That's more like a little girl, I thought, until she started wriggling her bottom around and jiggling up and down on my lap.

Her cheeks brushed my ear and I heard her whisper, 'You like me?'

A funny sort of question from someone you've only just met, but I was beginning to realise this was no ordinary place.

'You look like a very nice girl to me, but I'd rather you sat still and stop all this squirming around. You're hurting my legs,' I said.

She balanced herself on one of my knees and put her hand on my other leg, slowly drawing her fingers along my thigh.

'You like massage?'

I closed my legs to stop her hand going any further. 'You could rub my neck, that's a bit sore,' I suggested.

'Come,' she said taking my hand and pulling me to my feet.

Dan glanced in my direction although he looked more interested in a tall blonde who was curling her long legs around a pole, leaning her head back towards him. I winked to let him know I was alright, grabbed my stick and shuffled after the girl. She nodded to a bouncer who opened a side door that led into a run-down lounge like a waiting room at the dentists. Tightening her grip on my arm, she guided me past a few scattered sofas and chairs and through an arch. A board on a swing door announced: *Health Spa*. She held the door open for me and I walked towards a line of closed doors with glass windows and signs saying *Vacant* on them. She ushered me into the first one, changed the sign to *Occupied* and made me sit on a couch while she drew some brown curtains across the window. That felt more relaxing although too dark for me to see much.

'You my first customer so I give you massage for £30 instead of normal £50.' She had a foreign accent I couldn't quite place although it sounded similar to the Polish pilots I'd served with during the war.

I'd had a back massage for £10 only last year so her rate seemed a bit steep. 'That's more than I've paid before,' I said.

'If you regular customer here I do it for £25. I give you very special, happy ending.'

I knew what that meant and coming from a young girl like her it sounded quite shocking. It also told me there might indeed be a connection here to that specialist in happy endings, Vishal Sharma.

I held up my hands. 'No massage. No happy ending,' I said, reaching for my wallet. 'But I will give you £25 for a nice chat instead.'

She looked confused. 'Chat? What is chat? Never before asked for chat.'

'We talk. Get to know each other.'

I counted out the money and offered it to her. She looked around anxiously and then quickly tucked the notes into her bra.

'You must be cold dressed like that.' I took off my jacket. 'Here, take this.'

'No, this is what I must wear when I work. Why you want to talk?'

'I'm Harry by the way. What's your name?' I asked, offering her my hand.

She shook my hand lightly with her fingers. 'I am called Nadia.'

'Where are you from, Nadia?'

'I come from Romania.'

'Romania. I've never met anyone from Romania. Eastern Europe isn't it? What's it like?'

'Very beautiful country, mountains, beaches, forest.'

'Much to visit is there?'

'Many interesting things, castles, palaces, churches, old towns.'

I didn't really need to know all this but I could see she was relaxing now she was talking about her home.

'And which part are you from?'

'From the east, near border with Moldova. My family from there.'

'From Moldova? I definitely haven't met anyone from there. What made you leave such a lovely country and come here?'

'To work. There is no work for me in my country.' She looked at the floor, wringing her hands. 'I apply for job in UK,' she said, so quietly I could hardly hear.

'That's what I wanted to talk to you about.' I was beginning to feel a bit foolish talking to a girl dressed only in her underwear so I patted the couch next to me. 'Sit down.' She lowered herself slowly onto one end. 'You see, a friend of mine, not much older than you, has been offered a job to work in a bar like this one. She was working as a nanny for a Mr Sharma. You may know his son, Vishal?'

She stood up quickly, her small eyes staring at me intently. 'Your friend offered job by Vishal?'

'Yes. You know him? An Indian lad who can be a bit rough with women.'

'No, I don't know him.' She blinked rapidly and looked away.

'Pity. My friend doesn't know much about this line of work and she isn't sure she can trust him. Would you advise her to work here?'

Nadia looked shiftily around again. 'I arrive last month so cannot say.'

'I see, you're new. What did you do before?'

'Training. I train as teacher. Sports teacher.' She stood tall as she said that and I could see that she looked the sporty type with her slim body and short hair.

'What sports do you play?'

'Running. I was a runner.' The "r" rolled off her lips as though she was purring.

'There were some good runners from your part of the world in the old days. There was one who won all the medals in the Olympics soon after the war. What was his name now…?'

Quick as a flash, she added, 'Emil Zátopek. He won 5,000, 10,000 metres and marathon in 1952 Olympics.

I follow his training methods. Very strict, very tough.' Her eyes shone as she added, 'He was Czech. I want to win medal in athletics, like Zátopek. Romania only wins medals in gymnastics.'

'I'm not sure working here will help you to do that. How did you end up in this place?'

'No money for training so have to work abroad.'

'Couldn't you be a teacher here? There're plenty of jobs for good teachers, I'm sure.'

Her expression fell. 'I came here to be sports teacher. I was promised teaching job. But I have to work here first to pay off debt.'

'You haven't been borrowing money have you? That never did anyone any good.'

'Much to pay off so have to work very hard.' She looked at her watch, anxiously. 'Must go now and find next customer.'

I was feeling more and more uncomfortable about what this poor girl had let herself in for.

'Customer for what? What exactly is this job?'

'Hand job, with massage. They don't usually ask for – how you say – chat.'

The thought of her going back to that dance floor to entice more men into this so-called health spa, horrified me.

'How many of these jobs do you do every day?'

'Target is fifteen.'

'Each day?

She quickly turned and drew back the curtains. 'Time to go. No more chat.'

'I'll come back.'

'If you pay, I can chat,' she said.

~

I found Dan with a dancer on his lap, her cloth wrapped around both of them so I couldn't see what they were getting up to.

'Off that girl, young man. Time to go,' I said, tapping him firmly on the shoulder.

He shot up, looking guilty. 'To be fair, you had disappeared with one yourself,' he said, as we made for the exit.

'Just for a chat. No hanky-panky. We're not here for that.' I was feeling sick in the stomach and wanted to get out fast.

When we made it back to the street, I stood still taking in deep breaths to cleanse myself of that evil den.

'You alright?' Dan asked, taking my arm.

'Do you know what they do in there?' I asked him.

'Who?'

'The girls. That's no health spa. It's what my commanding officer referred to as a house of ill-repute. He warned us to keep out of them when we got to France as the Germans would have given all the girls the clap before they left.'

Dan whistled. 'They keep that quiet. It's not one of the better-known knocking shops in town.'

'You mean there are others like this?'

'Some, yes. As a bouncer, you get to hear about them.'

'I thought it was illegal. Why don't the police put their foot down and stop it?' I asked, shuffling off towards the taxi rank.

'As long as there's no problems, the fuzz don't bother

any of the clubs or bars. That's why they employ me. No rumbles inside, no trouble outside and the boys and girls in blue walk on by.'

'Well, we've got to do something,' I said, as I hauled myself into the back of a cab. 'I am going back there tomorrow. Can you come?'

'If you're paying, I'm playing. What time?' he said.

'Same as today,' I said. Dan had said it would be safer at lunchtime. It made it all the more shocking to know this was going on in broad daylight.

The taxi dropped me at the campsite on the outskirts of town where we had parked the camper and Dan continued on his way home.

Bituin waved from the doorway of the van. She looked relieved to see me. 'What you find out, Harry?'

'Enough to make my skin crawl,' I said. I didn't have time to tell her more because the phone rang.

'Hello, who's calling?' Luckily, I didn't say my real name when I pressed the button.

'Hello, am I speaking with Norman, please?' The voice sounded familiar.

'Norman?'

'Yes, Norman. This is Kumar who is speaking with you, assistant to Mr Sharma.'

The penny dropped. 'Oh hello Kumar. Yes, this is Norman. What can I do for you?'

'Good afternoon, Norman. I hope you are well and enjoying this fine weather.'

I had to stop myself from telling him that I was indeed enjoying the weather out and about in my campervan. 'Yes it's quite nice thank you. How can I help?'

'Mr Sharma was wondering when he might be receiving the agreement you discussed,' he said.

'You haven't had anything from my lawyer?'

'No, we are not receiving a thing from you since our meeting in London. Mr Sharma is becoming anxious that you return to him what is rightfully his.'

'I see. I will call my lawyer to remind him,' I said.

'Will you be letting us know when to expect the return of Mr Sharma's goods?'

I had assumed until this point that we were discussing Bituin when we talked of returning something to Mr Sharma. But it suddenly struck me that "Mr Sharma's goods" could be his computer. Now that I had seen what was on it, I could understand why he might be anxious to get it back.

'Yes, I will let you know.'

As soon as he was off the phone, I fumbled in my bag for Billy's number. He didn't answer when I called so I left him a message and my mobile number.

Bituin was looking anxious. 'I can't help overhear. You talk to man named Kumar? Mr Sharma had a man called Kumar.'

'Yes, that was him.' I had quite forgotten how little I had told Bituin about what I had been up to on her behalf. She was looking at me, expecting some sort of explanation. 'I am trying to talk to Mr Sharma into releasing you from your contract with him so you can find other work here.'

'Oh you so kind to me Harry. Treat me just like daughter.'

That gave me a warm feeling inside. 'There's another

daughter we have to help too. She has one of the jobs Vishal earmarked for you.'

When I told her about Nadia, she shook her head in disbelief. 'Poor girl. She got trapped. Why she not run away?'

'She mentioned a debt she had to repay. I am going back to find out more. I wouldn't be surprised if that… that computer thing we watched… what did Dan call it?'

'Business plan?' she prompted.

'Business plan, that's it. I wouldn't be surprised if that business plan is something to do with the debt she's been saddled with. You know what these commercial types are like, always borrowing more than they can ever repay.'

'You go back to club? You sure it's safe, Harry? Not a place for…' she hesitated.

'An old man like me? No it's not, and it's not a place for a young girl like her either.'

She gave me a hug which I took as her blessing for my plan. Not that I had a plan, just a feeling in my water that I was on to something.

~

I was tired from the exertions of my outing so I had a little nap in the dying sunshine of a warm, spring day. It was getting dark when I woke and Betty was in my head. I was sitting in a deckchair outside the van and Bituin was cooking up something inside. Stir fry by the smell of it: plenty of onions and chopped courgettes.

I told Betty I had met this girl who was down and out and needed help.

'Not another girl to take advantage of you. Where did you meet this one?' she asked.

I was hoping she wouldn't ask that. 'At a club. She's a sort of dancer.'

'Back to your old habits. You met me at a dance.'

'I know.'

'I've always wondered what would have happened if I hadn't lived further away than Margaret.'

We'd had this conversation several times before so I knew what she was driving at. I'd met Betty at a dance hall with her friend Margaret and we had got talking, as you do, and they both looked quite nice so I had asked if I could walk them home. If it was today, they would probably get a taxi home and I would have to go on the Internet to meet them again. But in those days you walked someone home; that's how you got to know them. Except that I was walking two of them home and I didn't get much of a word in. They were so busy chatting about this dress and that hairstyle that it didn't matter if I was there or not. You can imagine my relief when after about a mile, Margaret said: 'I live here so I'll say goodnight.'

'I live further on if you can manage it,' Betty had said. We were walking in the opposite direction to my house but I didn't mind. It gave me a chance to have a chat with her. I can't even remember what we talked about. Betty probably can. All know is that when we reached her house, she gave me a little kiss and agreed to meet me again. It was over two miles back, but I ran and skipped all the way.

Whenever Betty and I talked about that night, she always asked me the same question: if she had lived closer than Margaret, would I have walked Margaret home, given her a little kiss and asked to see her again?

I stuck to my story. 'I would have walked her home, of course. I couldn't just leave her in a dark road on her own, could I? But I'd have known your address from where we dropped you off, and I would have been calling on you the very next day.'

'Yes, so you've said. But when the three of us went out for a picnic together, you seemed to spend more time talking to Margaret than with me, even though we'd been together several months by then.'

'I didn't want her to feel out of place, like a gooseberry,' I said.

'Even after we were married, you kept asking her round for tea.'

'I thought you'd want to keep up with your old girlfriends.'

'Margaret wasn't a particular friend of mine. I didn't normally go out with her; it was just that none of my other friends were free the night of the dance. I told you at the time but you didn't seem to listen. Just kept on inviting Margaret round. And now you tell me you've got involved with another young girl?'

'Not exactly involved. She's got herself into a downward spiral and no-one is going to pull her out of it. I'd like to help her, that's all.'

'Do you remember how you helped Margaret that time she came round and said she felt stuck in a rut, always doing the same things. You told her to go and see the world, look for the bright lights; do you remember?' Betty asked.

I had forgotten about that, although I do remember Betty looking pleased when Margaret told us she'd got a job in London.

'Maybe you should tell this Nadia something similar. She's in a rut and she needs to get out and do something different.'

My phone rang. It was Billy.

'Glad to hear from you Harry. I've been worried about you.'

I'm alright. Listen, Mr Sharma is after that contract. Have you had time to do it yet?'

There was a pause. 'Where are you Harry? I sent it to your home address for your approval days ago, recorded delivery.'

'Ah. I'm not there. Taking a few day's holiday. With the family.'

'Holiday? What have you done with the Filipino girl?'

'She's the family. I couldn't leave her behind, could I?'

'Harry, I warned you about getting too involved in this affair. It sounds as though she is manipulating you. You haven't given her any money have you?' He sounded quite agitated.

'Billy, when you get to my age, you don't mind being manipulated so long as you enjoy it. Which I am. And she hasn't asked for any money.'

'She will. Believe me, she will. I have a suspicion she may be in league with this Mr Sharma and his friends to relieve you of as much of your wealth as they can.'

'Well they've picked the wrong person. There's not much wealth they can relieve me of.'

Eventually, Billy agreed to send Mr Sharma the

agreement directly. I didn't need to see it; I wouldn't understand it anyway.

'Let me ask you about something else,' I said. 'Can someone from Romania work in this country without a special visa?'

'They can now. Romania joined the European Union in 2009. Why do you ask?'

'There's a sports teacher, I know, who's ended up in the wrong type of work over here. Fallen in with a bad crowd. Can you help her find a better job?'

'There is a high demand for qualified teachers especially if she is prepared to work amongst disadvantaged communities. If she ticks the right boxes, I can introduce her to organisations that can help her,' he said.

'What sort of boxes do you mean?' I asked.

'Speaks reasonable English, doesn't have a criminal record, knows who the Prime Minister is, that sort of thing.'

'I'm going to see her tomorrow,' I said. 'I will tell her about the Prime Minister.'

CHAPTER 11
The Escape

I can't take Betty her cup of tea in the morning or give her a little peck on the cheek like I used to, but I still look forward to our chat first thing. It keeps us close together. Or so I thought.

'I feel as though I am losing you, Harry,' she said the next day. Just like that; no word of warning.

'Losing me? Whatever makes you think that?'

'I can't seem to get through to you any more. You've got so much on your mind, like you're back at work.'

Now she mentioned it, it did feel a bit like that. I had something to do, something to scheme about, find the best way forward.

'Don't you worry, this will all blow over soon enough and I'll be back home. It won't be long before everything is back to normal.'

'That's what you said when we got married,' Betty said. 'You said you'd be back soon but I hardly saw you for six years.'

I nearly said there was a war on and she could hardly blame me for that, but I didn't want to upset her any further. We got married in a hurry not for the usual reason but because one day in 1939, Mr Chamberlain told Mr

Hitler to get out of Poland. We knew war was coming but not quite that quick. The very same morning that I was sipping a glass of port at Betty's mother's house after our marriage at the registry office, I heard the Prime Minister say those fateful words on the radio: "This country is at war with Germany." He also said that anyone in the fighting services should report for duty, and that meant me. The port didn't taste so good after that. 'Sorry, but I'll have to be on my way,' I said to the few friends and family who had gathered to celebrate our wedding. I saw Betty's face drop but there was nothing I could do, was there? Orders is orders. I just said, 'I'll be back soon,' and I was off to my base to get our squadrons ready to greet the Luftwaffe.

I shifted my weight from one foot to the other, trying to keep warm in the fresh morning air.

'This little job won't take six years. Anyway this time you can come with me, can't you?'

'Yes I'll be with you, Harry, so watch what you get up to with those young girls.'

~

Bituin wasn't too happy that morning either; it seemed the mood of the women around me matched the drizzling rain outside. When we squeezed around the table inside the van for breakfast, she sat stirring her bowl of porridge in a bit of a daze.

'Anything the matter?' I asked when I noticed that she hadn't eaten anything and I was nearly finished.

'I worry,' she said.

'I'll be alright. I've been around long enough to take care of myself.'

'Not you I worry about, Harry. My mother and sister at home in Philippines.'

'What about them? What's happened?'

'Nothing happen but I don't send them money, not since… since I leave Mr Sharma.' She was nearly crying now and wiped her damp eyes with a napkin.

As I was paying for her board and keep, I hadn't realised she had money problems

'How much did you send them?' I asked.

'Mr Sharma pay £100 each week and I send £80 to my mother. Her only income, pay for my sister at college.'

'Why don't I pop into the bank today and send them that sum of money then? I've got enough.' One thing my father taught me was to get a good pension.

Bituin looked hard at me. 'You do that for me, Harry? You too kind already.'

'It's the least I can do. Some people give their money to save elephants and whales, even stray dogs and cats. Why shouldn't I help real people in need?'

She took a piece of paper out of her pocket with some numbers written on it.

'Here are bank details to send money to. Sadly they charge fixed amount for transfers abroad so better to send payments in one go.' I wasn't quite sure what she meant by that until she added, 'Cheaper to send three month together.'

'Oh, so you'd like me to send… let me see…?'

'£320 for April, May, June. Total £960. But only if you have it, Harry.'

'Yes, I can do that today when I go into town.'

It was then I remembered that Billy had asked me if I had given her any money. She did seem very organised about it.

She leant across the small table to give me a big kiss on the cheek. 'Thank you, Harry. You very, very good father to me.'

If I was being taken for a ride, at least I was enjoying it.

Dan arrived soon after and we called a taxi to take us back to the Bollywood Bar. He was wearing a dark suit and I could see he had freshly greased up his hair. He said he was going to ask the manager about a job as a bouncer because he thought he might find out more behind the scenes than he could as a customer.

'But I will be watching you,' he said. 'Remember what you told me, no hanky-panky.'

The rain had stopped by the time we were strolling along the little backstreet that lead to the club, but it was still a dull, blustery day that did nothing for my mood. I didn't like the thought of going back into that disgusting place to see young girls entice old men to do things they shouldn't. Dan chatted to the bouncers outside, whilst I gritted my teeth and went back into the Bollywood Bar. The tired Indian lady must have been resting because a fresh-faced young man in a flowing white robe stood in her place, beaming a welcome at me.

'Come in, sir and soon you will be enjoying the delights of our beautiful Bollywood dancers.'

I wasn't feeling so friendly. 'And you will be enjoying my £20 no doubt.'

'A small price to pay for our wonderful, exotic ladies,

sir. But I am thinking you have been here before?' He turned to the bouncer with dark glasses beside him who nodded and grunted. 'So I am happy to offer you special discount today. Only £15, sir.'

Once inside, I was temporarily blinded by the bright, multi-coloured lights and paused, blinking, uncertain where to go. A smiling waiter appeared from nowhere and I was grateful to follow him to a seat from where I could take in the scene. Men in suits sat at the bar or around tables, not saying much, their eyes glued to two girls wearing next-to-nothing who wound their long legs around a thin pole while strange eastern music jangled away. It didn't take long for the tallest of the girls to untwine herself from the pole and slink towards me. I swallowed hard and hoped Betty wasn't watching. She put an arm on my shoulder and I felt her fingers delicately stroke the back of my head, my neck and cheek. I tried not to enjoy it. Turning her back towards me, she winked over her shoulder and slowly bent from her waist towards the floor until all I could see was her bright red underpants and long legs. Wriggly her bottom like a fluffy duck, she stretched down to grasp her ankles in her hands and looked at me between bare legs. It would have been rude not to watch so I stared and wondered if I should clap.

She straightened herself up and turned towards me, forcing her lips into a smile. 'You like to see more?' She had a harsh, clipped accent.

I cleared my throat. 'That was very clever, but I was hoping to see Nadia.'

She dropped the smile straight away. 'I can show you good time also. You like massage?'

I played for time. 'Where are you from?'

She ignored my question. 'Come, I give you massage. With happy end.'

With that she took my hand and tried to drag me to my feet. It gave me a jolt and I began to cough, a little splutter that gradually grew into a choking fit that must have turned my face red. There were some peanuts on the table and I'd helped myself to a handful when I sat down. One of them must have gone down the wrong way. I heard myself wheezing and coughing above the sound of the music as first the waiter then one of the bouncers hurried over. The girl let me slump back into my chair and the waiter tried banging me on the back.

'Do you need an ambulance?' he said, bending his head towards my ear. I just barked like a dog when I tried to speak, so I shook my head instead. The waiter handed me a glass of water which calmed my throat down. It felt like everyone in the room had turned to stare in my direction.

'Maybe you over-excited him. He's too old for this,' I overheard the bouncer say to the girl.

'It's your peanuts that are too old, not me,' I managed to say.

At that moment the music changed its rhythm and a different set of dancers appeared on the dance floor. One of them ran over as soon as she saw me slumped in my chair.

'What happen to you, Harry?' It was Nadia. She knelt beside me as the tall girl rolled her eyes upwards and marched off.

'It's this damned cough. I'll be alright soon enough.' I gulped more water.

'You know him?' the bouncer asked.

'Yes, I take care of him,' Nadia said.

She sat next to me holding my hand while the place gradually returned to its normal business.

I took a sip of water and a deep breath. 'I've got some good news for you, young lady.'

'News for me?'

'We can get you a job as a teacher, a proper job, not sleazy work like this.'

She looked round anxiously. 'Cannot talk here. We go for chat. You must pay because they watch me but I give you very lowest rate. £20.'

Everyone seemed to want my money. Was I being such a silly old fool that they were all taking advantage of me?

The rotating lights flashed across our table and for a brief moment she was lit up like a bomber caught in anti-aircraft searchlights. For the first time, I saw the despair behind that fresh face and the fear in her bright blue eyes.

I remembered what Betty had said that very morning, "She's in a rut and she needs to get out and do something different."

'We go?' Nadia asked.

'We go,' I said, slowly getting to my feet.

We got to the Health Spa quicker this time as I knew the way and she was in a hurry. As soon as she shut the door, she turned on me.

'Who are you? Why you talk of new job? Who you work for?'

'Slow down, young lady. It won't do any good to get all agitated. I am here to help you, that's all. As I said last time, a friend of mine was offered one of these jobs and I

145

want to get to the bottom of what goes on here, because it's something fishy isn't it? It hasn't done you any good, has it?'

She bit her lip and narrowed her eyes. 'You are police?'

'No, no. I'm not police. I'm Harry, acting as a private person you might say. With your best interests at heart. That's more than I can say about whoever employed you here. It's Vishal, isn't it? Vishal Sharma.' My hand felt a little shaky on my walking stick, so I moved closer to the couch and sat down.

She was wearing a few more clothes today, with long tassels hanging down from her bra and tight shorts instead of pants. Maybe it was the colder weather. She drew the cloth tighter around her shoulders.

'Vishal not my employer. He brought me here and sold me.'

'Sold you? Have I understood your English right? You mean he sold you just like... like selling a second-hand car?'

'Yes except, I was a new car, not used until he brought me here.' Her mouth twitched and her hands twisted the ends of the cloth.

'Why did you let them do that?'

Instead of answering, she carefully opened the door, had a peep outside and quietly closed it again.

'Tell me about job,' she said.

'I've a nephew – great nephew actually – who works with disappeared people and he says he can find you a job teaching. Do you know who the Prime Minister is?' She looked blank. 'No, I didn't think you would, but we can train you in that sort of thing. I'm sure with a proper job you can soon pay off the money you owe for bringing you here.'

She had one of those expressive faces that moves about while she listens, and I watched it change from looking hopeful to despondent while I spoke.

'She say I must give back all the money that she pay for me before I can go. With interest.'

'Who's she?'

'Indian lady who owns club.'

'How much do you owe her?'

'£5,000 plus interest at 70%.'

I whistled. 'That's a lot of interest. How much have you paid off?'

She snorted. 'Almost nothing. I receive credit of £20 a day if I reach target; if not, much less. Rest is for them. I have to work here for years to pay off debt.'

'That's criminal. Why don't you walk out?'

'Doors are locked, windows barred. No way out.'

'How on earth did you get into this mess?'

That was the final straw. She held her hands over her eyes and tried to hold herself together, but, as I stood to comfort her, she collapsed on the couch and sobbed. She didn't make a sound but her body shook and the tears rolled down her cheeks.

In what seemed like seconds, it was over. 'I tell you too much already,' she said suddenly composing herself, wiping her eyes and cheeks with the cloth. 'Too much chat. £25 please.'

'You said it would be your lowest price today, £20. And I haven't had a massage.'

Don't get me wrong. I didn't want a massage, certainly

not with any happy ending. No hanky-panky was still the rule. I just wanted to keep her talking a bit longer and if I judged her to be one thing, it was a haggler.

'You buy chat, not massage', she said.

'But you stopped the chat too early and I want my full 20 minutes,' I said.

She looked at her watch. 'Ok I can massage for 10 minutes only.'

'To be honest I'd rather chat. Let me do the talking if you won't. You see I've met Mr Sharma, Vishal's father, and we have agreed he is going to get his son to mend his ways. I know he is not very nice to young—'

'Not very nice! He is a bloody bastard, that's what he is. I spit on his name.' She spat a stream of spittle onto the floor. 'You know what he did to me? He offer me job on Internet as sports therapist in health club. He send me ticket to London and when I arrive at airport, nice car pick me up and bring me to house where he tell me I have to give clients happy ending. When I refuse, he leaves room and sends in Cezar, big, ugly, crazy man.' She closed her eyes and shook her head. 'Why am I telling you this?' She took a couple of paces towards me and looked me in the eye. 'You must tell no-one what I have told you, Harry. They will hurt me very bad if they find out. You promise?'

'If you don't want me to tell anyone, I won't. But don't you think we should go to the police if they have hurt you?'

'Then I am dead, Harry. Cezar say he kill me if I tell anyone what he did to me. He is very crazy.'

'The police can protect you from thugs like that.'

'And my family at home? Cezar has brothers in

148

Romania. British police cannot protect my mother from them.'

'We'll find a way of getting you out of here, don't you worry,' I said.

I slid off the couch just as there was a sharp knock at the door.

CHAPTER 12

The Fire

Betty used to say, "Act in haste; regret at your leisure". According to her, I used to do a lot of hasty acting. It started when I returned home after the war and left the armed services to find work in Civvy Street. I jumped at a job building a new passenger aircraft, adapted from the Lancaster, our stalwart RAF bomber.

'It's the ideal job for me,' I told Betty, 'because I'm still working on planes but I don't have a commanding officer bellowing in my ear.'

But the airliner developed problems and contracts to buy it were cancelled. Just six months after I started, I was made redundant, back to square one having turned down a promotion in the RAF. Betty always referred to it as the "ideal job" after that.

That knock on the door, was similar. It gave me an opportunity that I took without thinking about the consequences. And it lead to some big problems.

'Fire! We have to evacuate,' a voice said. Nadia tore open the door and there was the bouncer, panting from his run to fetch us. 'To the fire escape, quick. Follow me.'

Follow him we did, Nadia by his shoulder, asking questions, me struggling to keep up at the rear. We soon made it back to the main area of the club. Black smoke was pouring through the entrance. Everyone had gone. The bouncer pointed to the fire escape behind the bar and we headed that way, just as two firemen burst in between us, reeling out a thick, orange hose towards the smoke. Once they turned it on, white foam gushed in a great plume towards the smoke, dampening down the fire. But that hose was now blocking my path to the door. I knew I couldn't stoop low enough to get under it and I certainly couldn't climb over it.

I couldn't think straight and froze to the spot. It wasn't a good place to die, I knew that. I could see the headline in the papers: *Ninety-seven-year old man burns to death in a brothel.* But I couldn't think what to do. The bouncer had disappeared in the smoke and the firemen were busy dosing the fire and hadn't seen me.

Thank God, Nadia realised I was stuck. She ducked her supple body under the hose and rushed back to me.

'This way better,' she shouted, tugging me in the opposite direction, back the way we had come.

Smoke was still filling the room, tickling my throat into a spluttering cough as I tried to make my old legs move faster. She led me towards the lounge door where the bouncer had stood. When we reached the wall, she hit a metal bar with her fist and an emergency exit door flew open. Cold air hit my face and filled my lungs, making the coughing worse as I tried to suck in the fresh air. We were out.

Once my head cleared I saw that not only were we out, but we were out on our own. We were in a side street, around the corner from the main entrance. We looked at each other and I knew what was going through her mind. This was her chance to be free, to climb out of the desperate pit she had fallen into, an unexpected opportunity to start her life over again. We both knew she had to take it.

'Run until you find a taxi. Tell it to take you to Sunnyside Farm camp site. At the reception ask for Harry Pigeon's campervan. Go to the van and tell Bituin I sent you.' She was repeating the instructions just as a bouncer appeared around the corner.

I gave her a £20 note. 'No chat, just go.'

'Wait there. Don't move,' the bouncer shouted.

'You're a runner,' I said to her quietly. 'So run.'

And she did. Like the wind.

The bouncer wheezed up to me, realising he had no chance of catching her.

'Why'd you let her go?' he asked.

'I didn't know she was a prisoner,' I said.

He squinted at me. 'You'll be coming with me to explain this, I think, sir.'

I didn't want to go with him. I just wanted to get out of this place as fast as I could, but he took a tight grip of my arm and steered me around the corner. It was a chaotic scene. Two fire engines filled the narrow street at the entrance to the club. On the opposite pavement, the dancing girls were huddled together, the bouncers forming a ring around them, which I knew was to keep them in, not to protect them from prying eyes. I could hear the Indian woman wailing as she rushed around giving instructions to anyone and everyone. Police were re-directing traffic and passers-by away from the area. One of them stopped us.

'You can't go any further. There's been an incident.'

'I'll be on my way…' I felt the bouncer's hand on my arm tighten as I spoke.

'I work here and this man is a witness,' he said.

'You'd better see my colleague over there,' the policeman said opening the barrier and pointing to another officer who was talking to Dan. At least I had found him.

'I believe you were the one to raise the alarm?' I heard the police officer say to Dan as we approached. He didn't have a chance to answer before the Indian woman rushed over to us.

'Where is Nadia?' she screamed at the bouncer.

'She ran off. She was with this gentleman.' The bouncer said something else in her ear which I didn't catch.

That quietened her down. Her eyes opened like saucers, glaring at me suspiciously. She seemed about to speak, but darted a glance at the policeman and held her tongue.

'Find her. Now,' she barked.

The bouncer disappeared.

'I take it all your staff are accounted for?' the officer asked. The woman nodded, keeping her eyes on me. 'I'll just report that to the fire officer. If you could wait here, sir, so we can finish your statement,' he said to Dan. 'Perhaps I can have a word with you after that, sir?' he said looking at me.

He marched off to the fire engine. The woman was still watching me and came in close so that no-one else could hear.

'You a client of Nadia?' She was so near I could smell the sweat beneath her long robes and see every line and crease in her brown face.

'I wouldn't exactly call myself a client, no,' I said, shuffling back a little.

'I am thinking your family don't know about your visits here?' She raised her eyebrows and I shook my head. 'Then we are not mentioning it either,' she said showing a set of fine teeth that told me she might have been a good looker in her day. 'Now, tell me where Nadia goes?' Her face became stern once more and she glanced around to make sure no-one was listening.

'I don't know,' I said.

'My doorman says you were giving her money when she ran off.'

'Only what I owed her.' I looked over at Dan who was watching us carefully. I didn't particularly want this woman to know we were together, but he mistook my glance.

'You alright, Harry?'

'Yes I'm alright, just explaining to this lady here that I don't know much about what happened.'

She looked hard at Dan and a look of recognition came into her face. 'Now I am remembering you both. You came in yesterday, together, didn't you? Did you see Nadia then?'

'Sorry to keep you, sir.' The police officer came back to save us from her inquisition and started on one of his own. 'You say you saw smoke in the toilet block?' he asked Dan.

'That's right. As I was saying, I was waiting to be interviewed for a job. I work as a doorman in local clubs and bars like this and I popped in here on the off-chance they had some work.'

'Which we don't,' the woman interrupted. 'We are not employing young people like you.'

'Well, I didn't know that, nor did the doorman on duty because he asked me to wait in the hall while he fetched someone. It was quite a wait, so I asked if I could use the washroom as they say in Hollywood. When I opened the door into the gents, smoke billowed out. That's when I raised the alarm.'

'So you didn't actually go into the toilet?' the officer asked.

'As soon as I saw the smoke, I thought that's a fire, not a secret smoker, and I shut the door, as I've been trained to do. Step 1, cut off the oxygen supply.'

'The doorman says you were in there for quite a few minutes before you raised the alarm,' the officer said, flicking through the notebook he was scribbling in.

'Ah, yes, that was down to my confusion over the doors. I went into the ladies by mistake. To be fair, the signs do look similar. Both of the little people were wearing what looked like dresses to me,' Dan said.

'Traditional Indian clothes. It's easy to see the difference,' the lady interrupted. 'Woman has headdress, man does not.'

Dan shrugged. 'Sorry didn't see that. I always get nervous before an interview.'

'There was not going to be any interview,' the woman insisted.

The officer coughed. 'So by mistake you went into the ladies before the gents. What time would you say this happened?'

Dan looked at his watch. 'It's 2pm now, so roughly 30 minutes ago; maybe 1.30?'

Half an hour, a lot had happened in that time. I wasn't

used to things going so fast. I just wanted to sit down, have a nice cup of tea and ask Betty what to do next.

No chance of that. The officer was flicking at his note book. 'And you sir, were you inside the club when the fire broke out?' His pencil hovered over a clean page and I felt the woman's eyes boring into me as I coughed and shuffled my feet, wondering what to say.

'No, I was just walking up the side street on my way to the bank when this door flies open and someone rushes out.'

'Who came out of the door, sir?'

I waved my hand towards the staff who were still standing shivering inside the bouncer's protective ring. 'One of those I think.'

'Right then.' He closed his notebook and I had to restrain myself from breathing out audibly. 'If I can have your names and addresses and where we can contact you should we have any further questions, that will be all for the moment,' he said.

'I'll write it down for you,' I said, noticing that the Indian lady was still listening intently.

The firemen seemed to have done their job as all the smoke had died down and everyone was standing looking at the building. Black, sooty foam was everywhere and I even felt a twinge of sorrow for the owners and staff of the Bollywood Bar who would have to clean up the mess.

I handed the policeman the sheet of paper with my details. 'You're a long way from home. Where are you staying in Bristol? Can you jot that down too please?' he asked.

I could feel the Indian lady trying to read the address

as I scrawled the campsite on the notepad. With a final stare, the woman left us and started shouting at her staff again. Dan and I took off as fast as we could.

'What's occurring, man?' Dan asked, holding my arm when he saw that I was finding it difficult to move quickly.

'Too much. I need to get back to the campsite real quick before her ladyship works out where a member of her staff has gone.'

Dan 's jaw dropped. 'You didn't did you?'

I nodded.

'Oh my god,' he said quickly, then more slowly: 'Oh. My. God. You got Nadia out. What are you going to do with her?'

'Get her as far away from here as possible, that's what. Then I'll have to do some scheming.'

'Scheming? Why don't you call the police and let them do the scheming?'

'Don't you start. It's not as simple as that. Anyway, what's all this about you going into the ladies? What did you get up to in there?' I asked.

'No I'm not a pervert, nor was I lost. I was checking the security. Windows all barred, no other exits. It's like a prison camp. Or it was.'

'How did the fire start?'

'I really don't know. The hand of God. Or maybe Krishna or Shiva. Not me.'

We were just about to call a taxi when I remembered the bank. It wouldn't take long and I couldn't go back and tell Bituin that her family still hadn't been sent any money. You'd have thought that in this day and age when you can send messages and photographs all round the world in a flash, that you would be able to send money overseas in no time at all. Apparently not. I was in that bank for a good hour, waiting for the clerk to sort out the paperwork and signing all the forms, before we got a taxi and headed for the campsite.

When we pulled into the site, I saw something that made me shrink into my seat. A van was parked outside the reception office, rear doors wide open.

It was a black VW van.

I quickly checked the number plate and looked through the office window. Three men were talking to the receptionist. Two of them looked like bouncers from the Bollywood bar.

I cursed. 'Dan that is an enemy vehicle. I need a diversion.' I said, pointing to the men inside the office and elbowing him towards the door of the taxi. 'Here's something for your ride home.' I handed him a £20 note.

'I see what you mean,' he said. 'Captain Courageous to the rescue. I think that van has got a flat tyre.' He slid out of the taxi, and crouching low, ran over to the rear of the van.

'Drive straight in,' I ordered our taxi driver.

He turned around. 'That notice says all vehicles have to call at reception.'

Out of the corner of my eye, I saw Dan fiddling with the rear tyre of the VW.

'Doesn't apply to taxis that are dropping off a senior citizen. I need some pills if you could hurry up, please.' I tried to look a bit faint. The driver shrugged and drove on.

Hopping out of the taxi, I knocked at the door of the van in case the girls were in a state of undress. There was no reply. I turned the handle. It didn't budge. It was locked.

The taxi was already turning around and heading back to reception. My campervan was down in a small valley and I could just see the black VW still parked on top of the slope in the distance. It started to spit with rain.

I needed to sit down but instead turned my face up towards the sky, blinking as raindrops hit my face. 'Where are they Betty? Where are those two girls? Don't say I've lost them too? Just like I've lost you and... and our little girl.'

That woke her up. 'Don't you know anything about women, Harry Pigeon? Girls always go to the toilet together.'

I heard a giggle from the direction of the wash block. It was faint but I could tell that girlish chuckle anywhere. Someone was amusing Bituin and I just hoped it was Nadia.

As I shuffled quickly towards the block, my mind was scheming ninety to the dozen. Whatever Dan did, he wouldn't hold off those bouncers for long. They would come looking for me. Campsites were made secure with only one way in and out so there was almost certainly no other exit. Maybe there was a pedestrian exit but I needed my van; it felt protective, like the shell of a tortoise. Which left only one option.

'Are you there, girls?' I shouted through the door as soon as I reached the toilets. Bituin nearly knocked me over, throwing her arms around me and squeezing me hard.

'There you are, Harry. We thought you never come.'

Out of the corner of my eye I saw Nadia standing to

one side, smiling shyly. She was wearing one of Betty's old green dresses that Bituin had altered. It went really well with her short blonde hair.

'Come here, young lady,' I said and I put one arm round her too. She started to say something but I stood back. 'No time for chat. We've a bit of an emergency on and need to leave as fast as ever we can. Here, help me back to the van. I'm a bit slow with only a stick.'

They took an arm each, hurrying me along the footpath over the grass towards my trusty van. I just hoped it would start after a couple of days in the wet. Thankfully, I saw that the VW was still on top of the hill. Dan had obviously done his job.

'You two, up on the top bunk, out of sight. We could be in for a rough ride so hold on.'

I squeezed their hands as they scrambled into the back of the van and heaved myself into the driver's seat. When I turned the key, the engine turned over a few times, then stuttered into life.

And stopped.

Damn, too much accelerator. I'd flooded the engine. The couple of minutes I had to wait before trying the ignition again seemed like hours. I took a deep breath and turned the key again, less right foot this time. The engine coughed and spluttered on two or three cylinders, and eventually got going on all four. We were off.

Once we'd got over the grassy field on which we were pitched, I turned onto the tarmac track that sloped up to the reception area.

'Treat it like a runway,' I said to myself. 'Get yourself straight and then full throttle.' I hit the accelerator pedal.

My van didn't exactly leap forward but it was gaining speed nicely by the time we hit the top of the hill. I could see the VW clearly by then.

Dan was in the thick of it, surrounded by bouncers. Angry, shouting bouncers. One was pointing at the rear wheel of their van, another was grabbing at him, pushing him away from the VW. They all whirled round when they heard me coming, ignoring Dan for a second. I was almost on them, tearing along well above the 15 mile an hour speed limit. One waved at me to slow down and another stepped forward, his hand out-stretched to stop me. I thought about running him down, or at least pretending to, hoping he would jump clear at the last minute, but I had a better plan. I slowed down, smiling sweetly, looking all friendly and winding down my window. But I kept going, nice and slow.

'Anything the matter?' I shouted, poking my head out of the window. The second he stepped aside to talk to me through the door, my foot was hard on that accelerator. I heard a bang as my wing mirror caught him, but I was through. They ran after me of course but even my old van could outstrip heavy blokes like them. I studied my rear-view mirror to see what was happening to Dan but I had turned past a thick hedge and lost sight of him. I felt bad about that. But no real harm could come to him, could it? No black van appeared in my mirror so he must have succeeded in letting their tyres down. They would be angry about that.

'You can come down now,' I shouted to the girls as I hurtled along country lanes. 'We need to get the satnav working.'

'Where we go, Harry?' Bituin asked.

'Somewhere with no night clubs and no black vans.' I said.

'What do I put into satnav?'

'Try Land's End in Cornwall.'

'199 miles. Arrive in 3 hours 46 minutes,' she announced.

'The way things are, I wouldn't be so sure.'

I was right about that.

Soon we were cruising down a motorway and the girls were chatting away in the back. Dan was uppermost in my mind because I had left him surrounded by a gang of angry thugs.

'Did Dan give you his telephone number?' I asked Bituin.

'No, but he phone you so I can find.' She got hold of my mobile and we worked out when he had called and in seconds, she had his number.

Amazing what young people can do these days. You can't teach them anything because everything has changed so much. My father taught me everything I needed to know about gardening, cleaning my shoes, shaving with a razor. My mother showed me how to wash behind my ears and iron my shirts. What can I teach the young people of today? Not a lot it seems. I had to have lessons in how to turn my TV on from a youngster. She was only seven or eight but she knew how to press the buttons on the controls and get the programme I wanted. It's no wonder children today take no notice of their parents and grandparents. They think we're stupid just because we can't make the TV work.

After we had pulled into a service station, Bituin took

over the wheel and I phoned Dan. He answered straight away.

'Harry, where are you? No don't answer that. The heavy brigade may come back and torture me for information again. The least I know the better.'

'You've been tortured?' I asked.

'Not physically, but mentally they did rather turn the screw. They threatened to report me to the police for malicious damage to their vehicle unless I spilled the beans. They probably knew my livelihood as a bouncer relies on me having a clean sheet, criminal record-wise. No red cards; not even a yellow,' he said.

He was gabbling and made no sense to me. 'Spill what beans?'

'About you. They made me tell them everything I know about you in return for dropping charges against me.'

'I see. Sorry to have got you into this mess.'

'To be fair, the bean count was quite low. It was a small-sized can to spill. I did manage to forget one or two things but actually, I don't know that much about you.'

'So what did you tell them?' I asked.

'You seem to be public enemy number one in their eyes, so I had to distance myself from you, pretend I was just your lackey. I said you'd hired me.'

'Hired you?'

'Yes, as a bodyguard. It fits my profession.'

'Well you did look after me, I suppose, and I did pay you a bit,' I said.

'One of them was very interested in your little computer. He claimed you'd stolen it from them and there was a reward for its safe return. I did say I'd seen a tablet in your possession but that you couldn't work it. I didn't tell them I'd unlocked it. That would be a definite red card offence for me.'

'Did they ask about anything else?'

'Just the small matter of two of their employees. They said you had abducted them and I should help them to find them. You haven't been reading John Fowles have you, Harry?'

'John who?'

'Fowles. He wrote about a butterfly collector who moved onto girls.'

'I think the girls are collecting me rather than the other way round.'

'Let the girls go, Harry. There's nothing you can do for them. These lads are serious ruffian material. They're coming after you,' he said and rang off.

CHAPTER 13
Nadia's Story

Dan's words kept repeating in my head. I wasn't quite sure what he meant by "serious ruffian material" but it didn't sound too friendly. I knew they had to be looking for me. Perhaps he was right. I should let the girls go. They could disappear quietly, get jobs on the black market, keep their heads down and it might all blow over. "There's nothing you can do for them," he'd said. He was right. They could look after themselves now. I watched Bituin drive. She was hurtling along faster than I would dare to go. She looked so perfect with her fresh face and bright eyes.

'Just like the blackbird in our garden.' It was Betty. I'd been thinking so hard, I must have woken her up. 'The one that used to stand on the edge of the birdbath, looking at the water, just like you used to stand on the beach at the seaside, wondering whether to take the plunge and get wet.'

I knew the one she meant. She was a beautiful bird, flawless, not a feather out of place. Betty would watch her from the chair by the window, motionless in case she took fright and flew away. She knew every move that bird made.

'All of a sudden, she would hop in, spreading and shaking her wings so that water showered down her back,' she said. 'Next, she would wash her beak, filling it with water to throw over her shoulder in case she'd missed a bit. Do you remember the day she came with a young one and taught it how to wash itself?'

She had called me in to see the show. That little bird had put more water on the ground than on him, but he soon got the hang of it. He took notice of his mother, not laughing at her behind his back like our modern children do just because we can't turn on the TV.

The very next day, I found the mother blackbird lying on my path, its neck flopped to one side, nipped in the neck by the neighbour's cat. I picked that bird up in one hand and I must admit I shed a tear or two. Full of life one minute, dead the next, all because that cat wanted a bit of fun. I heard her little one chirping in the hedge and wondered what he was going to do now his mother was gone. I told Betty they must have emigrated when she asked me why we hadn't seen them for a while. She guessed the truth, I'm sure, but she didn't want to face it either.

These girls were in the same boat as that young bird – at the mercy of anyone more powerful who wanted to play games with them. I couldn't just leave them, could I? Not until they could fly by themselves. They still had a few things to learn.

~

I turned to Nadia who was sitting on the seat behind me that folded down into a bed, her slim legs tucked up under her.

'Are you alright there?'

I'd hardly had time to speak to her since I watched her run into the distance, away from the Bollywood Bar.

'Oh yes, Harry. So much better since I meet you and Bituin. She tells me how kind you are to her. We are very lucky.'

'I do my best,' I said.

'You'll find me job as teacher, yes?' she asked.

'What was that?' I was finding it a bit difficult to hear what she said as she was on my deaf side and the battery of my hearing aid was running low and whistling in my ear.

'I'll come in the back,' I said, clambering between the two front seats, trying to stay upright as the van lurched round a corner. I flopped down beside her and patted her arm. 'That's better. Now I can hear you.'

'I ask how I find teacher's job.'

'I'll call my friend who knows about these things and he'll tell you what to do,' I said.

She looked a little crestfallen. 'Will it take long to find job, Harry?'

'Few weeks, maybe more. I'm not really familiar with these things but there's always bureaucracy to go through.' She bit her lip when I said that.

'Why? What's the matter?'

'I send money each month to my mother in Romania. They deduct from my earnings at the club to send to her. It pays her rent. She's evicted without it.'

'How much is it?'

'£20 per month.'

'Write down the name of your mother and her bank details and I will make the arrangements,' I said. Bituin must have mentioned my financial help for her to Nadia so I could hardly refuse, could I? At least she wasn't that expensive.

'Perhaps you can tell us how you fell into the clutches of this gang?' I asked as she scribbled down her mother's details. 'What made you want to leave Romania?'

'Long story,' she said.

'We have a long way to go,' I said.

'Then I begin at the start,' said Nadia. 'My parents lived in Moldova but when it became independent of Soviet Union, they moved to Romania. A few years later, in 1992, I was born.'

'So, let's see; you are 20 years old and Romanian,' I said.

'I have Romanian passport, yes, but I am really Moldovan. Very poor people, always invaded by this country or that, Romans, Huns, Poles, Turks, Russians, they all take turns to rule us. When independent, we forget how to rule ourselves and things go very bad so many leave, like my parents. My father was a journalist, a sports writer, and he tells me to become a sportswoman so I can be famous and rich. In Romania, they are good in gymnastics but I am good in running. I keep running, running, running every day.' The roll to her 'r' made 'running' sound like an engine revving up. 'No coaching for runners in Romania so my father give me book about Emil Zátopek.'

'Winner of the 5,000 and 10,000 metres and the marathon in the 1952 Olympics,' I said.

'Good, you remember our chat.' She was smiling for the first time since beginning her story.

'Oh yes, I won't forget our chat,' I said, trying to put the image of what she was wearing out of my mind. Betty's green dress suited her much better.

'I study his training methods and train very hard, always training every day. I am junior champion and move into senior events. One day, my mother tell me…' she paused and took a deep breath. 'My mother tell me my father has cancer. He cannot work so I must get job as I am eldest child. I become a cleaner, cleaning, cleaning not running, running all day. Then my father die and my mother tells me we have to earn more money to pay rent.'

I passed her my handkerchief as I could see the tears forming in her eyes. She dabbed at her face and blew her nose but managed to continue. 'Many people were looking for jobs abroad when we join European Union as other countries pay more than Romania. My mother has passport from Moldova, not in EU, so she ask me to work abroad to earn enough money for everyone. I look in newspapers and see many jobs but only one in sport. *Health Club Assistant. Work in busy club making customers fit*, the advertisement said. I think this is just right for me as I keep fit also if I work in health club. I become an athlete again. I apply and have interview with very nice lady. She ask only a few questions and says I can have job. She gives me a plane ticket and asks me to sign a contract saying I have to pay travel and other costs back from my wages. It is in English so I don't understand it very well.'

'This is how you got into debt?' I asked.

'Yes. How you say, I kick myself?'

I nodded.

'Yes, I kick myself,' she continued. 'I was so keen to take

job, I didn't read contract properly. When I board plane, I was so happy. At last I can do what my father wanted me to do. I can run and compete. And I can win. Even the strange-looking men who meet us at airport in London don't give me bad thoughts. They put me and other girls from Romania into small bus and drive to house in the country. Very nice house with drive to front door and garden all around. I think this is a good place to work, but they say it is for interview and training only. We here only to find which club to work in. They give us nice lunch with some wine, plenty of wine.'

She swallowed hard and coughed as if trying to get the words out. 'Then interview start with young Indian man.'

'I have a feeling I may know him.' I said, expecting the worst.

'Someone call him Vish. At first, I think this is charming man. Very handsome, very polite. He tells me he has many clubs to offer us but he has to match us carefully to right one. He ask me if I have done any massage. I say I only rub myself down in shower after running. He says that, if I like running, he can send me to health club, but only if I learn how to give special massage to clients. To have this job, I have to pass test.'

She swallowed audibly, turning away from me, breathing heavily.

'What sort of test?' I asked.

She swivelled back to face me, her eyes brimming with tears and spoke quickly. 'He lie on couch, pull up robe and tell me to massage between legs.'

'Unhappy ending,' I muttered.

'I'm shocked and say no, prefer different job. He says I

170

will not like other jobs. This one best for me. I say I want sports job. He hit my face and say maybe I like boxing.'

'So he sent you to the Bollywood?'

'Not yet. First my dream become worst nightmare. He call in another man to interview me for different job. I recognise him as Cezar who meet us at airport, greasy hair, bent nose, big hands. He say he will show me job he has to offer. He take off jacket and ask me to come near. I don't move so he undo his trousers and grab me by throat.' She put her hand on her neck as if reliving the experience.

I tried to spare her the pain. 'I can guess what happened next.'

'No I don't think you can. He put his hand on my mouth and hold me… hold me so I can't breath.' Nadia's voice rasped as if her throat was full of glass splinters. She was breathing jerkily, her eyes staring down, unable to meet mine.

'When he take hand off, he put me on floor and says he will kill me if I struggle. He put hand back over my mouth until I feel my eyes bulging from my head and my heart banging in body. I think I'm going to die. He take his hand away and tell me to lie still or he will stop my breath again. I am gasping, gulping air as he force open my legs. When I try to push him away, he puts hand over my mouth again and I have no more strength. I lie still and let him do what he want. I have to breath.' She was panting, tears streaming down her cheeks.

I didn't know what to say. How could this happen? In a country that claims to be civilised and the police are down on you if you so much as go a few miles an hour above the speed limit, how can a girl like her be violated so easily?

'I tell you this to explain why I took job giving massage. Vish come back and ask me to choose. Go with Cezar or work in health club. I have no choice. I learn to give quick, happy ending. And do Indian dance.'

I needed a break after Nadia's story. 'Why don't we pull over and have a cup of tea. There's a lay-by coming up according to the road signs,' I shouted to Bituin.

~

It wasn't a big parking area, just one of those small indentations at the side of the road, but it was enough for a quick cuppa. I tried phoning Billy while we waited for the kettle to boil on my gas stove in the van. He didn't answer so I left him a message to call me back as soon as possible.

Bituin asked me what the red light on the dashboard meant. Red lights are the one thing you don't want to see in an old van like mine so I shot forward into the driver's seat to see for myself. When I turned the key, there was a clunk instead of a whirring noise. Damn, the battery was flat or the starter motor was gone. I couldn't do too much about either on my own. There was nothing for it. I called the RAC.

'I'm afraid we are very busy this evening, sir,' the young lady said when I got through. 'Estimated response times are currently up to 3 hours.'

'Three hours! I can't wait that long,' I said.

'Are you in an emergency situation, sir?'

'Yes I am. I'm…' I paused. I couldn't really say I'd got two young ladies on board recently escaped from sexual exploitation and thugs were out looking for me, could I?

'Are you alright sir?'

'Yes, it's just that I'm ninety-seven years old and need to take some medication.' I lied about the medication.

'Are you alone in your vehicle, sir?'

I quickly realised that an old man alone on a busy road in need of medicine might make a difference.

'Yes I'm on my own.'

'I will put you on our emergency list, sir. Someone will be with you within one hour. Can you wait that long?'

'I can probably manage, yes.'

It didn't take an hour. I saw his flashing lights pull up behind me after about twenty minutes. He was a nice enough man but I felt shifty all the time he was there. I'd had to hide the girls up in the top bunk so I could appear to be on my own. They were very quiet up there but every time one of them moved, even slightly, the van shook a little. I noticed he frowned a bit curiously when it did, and once or twice I caught him peering in through the windows.

He called me over after he'd had his head under the bonnet for a while. 'It's the points on the distributor. All furred up so the charge going into the alternator isn't enough to keep your battery charged. I've cleaned them up to see if that makes a difference. Tell me if the red light has gone off now, would you?'

He revved the engine and I pulled myself up into the cabin. No red light. Phew, we would soon be on our way.

'Lucky you got an old 'un like me,' he said, wiping the grease off his hands. 'The young fellows only know about electronic ignition systems that come in boxes. I get phones calls from them all the time. "I've been called to an old crock," they say. "What's the round black thing with wires sticking out the top?" They've never seen a distributor before. So I have to take them step-by-step through the procedure.'

'We older men do have our uses, then,' I said.

'My wife might not agree with you on that one.' We both had a good laugh at that.

'Your van is good to go, sir, but I would suggest you replace the distributor with an electronic system if you can. Especially if you are going to be out driving on your own.'

It may have been my imagination but I thought he put special emphasis on 'driving on your own'.

He'd parked his van right behind mine, sticking out slightly to protect us from the traffic that was tearing along the dual carriageway. Just as I was watching him switch off his flashing lights to pull away, I saw a black van come past and slow down. It was a VW. I could see burley men in dark jackets inside and one was pointing at me and my van.

~

I'd been enjoying myself until that moment. I hadn't messed about with an engine for a long time. Although I worked in a garage from the age of fourteen on all sorts of cars like Bentleys, Jowetts, Triumphs and Rovers, I'd always been a motorbike man at heart. You can get at a bike engine from all sides whereas you need to be a contortionist to get your hands on some parts of a car engine under a bonnet. My brother was a motor bike fan like me and the two of us would spend hours pulling my old Norton to bits and putting it all back together. We would chat too, just like I had with the RAC man. Too long as it turned out. If I hadn't spent so much time chin-wagging with him, I could have been away before that black van caught up with me.

I dodged behind my van praying they hadn't seen us properly as they sped by. It took them a while to slow down but when I saw their emergency lights start flashing in the distance, I realised they had stopped and had perched their vehicle on the side of the busy dual carriageway like a big crow looking for road kill. I didn't wait to see what they would do next but scrambled up behind the wheel of my van. The engine was still running to charge the battery.

'We're leaving soon but stay up there for a bit longer,' I shouted to the girls.

The RAC vehicle hadn't moved and it blocked my rear view, preventing me from seeing what was coming down the busy lanes, so I couldn't pull out immediately. I watched the VW to see what they would do next. They couldn't really reverse towards me as the road was far too busy. No, they would probably wait for me to leave and then follow close behind me. What could I do then?

I saw a door open and someone jump out of the VW. The cat was coming after my little birds.

CHAPTER 14
The Capture

Two of them were running down the side of the road towards me. They must have thought my van was still immobile with the RAC truck stuck behind me. In a way it was; I still couldn't see to get out.

Whatever was that RAC man doing behind me? Why didn't he just go? They would reach me in a couple more minutes. I couldn't stay there and have our necks nipped.

I eased my van forward, past the line of his vehicle, hoping no-one was coming. A horn blared as a car swerved to miss me so I had to pull back in. The features of the men running towards me were clearer. One was wearing dark glasses: it was the Bollywood bouncers alright. Winding down the window, l leaned right out to get a view of the road behind.

The inside lane was solid traffic but the outside lane had a few gaps. The bouncers were shouting and waving at me now. Why didn't anyone let me out? They were just going to have to slow down or pull over. I was coming out.

My right foot stamped on the accelerator and I heard a little cry from the girls in the bunk above me as we shot forward and slewed left to give the traffic behind space to go round me. Headlights flashed in my mirrors and my van shivered as a Range Rover came past so close I could see the driver shaking his fist at me. I was out.

What would the VW do? Chase after me or wait to pick up their mates who were now stranded on the roadside? I wish I could have seen their faces when I drove away but I was looking too hard in my mirror at the cars behind. The VW stayed put as I tore past, but it wouldn't take long for them to regroup and come after me.

I let out a long breath. The manoeuvre was not something my advanced motorist instructor would have approved of, but it'd worked. For now.

'You can come down now ladies. I need some satnaving from you. Time for a change of route. We need to get off this dual carriageway. Take me to a quiet place on the coast. And keep your eyes peeled for a black VW van.'

'We being followed?' Nadia asked, looking around frantically.

'I'm not rightly sure. I may have shaken them off but just as a precaution—'

'There's one,' Nadia shouted. I was already on a slip road off the main route so I didn't have time to look behind me properly.

'Where?' I asked, throwing the camper round the roundabout so hard that I could hear tins and crockery crashing around in the back.

Nadia squealed. 'Behind us.'

I accelerated out of the first exit looking hard into my mirror. I glimpsed a dark van pulling in behind me.

It was a Mercedes. I've never been so pleased to see those gun sights on a front grill.

'Please do a U-turn as soon as possible,' the satnav said.

It kept trying to direct me back to the dual carriageway but I was having none of it, and I told the lady in no uncertain terms that I was not doing any about-turns. Bituin giggled and said the lady couldn't hear me.

'Turn her off then. I'll use a map. It'll soon be dark so it's time you had a drive.'

Bituin was eager to climb behind the wheel and soon had us flying along the country roads. No moon that night so it was pitch-black as we hurtled down narrow lanes with dense hedges towering on either side. Bituin's lips parted into a determined grin as she threw us around a bend and braked hard when she saw headlights coming towards us. We shot into a passing point to allow the other car past and then roared away as fast as my old van would carry us. There was no stopping her; it was do or die stuff. I wasn't worried about the VW catching us any more. Surviving the journey had become my main concern. I tried chatting to Nadia but she said she felt sick and stared out of the window at the dark foliage rushing by, occasionally brushing the window as Bituin took a hedgerow a little too fine. Finally, I breathed a quiet sigh of relief as the enclosed lanes gave way to more open landscape.

'There's the sea,' Bituin announced.

I recognised the area and guided us around the headland towards a campsite that I knew was tucked away in the valley back from the beach, a nice, quiet place where dogs and children had to be well-behaved and on a lead – well only the dogs had to be on a lead. A five-barred gate had been closed across the entrance into the site. I'd forgotten about that; you needed a code to get in. We were locked out.

Headlights shone in our rear-mirror and a car stopped behind us.

'Pull over, Bituin. Here's our entrance ticket,' I said.

As the car came alongside us, I leaned out of the cabin window and called over to the driver. 'Broke down on the way so we're too late to check in. We'll follow you if we may. I've been here before.' I wasn't lying about that. 'They won't mind.' I was about that.

The driver looked hard at my tired, old face and must have taken pity on me. We were soon through the gates, tucking ourselves in at the back of the site where no-one could see us from the road. It had been such a busy day that we all collapsed onto our bunks as soon as we could. I was out like a light and didn't even get a call of nature during the night.

~

As the sun rose over the valley the next morning, I was up, making sure we were parked in a good spot. The few campers that were on the site were clustered around the offices and the washrooms. Our field at the end was deserted except for us.

Bituin wandered towards me, yawning and looking up at the tall trees that overlooked the campsite. Big, black birds were making a heck of a din from their rookery way above us.

'Crows noisy this morning,' she said stifling another yawn. 'Storm coming.'

'Weather looks pretty fine to me,' I said, looking around at the clear sky.

'Not always weather that makes storm,' Bituin said.

She was right about that. Our storm struck later that day.

After breakfast, I went to make my peace with the man at reception. At first he seemed quite upset, pointing out a sign on the wall saying that, without prior permission, admissions were not allowed after 8pm. I explained that we couldn't see the office, let alone that sign, from the other side of the locked gate. He said that their terms and conditions were on their website, in full.

Now I don't know much about websites except that someone once told me they were like your back-side: everyone's got one but no-one wants to look at yours. I didn't think that would go down very well if I told him, so I asked him about the motorbike parked outside instead. I'd been admiring it on my way in.

'Isn't that Goldwing a lovely bike?' I said pointing through the window. I could tell immediately it was his because his expression changed and his face broke into a smile. 'I wish something as comfortable as that had been around in my day. I had to put up with a drafty old Norton.'

Then of course we were off, me reminiscing about the old bikes, him telling me all about the new ones. His name was Ron and by the time we'd finished, we were firm friends. And I'd forgotten to tell him there were three of us in the van, not just me as he put in his book. Just as well; I wanted to keep the girls under the radar for a while longer.

'One more thing,' I'd suddenly remembered my promise to Nadia. 'Where's the nearest bank?'

'There's a cash point in the post office, but it does charge you.'

'No, I mean a proper bank where you can talk to someone.' I was pretty sure those machines weren't clever enough to send money abroad.

'Nearest one's in the next village, two and half miles that way,' he said pointing up the valley away from the sea.

'Is there a bus? I don't think my legs can cope with walking that far.'

He laughed. 'No buses. Everyone drives a four-by-four round here.'

'Blast, I'll just have to get the van out again. I was hoping to have a day off driving after all our problems yesterday.'

He looked at me carefully, his eyes narrowing. 'When's the last time you rode a motor-bike?'

'Ooof, now you are going back a long way. I sold my Norton when war broke out; you couldn't get much petrol once rationing came in. 1940. That would be the last time, when I rode it to the garage and sold it.'

'I think you deserve another trip after all these years,' he said, looking at his watch. 'It just so happens I need to go to the bank today and this is probably as good a time as any. I'll give you a lift on the back of my bike.'

I probably did look a good deal younger than I was so I couldn't blame him for thinking I was up to clambering onto the rear seat of his bike. There was nothing more I would've liked either but I knew I wasn't up to it.

'What do you say? It's only a five minute ride.'

I looked wistfully out of the window at the rear seat of his bike. It looked more comfortable than anything I'd seen before with a high back to hold you on, like a child seat in a car, only bigger.

'To be honest, I don't think I can climb up that far,' I said.

For the first time since I arrived in his office, he stood up. I would have been more polite if I'd known how big he was. He just went up and up and up until he towered a good foot or more above me. I'd noticed he had broad shoulders but now I realised he was a giant of a man, the sort who makes the room go dark when he walks in.

'Let's give it a go, shall we?' He fetched some leathers from a cupboard and offered me a jacket. I think it was probably one of his because it came to the floor on me. Tossing his keys in the air and catching them, he strode outside, whistling. He was enjoying himself even if I suddenly felt my feet go very cold. What on earth was I up to? There was probably 1000cc or more in that engine. My old Norton only had 250.

He fiddled with the ignition while I tried to work out a way of getting up into the passenger seat.

He smiled at my hesitation. 'Here let me give you a hand.'

Like a huge crane on a building site, he grabbed me around the waist and yanked me off my feet. Swinging me up and round, he gently lowered me down into the seat. I was on a motorbike again.

He handed me a helmet. 'This is my wife's so I hope it fits.'

Jumping on the front, he pressed the start button. In my day, it would have been a kick-start, or more likely, several kick-starts. I was expecting a roar from the engine below but it was gentle purr like a big, happy cat. Until he turned the throttle, that is, when I could feel the vibrating power under me. As soon as he was on the road, boy, didn't it half go and I felt myself thrust against the back of the seat, hardly able to breathe as the bike surged away.

I was in my element. In no time at all, we'd zoomed up and down the hills, around the bends and we were in the next town, both grinning from ear to ear as we took off our helmets to go into the bank.

'You look as though you've lost a penny and found a pound,' Ron said.

I asked to speak to a bank manager, but instead I found myself sitting in front of a "customer advisor", filling out forms to transfer money to Nadia's mother in Romania.

'Fancy a coffee,' Ron said to me when we had both finished our banking business. I really wanted to get back to the campsite but it seemed only polite to go with his timetable, not mine and I hadn't been to a teashop at the seaside for a long time.

'What was the ride like?' he asked, once we were settled around an outside table with a good view of the ferry that crossed the inlet.

'Marvellous. I haven't enjoyed a ride so much since I used to race before the war.'

'You raced?'

'Not officially. There was this pilot officer, Tommy, who had a smart MG sports car and he was always bragging he was quicker than anyone on the road. His parents lived not far from mine so when we both had passes to go home for the weekend, I said I'd beat him back to the base. I even put some money on it.'

A waiter came over but stood by politely, not interrupting, so I continued.

183

'We met up in the marketplace and off we went, tearing through the town and out into the countryside. He had a bigger engine than me so he pulled ahead on the straight, but I just bided my time until we got to the bends. Down a gear, round the first turn and I was past him before he knew what was happening.'

The waiter coughed and asked if we were ready to order. He must have known my stories can take a while.

Once we'd ordered, I finished my story. 'The road was twisty from there on so I was laughing all the way to the guardhouse, where I had to dismount. That was my mistake. I'd agreed the finish line was the NAAFI, inside the base and I had to push my bike as fast as I could because I knew what was coming next. There was a toot-toot as Tommy drove past and piped me on the line. Officers were allowed to drive their vehicles around the base but ordinary men like me were not.'

After that, I thought he'd like to hear a few of my other stories about bikes. He chuckled at most of them until he seemed to get tired and started yawning.

'Best get back,' he said. I had a look at my watch and couldn't believe what time it was. The girls would be worried; I'd left them a couple of hours ago saying I'd be away a couple of minutes. We flew back in no time and I shook Ron's hand vigorously once he had set me back on the ground outside his office.

'You've made my day,' I told him.

'No worries. Nice to meet a fellow enthusiast,' he said.

~

I couldn't wait to get back to the van and tell Bituin and Nadia all about my little adventure. The door was open so I hollered, 'hello' as I approached.

There was no reply.

I almost tripped on an item of clothing. Something green and silky lay crushed under my shoe as I climbed into the van. It was Betty's old blouse that Bituin had altered. What was that doing there? Stupid of me, but when I picked it up, I couldn't help holding it to my cheek. The scent of Bituin's perfume hit my nostrils. Wherever she'd gone, she'd gone in such a hurry that she hadn't had time to take the few items of clothing she had. I sat for a long time stroking the sleeve of Betty's blouse wondering what had become of the two of them. I couldn't believe they had fled without good reason. One thing I had no doubt about. My little birds were in danger.

CHAPTER 15
The Police

'Maybe they're washing their hair? That can take a while.'

It was Betty. I was so relieved she was with me that I wanted to hug her. Except of course, I couldn't. Hair washing was always a palaver for Betty because she liked it to be really dry before she would show herself to anyone. "When it's all wet," she'd said, "it clings to my scalp and makes me look like a little old lady." She was still saying that when she really was a little old lady.

'Why have all these drawers been emptied out, if they're just washing?' I said.

'You're near the sea aren't you? They were probably looking for a costume to swim in.'

'Bless you Betty,' I said as I took out my walking frame and made for the washrooms. They were deserted. I headed to the beach.

It took me a while to walk to the sandy bay where I stood for a breather, carefully scanning the beach and rocky pools. Families huddled behind windbreaks eating fish and chips and children clambered over rocks, ignoring their mother's shouts to be careful. No sign of Bituin and Nadia. In the distance, tiny black dots like matchstick men jumped in and out of the waves. Maybe the girls were trying their hand at surfing. I started to walk towards the sea, feeling the strain as the sand got softer and wetter.

My phone rang. Where was it? Oh yes, I'd thrown it into the tray of my walker. I sat down to take the call. It was Billy.

'Harry, where on earth are you? I've been trying to reach you for days,' he said.

'Sorry, I'm in Cornwall with no signal on my phone and now I've lost the girls so I'm on the beach looking for them.'

'Girls? What girls?'

'Well there's the Filipino, the one you know about, and a Romanian I've had to take under my wing until she gets a teaching job. Do you remember, I asked you about that? Well, we managed to get her out of the terrible club she worked in so she's here with me as well. Except they've both disappeared for the moment.'

'You're going to have to walk me through this scenario a little slower, Harry. What club are you talking about?'

'Oh yes, I'm forgetting you don't know about that. We got the address from the computer, you know, the one we found in Mr Sharma's car?'

'No, I don't recall you mentioning any computer.'

'I wouldn't have taken it if I'd known it belonged to Mr Sharma. But I'm glad I did because there was this presentation on it about a scheme to exploit young girls into giving dirty old men a happy… '

I felt a tickle in my throat and starting coughing, slowly at first but it wouldn't stop and got worse. I fumbled around for the bottle of water I always have on hand for moments like these but dropped the phone instead. It was covered in wet sand when I picked it up.

Thankfully Billy was still there. 'Harry, Harry, are you OK?'

'Yes I'm alright,' I spluttered.

'I'm even more worried about you now. It sounds as though you have been drawn into a complicated and potentially dangerous situation. When are you coming back from Cornwall?'

'I don't rightly know. I've got to find these girls first.'

I was still wheezing but couldn't get the top off the water bottle with one hand.

'We need to meet up very soon to sort all this out. That will almost certainly involve the police, especially after what you've told me. You really are going to have to face that. I want to see this computer presentation. Have you still got it?'

Sand from the phone had got into one ear so I swopped it over to the other side.

'Yes, I've got it,' I wheezed.

I saw two girls strolling out of a café on the far side of the beach.

'If you're not coming back, perhaps I should meet you in Cornwall. I need a break from city life,' Billy continued.

The two girls disappeared into a gift shop.

'Right you are, Billy. Come this weekend. Got to go.'

I had a good old cough to clear my throat and swigged some water while I kept an eye on the gift shop. No-one re-appeared. Struggling to my feet, I headed towards the shops. The tide was coming in fast and the lifeguards were moving their viewing platform and equipment back up the beach. I could clearly see the people in the water now but there was no way of telling who was who from just their faces bobbing about in the surf, and when they left the sea they were all dressed in the same black suits that completely covered their bodies.

My walking frame clattered into a display of postcards in the entrance to the gift shop and nearly sent it crashing to the ground. Two girls span round at the noise. One had brassy blonde hair and the other was ginger. They looked at each other, sniggered and moved swiftly out of the shop.

I looked carefully in each shop and café, even the art gallery. I was getting desperate. Maybe Ron, the receptionist at the campsite had seen them. My legs were finished by the time I shuffled though his door.

'Hey up, Harry. You looks as though you lost that pound and found a penny,' he said when I sat down at his desk with a big sigh.

'I have,' I said, 'Except I haven't found a penny and what I've lost is worth far more than a pound.'

I had to confess to him that I'd forgotten to check-in two other occupants of my van to the campsite and that they had gone missing.

He frowned and opened his visitor book. 'Maybe they've wandered out to get some internet reception. There's none here and you know how they like to go online and chat to their friends every day. I'll have to charge you for the girls, mind. Even if they aren't here now, they were last night. That's £5 each per night, £10 altogether unless you want to pay for tonight as well?'

I wanted to tell him that they wouldn't be just strolling around on mobile phones because they were hiding

189

from wicked men who wanted to exploit them. Instead, I handed him a £10 note.

'There is one other thing you can do for me,' I said. 'Can you ask the other campers on site if they saw a black VW van come in here during the time we had our little trip on your bike, please?'

'Sure, I can ask. Friends of yours?'

'Thanks,' I said and shuffled out, pretending not to hear his question.

~

Having checked the van one more time and found it still empty, I decided I had to call the police. That involved going back to the only place my phone seemed to work: the beach. The tide was up and children, swimmers, surfers and lifeguards were now crammed together into a much smaller space. It was hard to hear myself speak above the shrieks of the kids and the pounding of the surf as I dialled 999.

When I told the operator my problem, he said he would put me through to my local police station. The woman from the police station took down my details and asked when I had last seen the missing girls. I pictured the two of them, sitting at the table in the van finishing their breakfast as I'd set off to reception.

'Approximately 9.45 this morning,' I said.

'You say they are both in their early 20's, so they're both adults. It's now 2.20pm so they've been away from you for not quite five hours. Would you say that's abnormal?' she asked.

'Well, yes. We've never been apart this length of time before.'

'And how long have you known these ladies, sir?'

'One of them for the best part of a month. The other one, let me think now...' I counted back to the day when I had first met Nadia on my fingers. 'One, two, three. Yes, including today, three days.'

'So you don't know these ladies very well, sir?'

If she'd known that I'd seen one of them in just her undies, she wouldn't have asked that, but I couldn't tell her all the facts on the phone.

'It's just not like them at all. I think someone may have made off with them.'

'Is that the sea I can hear near you, sir?'

'Yes, I'm on the beach.'

'Is it possible they went swimming? Have you reported this to the lifeguards?'

'They didn't bring any swimming things with them. We weren't expecting to be near the sea and I'm not even sure they can swim.'

'Just a precaution, sir. Please relay your concerns to the lifeguards so they can watch out for them. In the meantime I will report this matter on our system here and I expect someone will come over and take a full statement from you later today. Will you be at your campsite?'

'I may drive around to look for them.'

'That is up to you sir, although it is a little premature to start a search. Make sure someone is at the campsite to meet them when they do return, and keep your phone on so we can call you when we are nearby.' That was it; she rang off.

"Premature to start a search," was it? Too late more

like. I did as the lady at the police station told me and had a word with the lifeguard. He was a nice enough young man; his hair was in braids down to his shoulders like those West Indian singers and he was forever brushing it out of his face as the wind was getting up and he had to keep a watch out to sea. When I asked after an Asian and an east-European girl, he shrugged his shoulders and pointed at the water. It was hard to tell who was who. He gave me a chair so I could sit and keep a look out for them. It must have been the sea air that made me feel sleepy because the next thing I knew I was dreaming that my phone was ringing. I woke with a start. It was ringing.

'Hello, is that Mr Pigeon? It's the police. We're on our way to your campsite following up on your report of two missing women.'

I scuttled back as fast as I could to find them waiting in their car next to my van.

'Good afternoon, I'm PC Frank Swinton and this is my colleague PCSO Brenda Pierson.' He looked stern, tall with a gruff voice and not much of a smile. She was a chubby, young thing with a fresh, friendly face who scribbled notes in a pad and left the talking to Frank. I'd decided to tell them everything so I started at the beginning and told them about Bituin's arrival.

'You say that you offered to give shelter to this Filipino lady after she crashed her car into your gates. Did you tell anyone about this?' PC Frank asked. We were sitting around the table in my van as it had turned cold outside.

'I told Betty, of course. In fact it was her idea to help in the first place.'

'Your wife?'

'Yes, she's my wife. Or rather she was.'

'You're divorced?' Frank asked.

'No. Good heavens, no. Betty did mention divorce once but that was a long time ago. As a matter of fact, it was after I'd met a namesake of your colleague here,' I said, nodding towards Brenda who looked up from her pad. 'But we soon made up again. No, Betty's dead.'

Frank shifted his long legs that were cramped under the low table. 'I see. So you talked to your late wife but not the police?'

'I told them about the car, obviously. But Bituin was too scared to go back to her employers and didn't have any friends. So I hid her.'

'Hid her? Where exactly?' Frank was leaning towards me now and Brenda couldn't seem to keep her eyes off me.

'To begin with, she was in Betty's Memorial Room as I called it. No-one went in there as it was full of Betty's old things.'

'How long did this go on?'

'A week or more I think. It was touch and go at times especially when a policewoman came round. She was on the scent alright but I managed to move Bituin into my campervan – the one that we're sitting in now. That's what gave me the idea of having a little holiday until all the fuss had died down.'

'Mr Pigeon. Harry; can I call you Harry?'

'Everyone does,' I said.

'Thanks, Harry. You stated earlier that your motive for concealing this lady was that she would be abused if you returned her to her employers whose car she had taken. Is that correct?'

'Yes, and I didn't know the half of what was going on then. She was lucky to escape before they made her work in one of their sleazy massage parlours, like Nadia.'

Brenda looked up again, her eyebrows raised. Frank gave me a steady stare, trying to make me out, I suppose.

'We'll come to Nadia in a moment, if we may. I thought you said Bituin – is that how you pronounce her name?'

I nodded. 'It means a star in Filipino.'

'Lovely. I thought you said she was employed by Mr Sharma at the Indian Embassy?'

'That's right. Mr Sharma was the one who tricked me into chatting too long while he had my house broken into and searched.'

'What did the police say when you…' Frank saw me shaking my head. 'Oh, of course you wouldn't have told them would you?'

He was giving me another of his long, hard looks when there was a growl of a motorbike and Ron rode over the grass towards us, pausing outside the van to shout through the open door.

'Sorry to disturb, lady and gentlemen,' he said, nodding to my guests. 'I'm on my way out but before I go, I just wanted to tell Harry that someone did see a dark VW van drive in here this morning. It was when we were out. Came down to this field and left soon after.'

I struggled to my feet. 'We've got to get after them.'

Frank scrambled out from under the table and moved quickly between me and the door.

'Hold on Harry. After who?'

'The thugs who have got my girls. He's just given us the proof you need.' I pointed after Ron who was disappearing out of the field on his bike. 'That black VW van belongs to Vishal Sharma, I'm sure of it. It's been following me around ever since it appeared outside my house. It's come damned close to catching me a couple of times. Now it has finally got my girls, I know it has. I hate to think what they're doing to them now.' I was trembling, close to tears.

Frank took me by the arm. 'Don't excite yourself Harry. We'll put a call out and find this van. Do you have the registration number and model?'

I blurted out the details as far as I remembered them and Brenda went to the police car and fiddled with the radio.

'Brenda's reporting the details. All our patrol cars will be trying to trace that van now. Let's have a cup of tea, Harry, while you tell me the rest of the story,' Frank said.

I was shaking too much to strike a match to turn on the gas so Frank took over and put the kettle on. 'You said there's a computer with evidence of this gang's activities on it, is that right?'

'Yes it will tell you all about their business of bringing girls like Nadia in from foreign countries and selling them as slaves to sex clubs. She thought she was applying for a job as a sports teacher and she ended up giving massages,' I said and then added with emphasis: 'With happy endings.'

'Where do you keep your teabags, Mr Pigeon?' asked Brenda who had taken over the tea making duties.

'In that cupboard,' I said.

'Sorry, what do you mean by happy ending?' Frank asked.

Brenda rolled her eyes up to the roof and sighed.

'I didn't know either until—' I began.

Brenda interrupted. 'It's a wank, Frank. I'll put that in the notes so the sarg will understand too.'

It was Brenda's turn to receive one of Frank's hard stares. 'Can you show me this computer, Harry?' he asked.

'Yes, of course,' I opened the drawer where I had put it. 'It's gone. They must have taken that as well. I'm sure I put it in here. I wouldn't have forgotten that,' I said, frantically looking through all the cupboards and drawers.

'Do you forget many things Harry? You seem very fit physically but some people of your age aren't quite as – how shall I put it – mentally agile as they used to be.'

'Sometimes I do forget things. I used to ask Betty. She had a memory like an elephant. Now I write myself lists.'

I had stopped searching and stood staring out of the window. 'Mind you, that are times when even my list doesn't work. I was in Tesco's recently and I like to mark down not just the item I'm buying but the aisle where I can find it and the section it's in. On this particular day, I couldn't make head nor tail of it. Nothing was where it should be and I was getting really tired wandering around trying to find things. I leaned on my trolley and pulled out the mobile to phone Betty and ask her if I'd picked up the wrong list. I almost dialled it too before I remembered...'

Tears had filled my eyes so I paused. They were both staring at me, probably thinking I was crazy: crying over a shopping list. I took a few deep breaths to pull myself together.

'... before I remembered she couldn't answer the phone from over in the cemetery. I did get through to her though. "You silly old fool," she said. "They've re-organised the store, changed everything round." That's

196

when I remembered that they'd closed the store for a re-fit and I hadn't been in since.'

'Talk to you often, does she?' asked Frank.

'Oh yes. Most days we have a chat about something.' I sat down, sighing.

There was a bit of a pause. Brenda had put her pen down and Frank was watching me in that penetrating way of his.

'Do you mind if I go to the toilet?' I asked.

Frank looked around the van.

'No there isn't one on board; I'll have to use the campsite facilities. They're not far,' I said.

'I'll take you over in the car,' he said.

I wouldn't normally drive to the toilet but I didn't want to turn down the opportunity for a ride in a police car.

'A few years back this would have been a Jaguar, not a foreign car, but I don't suppose you've been in the Police Force that long have you?' I asked, as he turned the ignition key.

'Fifteen years now,' he said pulling away slowly. 'Jaguar is owned by an Indian company today so technically it's a foreign car too, although it is still made in England. And we're called the Police Service now, not the Force. Someone thought that was the wrong image.'

We've got a right one here, I thought. He even came into the toilet with me although he didn't need to go.

When we got back to the van, Brenda had obviously been having a nose around.

'Forgive me, Harry,' she said. 'But I couldn't help noticing there's not much evidence of young women living in the van. No sign of any clothing or make-up, for example?'

'That's because they didn't have much. When they came to me, Nadia was wearing not much more than her birthday suit and Bituin only had a small bag. I'll show you what they wore.'

I went over to the drawer where the girls had kept their things and pulled out a skirt. It was Betty's lovely blue one.

'My wife didn't often wear this colour. She preferred green.'

Frank peered into the drawer. 'Are these all your wife's clothes?'

'Pretty much, yes. Luckily Bituin brought more than she needed so we had some spare for Nadia. She shared Betty's tastes in clothes, I think.'

'Did she share her size to?' Frank held up one of Betty's dresses stretching it out to show how wide it was.

'Good heavens, no. They're both slim girls but it's amazing how they can tuck them in and hitch them up with a belt.'

Brenda chuckled. 'Me and my friends at school were good at that. Mum would always buy me sensible skirts to wear but as soon as I was out of sight of our house, I would hitch them up a few inches.'

And very pretty you must have looked too, I thought.

Frank took a deep breath and looked at his watch. 'I'm beginning to wonder if we're chasing shadows here, Harry. According to the reception of the campsite, you didn't check them in when you arrived. Has anyone else seen "your girls" as you call them?'

Brenda raised her eyebrows and watched me, pen poised.

I thought carefully about that question, running

through in my mind all the people who might have seen them. I'd been pretty good at keeping them hidden. I didn't want to draw Dan in.

'The RAC man may have spotted them but he was too polite to say anything.'

That did it. Frank wanted to know all about the breakdown and how I'd said I was on my own to get the RAC to come quicker. He was drumming his fingers on the table and frowning by the time I had finished.

'Right, Harry. That will be all for now,' he said, standing up.

'Where are you going to look?' I asked.

'Where are we going to look?' He had deep furrows in his brow as he repeated my question. 'To be honest, Harry, I'm asking myself what are we looking for here because there's not much sign that two young ladies lived in this van and, by your own admission, no-one has seen them. I'm just wondering if Betty hasn't misled you about them or talked about them in some way so that you think something has happened, when it really hasn't.'

My mouth fell open as he spoke and I could hear my chesty breathing. I'd been sitting here, wasting precious time with this… this excuse of a policeman who hadn't understood a word of what I'd been telling him.

'I see. You're saying that I've made it up, is that it?

'Harry, I need to be sure you are not deluding yourself as well as us before I commit resources to this enquiry. I've seen a lot during my time in the Police Force but nothing approaching a young, female car thief and a pole dancer riding around the country with a ninety-seven-year-old man in a campervan chased by a criminal gang.'

I wanted to scream at him but I managed to keep myself under control. 'It's the Police Service, not the Force, by the way. I can remember that much, although you seem to have forgotten. And she's not a Pole; she's from Romania.'

'Whatever. Look, we'll check out the other police reports you have referred to and track down this van. That'll validate your story. Or not. In the meantime, I want you to stay here at the campsite in case we need you for further questions. Is that OK?'

'I will be out looking for them as you are not going too. But I'll come back here if that's what you want.'

'No, that's not what I want. I want you to stay here. Right here. Is that understood?'

Once they had gone, I sat outside my van, mulling over events, tears welling at the back of my eyes. What would Betty say? I was in a right old mess with no way out that I could see. I wished I had brought the morphine.

CHAPTER 16

The Plan

'You're right. You're in a right old mess and you've got only yourself to blame. But that doesn't mean you can sit around moping. Why don't you do something?' Betty was awake and in one of her rare, decisive moods.

'It's not as simple as—'

'Why don't you do what you did in the war when you hadn't got what you needed?'

I knew what she was talking about. When our squadron of Hurricanes landed after a dog-fight, they had all sorts of bits missing that had been shot off by Messerschmitts. It was my job to find replacements from our stores so the mechanics could get the planes back in the air the next day. Sometimes the cupboard was bare. I hadn't got what I needed. Straightaway, I'd be on the phone to the other stations nearby. 'Have you got this piston or that propeller shaft?' and if they said yes I'd jump in the Bedford truck, switch off the governor that kept your speed to no more than 50mph and I was off. Whatever it took, I would collect the parts I needed and have them back to base for the mechanics to work on. Even if I had to break a few rules to do it.

Betty was right. If PC Frank Swinton wasn't going to

do anything, I would have to do it myself. If I'd sat round during the war, waiting for someone else to do something, where would we have been? We'd have had planes sitting on the ground waiting for parts while Mr Goering paid us another visit and smashed us all to smithereens. Frank may have tried to ground me but it would take more than him to stop me flying. Besides I'd realised where I should concentrate my forces. I was pretty certain I knew where that VW and my girls had gone.

I gave Betty a little salute. 'Flight Sergeant Harry Pigeon reporting for duty,' I said before quickly packing up the van: I was taking to the road.

~

I reckoned it was 150 miles and there were only three hours of daylight left. With my old eyes, I couldn't drive at night so my right foot was hard on the accelerator as I climbed up the hill out of the village and away from the coast. The satnav blinked beside me on the seat. Didn't need that for this journey; I knew where I was going. Besides I didn't know how to turn it on.

Exactly one hour into my journey, I pulled into a car park, grabbed my mobile phone and fumbled in my pocket for the piece of paper with Mr Sharma's number on it.

Khumar answered immediately. 'Good afternoon, Norman. It is indeed a pleasure to hear again from you. We have been waiting most patiently for your call.'

I bet you have.

'I have a message for Mr Sharma. I believe he has now

got back what he lost and I want to be sure he keeps to his side of the bargain.'

'I am sure when I pass this message on to Mr Sharma, he will be asking what bargain he has to keep his side of, Harry?'

'Tell him I would like to talk to him about his business plan. I know all about it. I think the authorities would be interested in it too, but I want him to explain it to me first. And tell him to look after those girls. There'll be consequences if any harm comes to them.' I had to shout to make my voice heard above the wind that was whipping around the van.

'I am happy to convey your messages to Mr Sharma but, once again, I know he will be asking me what girls and what consequences you are referring to, Harry.'

'He will know what I am talking about. Ask Mr Sharma if he can meet me tomorrow.'

'I will certainly ask him, Harry. Are you suggesting a meeting at King's Cross station once again?'

'No. Bristol,' I said.

'I am calling you back, Harry.' He put the phone down.

I was tired already so it was an effort hauling myself up into the cab and back on the road. Sitting in the van, peering hard through the windscreen, I felt lonely again; no eager voices chatting to each other; no satnav lady saying "at the roundabout take the second exit." Just the noise of the engine and my own thoughts to keep me company. But, funnily enough, I found a certain strength in being alone. There was something I had to get done and only I could do it.

Billy didn't answer when I phoned from the service

station, nor did Dan, so I grabbed a greasy looking pasty and got back on the road. It was motorway now so I could relax at the wheel while I munched my food. Nowadays, you're not supposed to eat while driving but I didn't have time to stop.

My mobile rang. Not supposed to answer that while driving either but there was nowhere to stop, so I tried to press the reply button with one hand and steer with the other, but my fingers were too clumsy and I dropped the phone onto the seat beside me.

'Hello, hello,' I heard someone say.

I leaned over as close as I dared to the phone, my head on one side so I could keep an eye on the road.

'Is that you Dan?' I shouted. 'I'm driving so can't talk long. I've lost that computer. Can you remember what was on that presentation?'

'Say that last bit again, Harry. You sound as though you're calling from the open cockpit of a bi-plane.'

'I need to know what was on that computer presentation. Can you remember much of what it said?'

There was a pause and I thought I had lost him, so I shouted: 'Hello, hello. Can you hear me?'

'I can hear you, Harry. I was just checking something. I may have a copy of it but it's taking too long to find. I will have to call you back. I don't want you to crash that plane.'

'I'm in the campervan, not a cockpit. It's quite important.'

He was gone and I needed to concentrate on my route as there were signs ahead. I was nearly back in Bristol.

'This is when I need you, Betty,' I said out loud. 'Have a look at that roadmap and tell me where that campsite is.'

'It's no good asking me now, as you know full well,' she said. 'But why don't you follow that sign with a tent and a caravan on it?'

She was right, again. Being right was one of Betty's little jokes – at my expense of course. She would say to one of her friends: "When I met Harry, I knew he was Mr Right. Then she'd pause and start smiling before continuing, "It was only later that I found out his first name was Always." That made her chuckle; not that you would have heard a loud cackle or snort like some people make. No, Betty had a quiet laugh.

I followed the signs to the campsite. It was one of those upmarket sites with flower-beds along the approach road and no potholes so I was glad that I arrived before the check-in deadline and I didn't have to break the rules to get in. The woman at reception looked at me strangely when I checked in just myself, but advised her that I hoped to pick up a couple of young girls to stay as well. I quickly asked her for the telephone number of a local taxi company and left to park up my van.

~

The taxi driver also gave me a strange look when, later on, I asked for the Bollywood Bar. So I asked him if he had ever been there.

'Oh no, sir,' he said. 'I am a married man with a family.'

'What goes on there to put you off?' I asked.

'It is for single men, sir, who want to see pretty women dancing. My wife, sisters and daughters are pretty enough. I don't need to go and look at other women.' He had a point but it was interesting that he didn't seem to know what else went on there.

Just as we arrived at the street where I wanted to get out, my phone rang.

'Hang on a moment, Billy. I have to pay the taxi man, but I do need to speak to you,' I said struggling out of the back seat and fumbling for my wallet.

'Sorry about that Billy,' I said catching my breath as the taxi sped off. 'Now, young man, I need your help. I'm certain I'm on to this gang that are kidnapping girls and making them work for next to nothing, doing the sorts of things that their mothers and fathers would not want them to do. So can you come to Bristol and help me catch them red-handed?'

'I will come to Bristol, Harry, but on the condition that you involve the police in what you are doing. I've told you before, this is not a matter for an amateur sleuth. You need to inform the authorities and let them deal with these criminals through official channels.'

I wasn't sure what a sleuth was but I reassured him I had already been to the police; however we had to give them a hand because they didn't seem to be up to the job. He agreed to catch a train the very next morning. The first part of my plan was in place.

I didn't think the next bit was going to be quite as easy as it turned out. I walked up the small street that ran along the side of the Bollywood Bar. There was the very fire door that I had come out of with Nadia when she had run away. I examined it closely: it was shut tight and I couldn't hear any noise on the other side. The street was deserted and there was no sign of life at the corner when I peered carefully round. No bouncers outside the front door. No bright lights advertising exotic dancing. It was closed. A notice pinned to the door explained why:

The Bollywood Bar is very sorry to
close for internal redecorating.
It will be opening again very soon.

I was about to leave when I saw a second notice, quite small and in smart typing. It was a strain to read in the dark but I made out the sense of it:

The Bollywood Health Club and Spa is open,
by appointment only, for existing customers.

I hadn't got a pencil to write down the telephone number so I thought I would try ringing it there and then.

'Bollywood Spa. How can I help?' It was a young man's voice.

'I'd like to make an appointment, please, for tomorrow.'

'We are opening from 11am to 5pm sir. Who is your preferred masseuse?'

'Nadia at 2pm.'

'Can I take your name?'

'My name is uh… it's Norman.' My old brain had to think a bit quick to remember who I wasn't, if you know what I mean. 'How do I get in? The main door seems to be shut.'

'We are opening in the street to the side for appointments only, sir. Just give your name to the person on the door.'

'Thank you. Oh, and someone else by the name of Billy will be with me.'

'Then he will be needing an appointment to enter. Shall I also book him for a massage, sir?'

'Yes. I've heard you have someone called Bituin working for you, now. Is that correct?'

There was a rustle of paper. 'She is not on the rota tomorrow, sir. Katrina is free. Can I book her for your friend?'

'Yes, she will do,' I said and that was the end of the call.

I'd found Nadia. Easy as that. I was sure Bituin was with her. Now I had to get Mr Sharma and son there in order to spring my little trap.

On the way back to the campsite I called Kumar. As usual, he answered after one ring. He must spend all his day watching his phone, waiting for it to make a noise.

'Good evening, Mr Norman. I was soon to be calling you. Mr Sharma would like to know at what time to meet you?'

'2.15pm sharp at the Bollywood. The Bar is closed so tell them to go to the side entrance into the Health Club. Tell Mr Sharma to bring his son, Vishal, with him. I have seen his plans and I want to put some money into his business.'

'I am making all the necessary arrangements to make sure they both hear all you have to tell them, Mr Norman,' Khumar said and rang off.

Next, I called Dan who had left a message to say he had some good news, so I arranged to meet him the next morning in the city centre. My old van was a welcome sight as I climbed the step and unlocked the door. As soon as my head hit the pillow I was asleep.

~

The next morning, I woke early, my mind buzzing with the details of my plan. All I had left to do was organise the police to turn up at the right time. I called Frank. He seemed quite anxious when I told him that I had moved on and not at all impressed that I'd found the missing girls.

'Look, don't you worry about me and what I'm up to,' I told him. 'Just come to the Bollywood Spa, Bristol at 2.30 this afternoon and you can meet these mystery girls, as you like to call them. They'll tell you all about the nasty people who have turned them into slaves. I have invited the leaders of the gang along too, so you can catch them red-handed.'

There was a pause and I could hear him breathing out heavily. 'This doesn't work like the movies, Harry. You are out of my jurisdiction now so I will talk to my colleagues in Bristol. I'd like you to report to the police station there as soon as possible so we can investigate this properly.'

So I could sit through another two hours of pointless questions while those thugs abuse my girls? Not likely! 'I'm meeting my lawyer in the morning who is coming specially from London, so like I've said, can you or the Bristol police come to the Bollywood Spa at 2.30 please? The timing is important so don't be late.'

There was another pause and then some clicking on the line. 'Where exactly are you now, Harry?'

I wasn't going to fall for that one. 'I'm out and about so I'll meet you at the Bollywood, 2.30. OK?'

'OK, OK. Someone will meet you there. Where are you staying, Harry?'

I ignored that question. 'Tell them to come prepared for trouble. We are dealing with people who are not always too friendly and I wouldn't want anyone to get hurt.'

That did it. His voice sounded really agitated now. 'Harry, just stay right where you are and we'll be with you very quickly to sort this all out.'

It sounded as though he knew where I was. 'Sorry Frank, I have to go out. See you at 2.30.' I put the phone down sharpish. It was time to move on.

~

I managed to get a taxi to pick me up at the campsite and asked for the harbour-side.

'Are you exploring the old city today, mister?' the driver asked. He looked a bit like my namesake Harry Belafonte except he had plaited hair down to his shoulders. I noticed a small photo on his dashboard of a dark-skinned man with wiry hair and a bushy beard, a gold crown on his head, his chest covered in medals. I recognised him immediately even though I hadn't seen his picture for years.

'Are you from Abyssinia?' I asked.

He chuckled when he saw who I was pointing at. 'No man, I'm from Jamaica but this is my King.' He picked up the photo and bowed his head.

'I think you'll find he was an Emperor,' I said. 'I travelled on a troopship all the way to RAF Khormaksar in Aden to help him. Hottest station in the RAF, 100 degrees in the shade.'

He turned right round to look at me. 'You fought for the Emperor Haile Selassie?'

'We were deployed but didn't fight until it was too late. We got Mussolini out in the end though.'

'Respect, man. That deserves a free tour. I'll show you where ships sailed from here to Africa on a regular basis. Not with troops on board though.'

'When was this?'

'I am talking before your time, when the English kings were from Germany and all named George. Trading ships they were, full of what they thought the Africans needed – blankets, guns, alcohol. What they wanted in exchange was slaves.'

He had my full attention now. 'Slaves?'

'Yes, my forefathers were taken from their homes and forced to sail on ships from this very harbour all the way across the Atlantic to the West Indies to work on the plantations. They filled their holds with black people for over 100 years. Do you know how many slaves were carried in ships from this harbour?'

He was in his stride now, waving one hand in the air, watching me in his mirror. He didn't wait for my answer.

'500,000, my friend. Half a million of my people in ships from this very city. If they survived, which many did not, they were sold for £20, maybe £30 if they were young and fit.'

Some things don't change, do they? I'd paid a similar price for Nadia, although that was for half an hour, not for life.

Driving down the waterside of the old harbour he continued his commentary, 'The first ship that sailed from here to take slaves to Jamaica was called *The Beginning.*'

The beginning and now a happy ending, I thought.

~

He dropped me at the café where I had arranged to meet Dan, but he wasn't there. I took a seat outside with a good view and listened to the distant strains of a busker in the busy square. My phone rang. Billy had arrived at the station so I asked him to meet me in the same café.

Dan came panting up as I finished the call, wearing a dark coat with a hood that he kept up over his head.

'Sorry I'm late, Harry,' he said glancing round. 'Do you mind if we go inside? It's a little exposed to the public eye out here.'

'Are you still worried about those bouncers?' I asked as he led me into the dingy interior.

'Having been up close and personal with them, yes I am. They are rough, tough and sadists to a man.'

'Can I get you a coffee or something?'

'Charming as I've always found your company, I am just going to give you this and disappear.' He briefly flashed a small stick the size of my thumb in front of my eyes and then put it back into his pocket.

'Whatever's that?'

'It's a memory stick. Plug it into a USB port and you will find what you need.' He might as well have said that in Chinese for all the sense it made to me.

'Ask someone who knows about computers and they will show you how to open it. When I unlocked your...

er… your wife's computer, I took the precaution of backing up the data in case I wiped it in the process. I put it all on this stick. Keep it where you won't lose it.'

He handed it to me, and I carefully found an inside compartment in my jacket pocket and slipped it in there.

'It's the presentation you asked me about, Harry. The business plan about trafficking. I had to do something with it or even my conscience would have been uneasy. Make sure it gets into the right hands. Goodbye, Harry, and good luck.'

With that, he put the hood back over his head and strode quickly out of the café. I looked around, fingering the small object in my pocket, not really believing it could do what he said. If it did have that presentation on it, that was all I would need to convince PC Frank of my case and have those crooks arrested. I ordered myself a fresh pot of tea with some scones and marmalade to celebrate.

CHAPTER 17

The Slave Trade

No sooner had I got my teeth into my scone, when I heard from Betty. 'Don't get carried away, Harry. You be careful you don't end up in hospital, like I did.'

She always did blame me for the time she broke her leg. Granted I did book us into a little cottage up north with lots of steps and a slippery floor, but I couldn't tell that in advance, could I? I wasn't to know she was going to trip and fall. The thought of her sprawled on that stone floor, leg all twisted and crying in pain quite put me off my scone.

'I just wanted us to have one last holiday away from home,' I said. 'I wasn't to know it would end with you in a strange hospital bed, miles from home.'

'No, and you don't know the problems this little scheme of yours will lead to, either, do you?' Betty always did see the gloomy side of life. Didn't half knock my confidence, I can tell you.

I was about to remind her that it was her idea to do something, when I saw Billy waving at me from the street outside. With his oriental look and casual clothes, you could have mistaken him for a tourist as he made his way between the empty tables towards me.

'Hi, Uncle Harry.' He hesitated and quickly looked around. 'Or should I call you Norman?' he whispered.

I wiped the marmalade and butter away from the sides of my mouth. 'Better give the impression you're a professional in front of the police and call me Mr Pigeon. The girls know me as Harry.'

'What girls?' he asked, pulling up a chair and waving to the waitress.

'I've made an appointment for us with two of the girls at the spa. I'm booked in with Nadia and you're seeing someone I haven't heard of before called Katrina.'

'And what is the nature of this appointment, Harry... sorry, Mr Pigeon?'

'They think it is one of their usual appointments.'

'Which is what exactly?' he interrupted.

'It's just a massage but when she gets into it, she will make it clear that she can go further.'

'Stop, stop. I need to get my head round this. I have an appointment to go to a massage parlour that is actually a brothel to meet a girl you don't know called Katrina. Is that right?'

'Pretty much, yes but it's all part of a plan to prove to the police that this is going on under their very noses. They think I am making it all up. Can you believe that?'

'To be brutally honest, actually, yes I can.'

That stopped me in my tracks. First Betty, now him, sowing doubts in my mind. I was close to tears and I think he noticed because he put his hand on mine on the table.

'Sorry, Harry. It sounds like fantasy because you haven't told me the full story. Let's start again, shall we?'

215

'This may convince you, if I can't.' I pulled Dan's gadget out of my pocket and watched the eyes in his moon-shaped face open wide, making him look even more like an owl. 'All we need is a computer and you can see the proof of their slave racket for yourself.'

'Fortunately, I packed my laptop so we can take a look,' he said, tapping the grey rucksack at his feet. 'But not here. From memory, the public library is not far and it has a reading room that we can use.'

He was right: it was a short stroll to the library, an imposing-looking building from the outside and even more grand on the inside. It was just like being in a cathedral with white columns going up to a high, domed ceiling. There was hardly anyone there so we had a long desk all to ourselves. Billy fished out his round, rimless glasses, perched them on his stub of a nose and, in hardly no time, he had his tiny computer up and running and there, glaring at me again, were those shocking words:

Investment Opportunity In The Human Asset Business

Billy read faster than me, so he flicked through the pages quickly. I stopped him on one that was headed *Total Market*, when I saw the figure 500,000.

'What's this about?' I asked.

'It claims that 500,000 new women and children are trafficked into the sex trade every year.'

I couldn't believe it. Half a million people made into slaves every year.

'Do you know that is exactly the same as the number of slaves put into Bristol ships over a 100-year period. My taxi driver told me. Look at the fuss that's made about that. This lot are ignored,' I said.

Billy was nodding. 'Half a million was also the total number of slaves originally imported into what is now the USA over several hundred years. That number grew of course as they reproduced and there were many more slaves in the Caribbean and South America. Today, according to this presentation, there are in excess of one million slaves, or "human assets" as it calls them, operating in the sex trade around the world. Slavery is just as big a business as it was back then, if not bigger.'

'Do you think it's right?' I asked.

He scratched his head. 'In all probability these are reasonable estimates. The figures come from reliable sources according to the referencing. Whoever wrote this did their research. It has the feel of an MBA presentation.'

'Just what Dan said.'

'And who might Dan be?' asked Billy.

'He's the clever young man that got this off Mr Sharma's computer for me.'

'Ah, obtained illicitly, I presume, so it may be inadmissible as evidence.' Billy rubbed his chin and flicked forward to another page. 'Fascinating reading though. Look at this table. It shows that the average price paid for a trafficked sex slave today is £1,200 compared to the annual revenue each one generates of £26,000. That's a very healthy margin of profit in only one year. No wonder the author has taken the trouble to prepare a business plan to expand their enterprise.'

'What exactly is it that they are proposing to do? I'm not too familiar with these things,' I confessed.

'Let me have a more thorough read and I will tell you,' he said.

It was time I went to the toilet so that suited me. I looked at my watch. 12 noon. Plenty of time before we sprang our trap. All of a sudden it seemed small beer compared to the scale of what was going on around the world. Still you have to start somewhere.

Billy was scribbling in a note pad when I returned to the desk. He leaned back in his chair, puffing out his cheeks.

'At first glance this reads like a standard investment proposal. It analyses the market, demonstrates that there is considerable potential to make large profits and asks punters to invest some money in the venture for a very attractive return.'

'But it's not a standard business is it? Surely it's illegal to do this sort of thing?' I said, dragging back a chair so I could sit down.

'You would be forgiven for presuming so. However, the author of this document claims to have found a loophole. That's his USP – sorry – unique selling point. He believes he can operate in a way that will be overlooked by law enforcement agencies in this and other countries.'

'Do you think he can?'

'It is clever, I must admit. Let me try and explain.'

I fiddled with my hearing aid. I didn't want to miss any of this.

'What he describes as the "human assets business", more commonly known to us as trafficking, can be divided into stages: first, acquisition of the person; secondly, moving them to another place, usually a foreign

218

country; thirdly, exploitation as a sex worker or in some other form of forced labour. The author of this document has developed a very efficient process for the first two stages, it would seem. Historically, people were acquired by coercion and smuggled across borders in the back of a truck or the boot of a car. Now, the free movement of labour between increasingly porous national boundaries has made it much easier.'

'Nadia just applied for a job and was flown here. Is that what you mean?' I asked.

'That would certainly fit with how he describes the operation. They lure girls from the poor countries of Eastern Europe and Asia with the prospect of jobs or marriage in more prosperous countries like the UK. They lend them the money for their travel and work permits if they need them, so there is no coercion involved. Young women come willingly believing that they will soon be walking along streets paved with gold.'

The memory of what happened to Nadia soon after her arrival came flooding back to me and, I know it sounds silly for a grown man like me, but I had tears in my eyes as Billy went on.

'Their situation changes catastrophically when they arrive. The girls find out that the promised job is selling themselves on street corners and their prospective husband is a pimp who is running a team of prostitutes. Moreover, exorbitant interest rates on their debts from the costs of getting here ensure they never pay them off. Threatened physically and mentally, they are trapped and often take to drugs and alcohol to escape from the pain of their miserable lives.'

Billy wasn't looking at the presentation or his notes any more and I realised he had come across this kind of thing before in his own work, tracking down missing youngsters. Taking a few deep breaths, we sat in silence for a moment or two.

'So how is he going to make all this legal?' I finally asked.

'He's greedy it would seem. At present his operation stops at stage two. He sells trafficked women on to clubs, brothels and pimps who write him a cheque for a few thousand pounds in return for a 'human asset' who works for no pay, just their basic costs of food and accommodation.'

'Just like the slave ships did,' I said.

'Indeed, just like the slavers of old. There is a list of addresses of his customers who buy these modern slaves appended to the presentation. Presumably the Bollywood Bar is one of them.'

'Yes, we found it from the postcodes.'

'What he is now proposing is called "vertical integration" in management-speak. He wants to take control of operations further down the supply chain.' Billy must have seen the blank look on my face because he paused and looked at his notes. 'According to the presentation, when they sell a slave into the sex trade in Western Europe they make around £3,000 for each one. Each of those slaves goes on to make an average revenue of £70,000 each year for their owners by performing over 3000 sex acts. That's about ten per day at £20 each. It doesn't take a genius to realise that there is a lot more profit to be had from the end-users of this business than from the middlemen in the supply chain. The problem is that the risk is also higher.'

'What sort of risks are you talking about?'

'Procuring and committing sex acts is illegal in most of Western Europe, the main exception being the Netherlands. The ultimate risk is a custodial sentence for the owner and the forced closure of their business.'

'Surely getting these girls here and selling them is against the law as well?'

'Certainly. Trafficking for sexual exploitation is a crime in most countries. But it is hard to uncover and prove. Traffickers can hide behind legitimate-looking job agencies and often do have a few real jobs on their books as cover. If they are caught, they can just plead ignorance of the real fate of their clients and claim they thought it was a genuine job offer.'

I looked at my watch. Time was ticking on but I did need to understand this before we confronted the Sharmas.

'So why would they want to risk going to prison even if they could make more money?'

'That is the clever part of this proposal, the USP I mentioned earlier. The author is planning to open a chain of outlets offering a range of exotic massages that appear to be legitimate, oriental health treatments.'

'That's not what's on offer at the Bollywood,' I said.

'I did say *appear* to be legitimate. The proposal is to cloak sexual services in the language of traditional medicines that work on the flow of energy within the body to ensure it is in balance. Mr Sharma's Indian ancestors, not to mention my own Chinese forefathers, have been practicing this form of healing for over 4000 years so it has the legitimacy of history going for it. Go to your GP and he will give you some pills. Go to a Chinese or Indian doctor and he might propose a change to your diet or some herbs. Or a massage.'

'I bet it's not the sort of massage on offer at the Bollywood,' I said.

'Actually it might be. One of our most important energies is our life-force or sexual energy. If that's misaligned, you may be advised to redirect it through orgasmic release.'

'Back to happy endings,' I sighed.

Billy looked at me over his glasses. 'I see you are well versed in the vernacular of this industry, Harry.'

'I've picked up a bit of the lingo. Are you telling me that this type of massage is legal?' I asked.

'No, in the UK, offering any form of sexual activity for sale is deemed illegal, and that includes orgasmic massage. But in practice, no-one is going to be prosecuted if it is dressed up as part of a traditional healing practice. As I said, it's a clever proposal.'

Billy was right: it was smart. I couldn't help thinking that a young whippersnapper like Vishal was not the only one behind it; an older mind like his father's must be involved.

'So why does he need money from investors?' I asked.

'The plan is to operate a chain of health spas offering traditional oriental massage – wink, wink, nudge, nudge – in major cities around Europe. They will either be new or they may acquire existing businesses. Either way they will need investment to start up. They may already have bought into the Bollywood as it seems to have adopted parts of their business model.'

I looked at my watch. 'Talking of which we need to make a move. We are due at the Bollywood at 2pm sharp,' I said.

'Oh yes, I have an appointment with – what was her name?'

'Katrina, but don't get carried away. It's not to release that pent up energy of yours. It's just a ruse to get us in there.'

'To do what exactly, Harry?' Billy fiddled with his computer and the screen went blank.

'To do nothing if we don't get a move on because we'll be too late. I'll tell you on the way.'

We didn't have far to go, but my old legs had had more than enough exercise for one day so we called a taxi. Billy didn't look too happy when I told him my plan but he couldn't think of a better one and the police were coming. That part at least pleased him.

As it turned out, it didn't please me.

I should have known something was wrong as soon as we arrived. There were two bouncers on the little side door that had been opened for access to what the sign on the wall now called the *Bollywood Health and Wellbeing Centre*. As soon as they saw me, one of them shot inside, leaving the other to greet us with a false-looking smile. He looked at a list when I gave my name and he ticked me off. When I introduced him to Billy, he shook his head and said there was no appointment for anyone by that name and so he could not be admitted. I knew full well he was lying, so I said I wasn't going in on my own and asked to speak to the manager. He got on to his walkie-talkie and spoke to someone in a muffled voice.

'We'll sort this out inside, sir, if you don't mind following me?' he said finally, with his false smile back on.

Following him through the door, I saw they had put up a partition to separate off the dance floor and bar so that we were led straight into the waiting room area where we were invited to sit on a leather sofa. I took one of the wooden chairs instead; oldies like me avoid low seats in case we can't get up. The first bouncer re-appeared and stood watching us with his arms crossed while the second one mumbled into his walkie-talkie again.

Billy looked around and gave me a worried frown. 'This doesn't feel good, Harry.'

My stomach was churning too. 'It'll be fine, you wait and see.'

We sat in silence for what seemed like an age. I looked at my watch. It was 2.15pm and still no sign of the girls.

'I think we should leave and let the police sort this out,' Billy said to me under his breath.

I was about to agree when there was a knock on the door and in walked the police. Things were happening in the wrong order. Where were those girls?

Two of the policemen wore heavy, bullet-proof jackets and had guns in their belts. The third one was dressed in a more normal blue uniform with a peaked cap. He was thin with beady little eyes that quickly searched the room before settling on me.

'Mr Pigeon, Harry Pigeon?' he asked.

I struggled to my feet. 'Yes, that's me. And this is my lawyer.'

The officer nodded and turned to the bouncers. 'Thank you. We can handle this now.' They didn't need a second invitation and both scuttled outside.

He fixed his beady eyes back onto me. 'Mr Pigeon, serious allegations have been made about you in relation to the kidnapping of two women. You do not have to say anything. However, it may harm your defence if you do not mention when questioned something which you later rely on in court. Anything you do say may be given in evidence.'

Billy jumped up. 'Are you arresting him, officer?'

'We are taking Mr Pigeon to the station for further questioning.'

CHAPTER 18

The Custody Suite

The good part to that afternoon was the ride in the police car. They even used their siren to get out of a traffic jam. It reminded me of the time Betty tried to learn how to drive. Some beginners really don't know what to do when they see that flashing blue light appear in their mirror. Betty certainly didn't. She was very nervous behind the wheel. It was me that made her nervous, she said, but we couldn't afford lessons so I said, tough, she would have to put up with me as her instructor. We were driving steadily along a busy road when we both heard the siren behind us. Her first thought was to jam on the brakes and stop in a narrow road opposite a traffic island.

'Drive on! He can't get past,' I shouted. Up comes the clutch a bit too quick and she stalls, a car full of angry policemen stuck behind us, siren wailing. She re-starts and kangaroo hops up the road. As soon as the police car shot past, she stopped, got out of the car and walked home. That was the end of the driving lessons.

~

When I arrived at the police station with Billy, I felt a bit like a celebrity at first. One of the policemen in padded jackets opened the car door for me and the other led me into the building on Billy's arm. The lady at reception smiled as they took me towards a sign saying *Custody Suite*.

That is where the bad part of the afternoon began. Any hint of a smile was soon wiped from my face when they handed me over to someone called the custody officer. I told him they had arrested the wrong person and they should go back to the Bollywood, find my girls and bring in the Sharmas. Completely ignoring what I said, he went about his work like a robot. He started reading from a script about my rights to have access to a free lawyer, to receive medical help, order food and drink, tell family or a friend where I was, go to the toilet and so on. He even offered me a little book to read; I gave it back quickly when I saw the title: *Police Codes of Practice*. I thought he would never stop so I repeated that he was just wasting our time while the real criminals were running loose and abusing women. He said I had to hand over all my possessions including my wallet, watch and mobile phone and when he asked me to take off my belt and my shoes, I didn't know whether to laugh or cry. When I gave him my walking stick, I told him to handle it with care in case it went off by mistake. He didn't even smile but he did check the end to make sure it wasn't hollow before he started to pat me all over with his rubber gloves on.

'Good thing I'm not ticklish,' I said.

Next, he took me to a cell. I don't suppose many ordinary people have been in a police cell. Well believe me, they wouldn't want to be there for very long. Not that it was scruffy or dirty. I've seen a lot worse in a cheap B&B. The

227

walls were a nice shade of yellow, not the smoky pub-ceiling colour that I was expecting. Against one wall, a padded blue couch looked comfortable enough to make do as a bed, if a little narrow. It was the sound of the key turning in the lock that made that room so depressing. The door was made of thick metal and the small window near the ceiling was covered in bars. No way out. I was in there until someone chose to let me out. Powerless, locked in like a caged animal.

I pressed the button on the wall and asked to go to the toilet. I had to have a change of scene. After the officer had taken me to the facilities, I asked him if I could speak to Billy and he said he would ask. Back in my cell, I didn't know what to do with myself. When I looked at my watch, my wrist was bare; I didn't even know what the time was. It was worse than a dentist's waiting room. There weren't even any magazines to read.

I pressed the button on the wall again.

'Could I have some tea and biscuits please?' I asked when a young man eventually answered. 'So long as it's not after four o'clock. I don't want to have biscuits too close to my evening meal in case they ruin my appetite.'

'Very sensible. That's probably why we don't offer biscuits in the Custody Suite, or tea.' The line went dead.

I sat on the bed, racking my brain about what to do next. A key sounded in the lock and the door swung open.

'The custody officer says you can see your solicitor now,' the officer said, inviting me out of the cell. He led me along the corridor to a door marked *Interview Room 2*, where I found Billy pacing up and down like a father expecting a baby.

'Harry, are you alright?' he said, taking my arm.

We were in a small room with no windows and a table in the middle with a few chairs scattered around, just like the ones you see in the films where the police question suspects.

'I would be if I could get a cup of tea and a biscuit,' I said.

'I'll see what I can do,' the officer said and disappeared.

Billy sat opposite me at the table. He was looking carefully at my face so I gave my mouth a wipe in case there were any bits of food or spittle hanging from it. Betty always used to check that for me before I went out.

'Have you any idea how you have gone from hero to zero like this?' he finally asked.

'I wish you'd tell me,' I said.

'You have to be straight with me, Harry. Was there any element of coercion in your dealings with these women?' I had to think about that because I didn't know what he meant. 'Did you in any way force or unduly influence them to stay with you?'

'Why bless you, no. How can an old man like me force young people to do anything they don't want to?'

'That's exactly what I'm wondering. Why do they believe you are capable of abducting two fit, youthful women? Didn't you say one was an athlete?'

'A champion runner. Goes like the wind.'

'We'll find out more when they question you.'

'When will that be?'

The door opened and the weasel-eyed officer walked in, flicking through papers in a blue folder.

'About now,' Billy whispered. 'Remember, keep calm and look at me before you answer. If I shake my head, don't say anything. You don't always have to tell them everything.'

'Mr Pigeon?' the officer began.

'Call me Harry, everyone does,' I said standing up, offering him my hand which he ignored.

'Please sit down, Harry. My name is Inspector Ralph Norris. There's a few questions I would like to ask you about your relationship with some young women. It will be recorded,' he said, pointing to a microphone on the table. 'Are you happy for your relative to stay?'

'Yes, he's my solicitor. A very good one he could have been too, except that he decided to help young people on the streets.'

Billy coughed and the inspector pulled a photo from his folder and laid it on the table in front of me. 'Do you know this person?'

She was looking grim without her normal smile but I would recognise that lovely face anywhere. 'Yes, that's Bituin. Do you know where she is? Is she safe?'

He turned the photograph over and read the reverse before returning it to the folder. 'Where did you meet her?' he asked.

I put my hand to my ear in case my hearing aid was off. 'Did I miss something, only I didn't catch the answer to my question?'

Inspector Ralph fixed me with his little eyes for a second, then glanced at Billy who was writing in his notepad. 'I'd like you to answer my questions before you ask your own,' he said.

'Look I am more than happy to tell you everything that I know, but first I want to find out what has happened to those girls. I can't concentrate, I'm so worried about them.'

He poked his head into the folder again and pulled out another photo. 'Do you know this person?'

Nadia looked like a criminal with her cropped hair and unsmiling face but I was relieved to see she had a decent set of clothes on. 'Of course I do. I helped her escape from those thugs at the Bollywood until they snatched her back again.'

He put the two pictures side by side on the table. 'Are these the girls whose welfare you are concerned about?'

'Yes, that's them. Where are they?'

'Are there any others?' The officer continued to ignore my questions.

Billy looked at me with his eyebrows up. 'No, those two were quite enough for me to handle. There were no others,' I said, looking at Billy who had closed his eyes.

'I can assure you that they are both well. Relieved to be free again, I would imagine.' He gave me that fixed look again.

'I should say so. They wouldn't have liked being in that van.'

'Indeed not,' he said, still staring at me before glancing towards Billy. 'I understand from the earlier police report that this young woman crashed her car into the gates of your house and then disappeared. Can you tell me anything about her disappearance?'

I looked at Billy who nodded. 'Yes I can. I hid her in my house, and then when the police came snooping round, I put her in my campervan.'

'And did you lock the door of the campervan?' he asked.

Did I lock it? I had to think about that until the events of that day came flooding back to me. 'Yes I locked it so the policewoman couldn't get in.'

The inspector glanced across at Billy again, 'According to PC Miller's report, this young woman was sighted by your neighbour but disappeared again. Can you tell me anything about that?' he continued.

'Who's PC Miller?' I asked.

'The policewoman you referred to, the one who searched your house but not the locked campervan,' he said.

'Oh, you mean Cecilia. She had me worried for a while especially after she talked with Doris who had seen Bituin when she ran away.'

'She ran away? Why did she run away if you were protecting her?' he asked, pointing at Bituin's photo.

I saw Billy shaking his head, but I had to say something.

'She ran into the field but soon came back when I went to fetch her from the old stable,' I said.

'Did you then drive her to Wales and to Cornwall?'

'I didn't do all the driving but yes, that's where we went.'

'Can you tell me why you did that?'

'So they wouldn't find us, that's why. But they followed us all the way. I shouldn't have left the girls alone when I did but I did so want a ride on that bike.'

'Tell me how this young lady came to be in your campervan?' he asked indicating Nadia's picture.

'Like I told your colleague, she was desperate to escape after what they had done to her, so when the fire in the club gave her the chance, I naturally encouraged her.'

He flicked over another page. 'Yes, you said that she was interested in changing her job to one that you had found for her, a teaching job I believe. Can you tell me more about that? Where was this job and how did you find it?'

I saw Billy shaking his head again and I didn't want to get him into trouble by saying it was partly his idea. 'She wanted a job teaching sports so she could get back to her training to be a runner. That was her dream, to be an athlete.'

'And you told her you could help her?'

'Certainly. I still can once she is out of that terrible situation at the Bollywood. So long as she remembers who the Prime Minister is, she ticks all the boxes,' I said glancing at Billy who was grimacing and shaking his head.

'But you had no particular job for her to go to?'

'Not as such, no. I just wanted to get her away from where she was.'

'And I believe you paid her some money? Can you tell me about that?'

One thing I do remember is where my money goes so I could tell him all about that. '£25 for our first chat, £20 for the second, £20 for the taxi when she ran away from the club and £40 a month for her mother.'

Billy was staring at me with his raised eyebrow look as the inspector droned on.

'And according to PC Swinton's report, you told him that you concealed both women when the RAC were called to your vehicle and also when you arrived at a campsite. Is that correct?'

'Correct.'

It was gradually dawning on me that he had got the wrong end of the stick so I thought it was time to put him straight. I cleared my throat and tried to speak like my father when he had something important to tell us at teatime.

'If you are thinking that I deliberately kept these two ladies in my van against their will, then you'd better think again because that is not how it was. They came with me to get out of the slave trade which is still going on here right under your nose. It's just as bad as it was in the olden days. Why don't you do something about that instead of questioning innocent people like me?'

My voice may have got a bit louder than I'd intended and when I stopped there was a deafening silence. No-one said anything for a while. The inspector just gave me that quizzical look of his and then glanced at Billy who was watching me over the top of his glasses.

'Perhaps I should explain why we have brought you in for questioning.' He opened up his folder and showed me the photos again. 'You see, these two women have made statements that indicate that they did not choose to come with you in your campervan but that you used coercion and enticements to abduct them away from their respective employers.'

You could have knocked me down with a feather when he said that. I couldn't speak. How could they think that? I saw Bituin standing on my doorstep that first night, peering into my little home to see if it was safe to come in. Did she really think I'd locked her up to kidnap her? I thought we'd understood each other. Maybe we hadn't. Perhaps Nadia hadn't understood me either. Maybe it was me, getting old, or their poor English that had got us into this mess. I felt my hand begin to shake.

Billy came to my rescue. 'Can we see these statements, Inspector?'

'You will have full disclosure in due course if and when charges are made. Suffice to say they were obtained here recently.'

'Have you verified there was no coercion involved?' Billy asked.

Judging by the expression on his pinched face, the inspector didn't like that question. 'Certainly not from my officers. Both of these women came forward independently with their complaints, so I have no evidence of undue pressure.'

Billy and I sat there, twiddling our thumbs, while he scanned through his papers again. I had lots of questions for him but Billy put a finger to his lips so I kept quiet. Eventually, he turned to Billy and spoke to him as though I wasn't there. 'I won't be making a formal arrest at this stage. We need more time to assess the facts. It's a complicated case with evidence in the hands of two different Police Forces.'

'Services, not Forces,' I mouthed, silently.

'In view of your client's age and some of the interview material, I am asking a psychiatrist to review his mental health as the next step.'

With that, he picked up his file and left the room.

CHAPTER 19

The Counter-Attack

The custody officer appeared with a form for me to sign about the interview. I went to stand but only got halfway up when I staggered and had to sit down again. My old legs weren't responding as they should.

'You alright, Harry?' Billy shot around the table to stand by me, looking worried.

'Does he need medical attention?' the custody officer asked.

'No, he needs his walking frame,' I said, sharpish. I was tired of this place and their endless questioning and investigating.

Billy and the officer had a confab about what to do next, the upshot of which was that they agreed Billy would go back to the campsite and fetch my walker and a few other things "in case he has to stay here tonight," as the officer put it.

Back in my cell, I looked at the thin bunk bed. Surely, I wasn't going to have to sleep on that? How could I spend a penny in the middle of the night if I couldn't open the door? Sorry, but us older folk have to think of things like that.

A familiar voice came into my mind. 'Now you know what it's like, Harry Pigeon.'

'Betty! I knew you wouldn't desert me.'

'No I wouldn't. I know how it feels to be on your own when you've been arrested,' she said.

'You? Arrested? When were you arrested?'

'When you were driving your big truck around Belgium at the end of the war. I did mention it when you came home but, as usual, you weren't listening.'

I remembered it then: how she was in town, shopping, soon after our baby died, put some things in her bag and left the shop without paying. Someone had been watching her; said she looked suspicious because Betty was in a bit of a daze, so they followed her out and challenged her. Betty said she had nothing in her bag but when they searched it they found some clothes: baby clothes. Today, they might understand that she hadn't meant to take them; she didn't even have a baby anymore. But in wartime you couldn't get away with anything and they began prosecuting her for stealing.

'What was it like?' I asked.

'Actually I quite enjoyed it. I got some attention for a change. Those policemen were in and out of my cell like yoyos. Did I have enough food? Could I drink a coffee? Did I want a blanket? They couldn't do enough for me. 'Specially when they found out my husband was abroad. I was a bit disappointed when they released me to go back to work in the munitions factory.'

'That must have been in 1944 when you were, what, 24 years old? You were quite a looker then. No wonder those leery old men couldn't keep away from you.'

'Not so much of your "old". There were some young'uns amongst them. One even offered to look me up afterwards, make sure I was alright. Seeing as how my husband was away for months and months and never took the time off to see me.'

'Well the bobbies are not exactly falling over themselves to look after me,' I told her.

'You'll soon find something to occupy your mind. Just like I did.'

~

I sat wondering about Betty's advice when a rattle at the door interrupted my thoughts. The custody officer's face appeared in the small window and the door swung open.

'Any chance of a cuppa? I never did get one,' I said.

'I need to take your fingerprints,' he said, beckoning me to follow him to the office where he poked a small stick in my mouth.

'It won't hurt. I need a sample of your DNA,' he said.

I reminded him about that cup of tea. I also asked him if I was allowed to make a phone call to a relative and, when he said I was, I asked him if I could have my wallet back to look up a telephone number.

I was thinking about what happened to Betty. Her case was eventually dropped when the police had finally become sympathetic to her cause.

Once the officer had handed my mobile and wallet back to me, I found the number and dialled quickly. 'Hello, is that Brian?'

'Uncle Harry! Where have you been? I've called round a couple of times but you're never in.'

I lowered my voice. 'As a matter of fact, I am spending

some time with your colleagues in the west country, and not by choice either.'

'You're with the police?'

'Yes, you could say that. I'm being detained for a while at Her Majesty's pleasure.'

'Not drunk and disorderly,' he chuckled.

'No, but I do need some advice from you. Are you at work?'

'I'm not, but I have to warn you that I can't directly intervene on behalf of family in police matters. Nepotism is frowned on.'

'I wouldn't dream of compromising your work. You're a professional, I know. All I want is an answer to a general question about witnesses.'

'Shoot. I can do general stuff,' he said.

'What would make someone tell a lie about what has happened to them? I mean, accuse someone of actually trying to harm them when they were only trying to help?'

'Maybe a case of a misunderstanding between the parties?'

'No, I don't think so. This is deliberate lying to the police.'

I heard a sucking noise on the line. 'I can only answer this hypothetically without reference to your specific case, OK?'

'Yes, fine.'

'First, you have instances where someone perverts the course of justice by giving a false witness statement to either protect someone or to harm them. You may remember the case of the wife of a prominent politician who falsely took points on her licence by claiming she was driving their car when it was caught speeding.'

'You mean the woman who changed her mind when she found out her husband was being a naughty boy with another woman?'

'That's the one. So in that case she changed her evidence to what turned out to be the truth in order to get revenge on an unfaithful husband. As a result they both went to prison.'

I didn't think that applied here. 'Any other reasons?'

'The second major category would be intimidation of witnesses. We often see this in cases of domestic violence, sexual offences and particularly where cultural issues such as race or religion are significant. So during the Troubles in Northern Ireland, there was a considerable increase in the incidence of unsolved crime because witnesses either kept silent or gave false evidence.'

'Terrible wasn't it. All that kneecapping by bullyboys who got away with it,' I said. Betty would make me turn the sound down when it came on the news because she didn't want to hear about it. There was a bit of Irish in her father who earned some pin money boxing in the marketplace and after a few drinks he had a habit of going home and practising on his own family. She'd seen enough of beatings that went unpunished.

I caught sight of the custody officer out of the corner of my eye talking to a bearded gentleman, nodding in my direction.

'Thanks. You've been very helpful.'

'Hang on. What's all this about?' Brian asked.

'I'll tell you later. Don't worry; your brother Billy is

taking good care of me,' I said, switching off the phone, wondering who the newcomer was. He was taking off his raincoat and opening up a scruffy, brown briefcase. I was taken back into the interview room where the custody officer explained that they had managed to find someone called Dr Schneider to assess my health. He said they had to do this before they could consider my release and that they had been lucky to find someone at such short notice at the weekend. I would have preferred Billy to advise me on this latest development but it seemed that they weren't going to let me out until this man had seen me so I agreed we should get it done, there and then.

Dr Schneider was not someone I took to immediately. He had these bushy, black eyebrows that shot up and down above his glasses when he spoke and he had a distracting habit of saying a long "erm" before every question he asked; maybe he was just nervous. He was also forgetful. He asked me who the Prime Minister was.

'When I was a boy we had Lloyd George. Lovely voice he had. Churchill had a good one too, his voice on the radio got us out of bed in the morning ready to fight another day during the war. That was Mrs Thatcher's problem. Her voice. It was too much like my old headmistress, telling me off for being naughty and you don't want that when you're a grown man, do you?'

Dr Schneider nodded and said, 'Erm no, but who's the Prime Minister now?'

'The name's coming to me,' I said. 'He doesn't have a good voice either. A bit posh but not at all distinctive which is why I can never remember his name. Funny isn't it how some names stick and others don't?'

When I told him I talked to Betty every day, he asked me if I heard any other voices in my head. None that give me orders like she still does, I said. That got him scribbling in his book. He asked me if Betty had told me to keep Bituin in the house. I said I suppose she had because, when I thought back to that very first day when Bituin had arrived, Betty had told me to treat her like a daughter. That's what triggered it all; I probably wouldn't have been so hospitable if Betty hadn't said that. So I told him yes, it was Betty's idea. From that moment, the doctor only wanted to talk about the dead. He was straight on to our little baby who died and then he went on to ask me how I felt about my mother. It was quite a grilling I can tell you. Soon after he'd finished, Billy came back.

'He thought I was trying to get off the hook by blaming the dead,' I said when I told him about the doctor's visit.

Billy had his head in his hands. 'No Harry,' he mumbled into his chest. 'He probably thinks you have voices in your head that tell you what to do. They section people like that, lock them up in a secure home for the mentally ill.'

This whole business was getting me down. I began struggling to my feet to have a walk around and think. Billy grabbed my walking frame that he'd brought back from the campervan.

'Here, use this,' he said.

It made me feel good just to hold on to those handles. My walker was like an old friend. We'd been doing things together for quite a while. Must have walked a fair few miles, hand in hand as it were, in all sorts of difficult spots: up and down rough steps, in and out of ditches, up and over fences. I could always rely on my walker to keep me going. Some people get into a wheelchair as soon as they feel their legs going. Biggest mistake they can make because as soon as they sit down to be pushed around, they've given themselves over to someone else to decide where to go and how fast. They've lost their independence the moment they put their bottom in that chair. I held on to the grips of my walker and breathed deeply a few times. I wasn't ready to give up just yet.

At that moment, the inspector and the custody officer came into the room. I thought they'd come to put me back in my cell so I was quite surprised at what happened next.

'We've been reviewing your case with the other services involved,' Inspector Norris said putting his blue folder on the table. 'There are a number of incidents with a bearing on this matter that cover a wide geographic area. We have therefore decided to refer the case back to the police authority where it all began. From now on the Norfolk Constabulary will co-ordinate the investigation.'

I was pleased to hear that. That was who Brian worked for. I was even more pleased about what he said next.

'That means you can go home.'

I let out an audible sigh and sat down on the seat of my walking frame, remembering to click on the brakes so I didn't shoot across the room. Inspector Norris turned to Billy and started speaking as though I wasn't there again.

'He will be on police bail which means he will have to report to the local police station when required to do so. He may or may not be charged once they have completed their investigation.'

Billy nodded and smiled. 'I understand. Did you get

that Harry? No more gallivanting about the countryside for a while.'

There was more form signing to do but eventually I walked out of the police station, not quite a free man, but it still felt good. Looking up at the black night sky where a few stars were peeping through, I nodded to Betty. I had a lot to talk to her about over at the cemetery. I would need to take a sandwich with me.

~

Billy and I were both too tired to talk much that night so we collapsed into our beds in the campervan, ready for an early start the next morning. It was hardly light when we left the site so Billy took the first stint of the driving. It gave me the chance to ask him the question that had been burning in my brain all night.

'Why do you think those girls made those accusations against me?'

'Presuming it was not just some misunderstanding between you—' I was about to interrupt him but he took one hand off the steering wheel and held it up to silence me. 'Which I admit seems unlikely. So the other, most likely motive would be fear. They seem to have fallen in with a criminal gang, who are almost certainly coercing them into making false claims against you.'

'Why would they want to do that? I can understand they would want to silence the girls from giving evidence against them, but why get them to turn on me?'

'To discredit any evidence you have against them. They know the computer was in your possession for a while, and they know Nadia has talked to you about the real nature of her work.'

Suddenly, it all became clear, except for one thing. I knew that Bituin had already stood up to their physical threats.

'What do think they are doing to her?' I didn't really want to think about it but I had to ask.

'I shudder to think, Harry. They are not the types to play by gentlemen's rules. Even if she is able to stand up to their threats against herself, she is probably looking over her shoulder at the safety of her family back home.'

Looking over her shoulder; that was one thing our boys in the Hurricane or Spitfire couldn't do very easily because they had to focus on what was ahead of them. That's why we lost so many: they didn't see the Messerschmitt behind them until it was too late. That's what was happening here.

'Of course!' I said. 'Bituin mentioned Vishal had threatened her sister back home and Nadia said something similar about her mother. We'll have to fit some rear-view mirrors.'

'Come again, Harry?'

'Rear-view mirrors. That's how I helped to save our pilots. I found them some mirrors.'

'You're going to have to talk me through this one a little slower,' Billy said.

'Simple when I think back, but it wasn't so easy during the Battle of Britain. Everything happened so fast. Most of our pilots were so young they had only just finished training and they were getting caught out in the dog fights by not seeing what was coming up behind. I went around the car dealers and bought up a whole load of rear-view mirrors. Once they had those in the cockpit, they just had to glance up to make sure they weren't being followed. They felt a lot more secure after that. They could concentrate on what was in front of them without worrying about what was behind. We have to do the same for my girls.'

'What, fit them out with mirrors?' Billy chuckled.

'Yes, except this time it can't be me that fetches them, can it? According to the inspector, I have to stay at home. You'll have to go.'

'You're asking me to buy some mirrors?' Billy was struggling with the gears again, making a mess of changing down as we went up a steep hill, but he finally managed to get into second.

'No, no, of course not. You will have to make sure the girls' families are safe, make sure they can't be threatened. Then Bituin and Nadia can tell the truth. They'll feel secure, like my young pilots.'

Maybe he was thinking about what I'd just said or maybe he was concentrating on making it to the top of the hill, but Billy went quiet for a while after that. It wasn't until he was coasting down the other side in top gear that I explained the plan that had just come to me. He wasn't at all keen to begin with but we had a four-hour drive to talk it over and by the time we got to my house, we had it all sorted out. We were ready to launch the counteroffensive.

CHAPTER 20

Lilly

The very first morning that I was back in my home, I stood on the doorstep and talked to Betty.

'Hello, I still love you,' I said.

'Don't forget to wash your pyjamas,' she said. 'You'll need spares if they put you back inside.'

That was a cheerful start. 'Don't worry, we're launching a counteroffensive, just like Monty did.'

'What's he got to do with it?'

I could have told her that General Montgomery was our best general in World War II who beat Rommel, Germany's best general, because he was meticulous, no silly do-or-die attacks, just a steady build-up of forces until he was ready and sure of winning. He wouldn't have been rushing round like a headless chicken as I had been. No, he made sure he knew what the enemy was up to before he made his move. Our codebreakers knew when German convoys were shipping Rommel's fuel across the Med and our bombers cut off his supply line until his panzers were stuck in the sand, out of diesel.

But I said nothing about that. She would have closed her eyes before I'd finished.

'We've planned things properly this time,' I said.

'Billy is catching a plane tomorrow to make sure the girls' mothers and sisters are safe. He'll bring them back here if he has to.'

'How is Billy paying for all this travel? He never earned a decent wage according to his father.'

'I've been to see the bank manager who said our little bungalow is worth a small fortune and I can have some of that money now. It'll be no good to us when I'm with you.'

'That's not what you used to say when I asked for anything new. It took us ages to save for that new cooker,' she muttered.

'When I told the bank manager I didn't believe in borrowing, he said this wasn't really the same as taking on a debt. He told me it was unlocking the cash value of an asset that I already own. I'll never have to pay it back. Not until I'm dead.'

'You'll find it even more difficult to repay then. Anyway, never mind all that. How are you going to catch these men who are ruining girl's lives? I've heard how you are going to get yourself out of trouble. But how are you going to stop them abusing any more young women? If they are still doing what you say they are, you should be able to catch them red-handed.'

Like I've said, Betty didn't often come up with her own ideas. She was more of a commentator on other people's ideas. But now and again, she managed to hit the nail on the head. We had to catch them red-handed; of course we did.

Just at that moment, I caught site of Doris approaching the bungalow on her mobility machine.

'Not fixed these yet, I see,' she called, pointing at the bent gates.

'No, they're still not working very well.' I pushed my walker along the pathway to meet her, grateful that the jammed gates had stopped her driving in.

'We would have mounted a proper watch on your property if you'd told us you would be away that long,' she said.

'Sorry, I didn't know myself. It's just that one thing led to another.' I kept to my side of the gates and made no effort to open them.

'What sort of things?'

'Oh this and that. Nothing serious.'

'And when are you off again?'

'Not for a while. I've been told to stay at home for a bit.' As soon as I said that, I realised my mistake. Pity you can't take back words like you can clothes that don't fit.

'Told? Who by?'

'Oh, just a relative. Worried about my health.' I made a little cough.

'Quite right too. You're far too old to be driving around in that contraption,' she said, indicating my van.

I nearly told her that my recent journey in that contraption had made me feel young again, but there's no point in arguing with someone like Doris.

'Anyway I can't stop now. Come round for tea this afternoon and tell me all about it and I will sign you up for Neighbourhood Watch,' she said turning her machine around. 'About four o'clock alright?'

I was desperately trying to make up an excuse to decline her invitation, but she was driving back along the road before I could speak. Tea with Doris; just what I didn't need. The last time Betty and I had taken tea in her house, my finger got wedged in the tiny handle of her teacup. When I yanked it out, I splashed tea onto my trousers and the table. Very embarrassing it was, as Betty reminded me many times.

I hurried back into the house to phone Billy before he caught his plane.

'One more thing,' I said to him. 'We've got to catch them red-handed.'

It turned out to be a very expensive phone call. Billy said my idea sounded dangerous but he would talk it through with his brother, Brian. When I said that Brian had told me he couldn't use his influence in favour of a family member, Billy chuckled.

'Why do you think your case has been transferred back to Norfolk then? What he said on the phone was to protect himself, but there are wheels within wheels. I'll see what I can do. Now I really must go or I will miss my plane.'

He rang off and I sat back in my chair, thinking things over. It was out of my control now and I didn't like the feel of that. That's when things often go wrong, when you leave too much to others. Betty wouldn't agree, I know. She said that things go wrong when you leave others to do something and then continually badger them to make sure they've done it. I should trust other people more, she said. I just had to hope that Billy would manage without me.

~

I must have nodded off because I was woken by the ringing of the phone. It was Doris.

'I have to cancel our appointment this afternoon.' I was relieved, but she sounded even more curt than usual.

'Nothing the matter I hope?'

'I think you know what the matter is. If not, read the local paper. That will tell you what the matter is. Neighbourhood Watch discourages any form of contact with suspicious characters.' She put the phone down.

What on earth was she talking about?

The paper was still on the mat where it had been delivered that morning. I usually read it after breakfast but I had been busy. As I stooped to pick it up, I caught the headline on the front page:

LOCAL MAN, AGED 97,
QUESTIONED OVER GIRL ABDUCTIONS

What a coincidence, I thought, when I saw that headline. Here was someone of my age suspected of kidnapping young women. When I read on, my jaw nearly hit the floor. It was not some stranger they were accusing of locking up a girl in his house: they were talking about me, Harry Pigeon. And apparently I had been cruising around looking to tempt other women into my campervan! The very thought made me seethe with rage.

I thought we lived in a democracy where you were innocent until you were proved guilty. That's not the impression you got from that newspaper article. Reading that, and only that, you would have frog-marched me straight off to prison for the rest of my days. It even questioned why I hadn't been locked up already, why I was being allowed to still live at home in my own house. No wonder Doris had cancelled our tea.

I scoured the article to see if there was a name at the bottom. Nothing. Anonymous. Newspapers always sheltered behind that. Well, they weren't going to get away with it this time. I looked up the phone number of the paper and when I finally got past all the recorded voices, I spoke to a human being.

'Hello, newsdesk.'

'Good morning, this is Harry Pigeon.' I just left it at that to see if the mention of my name would panic them a bit. It didn't.

'Yes, Mr Pigeon, how can I help you today?' the young woman's voice said.

'Don't you read your own newspaper? I'm on the front page.'

'Oh really? How can I help?'

'I want you to take it all back and print the truth. Did you write this rubbish about me?'

'Which article are you referring to, sir?'

'The one about the old man who is supposed to have abducted young girls.' That got her attention.

'Just a moment, Mr Pigeon.' There was a click and then some music, followed by a man's voice.

'Hello, Mr Pigeon. I'm the news editor. I understand you want to talk about an article in today's paper. I'm afraid we can't discuss individual stories on the phone.'

'Can you come and see me then? There's a lot more to this story than you've written.'

'I would imagine this is about to go sub judice so we will be blocked from further coverage,' he said.

'You mean you can print their side of the story but not mine, is that right? There's a lot more girls who will suffer unless we expose this slave gang now,' I said, wondering what sub judice meant.

'Do you have anything on this slave gang that does not relate to your particular case?'

'Do you have a lap top?' I asked.

'Yes. Why?'

'I can show you something on that if you send someone round.'

'I'm not sure I've got anyone free today.'

I could hear the uncertainty in his voice. What he meant was he didn't want to risk sending anyone round to meet a kidnapper like me.

'I'll come to you and show it to you in your office.'

That clinched it. I called for a taxi and grabbed my walking frame and coat.

~

Half an hour later, I was sitting in the office of the voice on the phone, which belonged to a man called Ted Mason who turned out to be quite polite and helpful.

I sat and watched as he flicked through the presentation on the *Human Assets Business*.

'Where did you get this from?' he asked without taking his eyes from the screen, writing a few quick notes in a pad as he pressed buttons on his computer. It was good to see someone still using a pen and paper.

'From the father of the person who wrote it,' I said, not wanting to give away too many names just yet.

'And you think it is about a slave ring?'

'Don't you? I know it calls it other things but it was pretty obvious to my lawyer.'

His face fell. 'So you'll be using this as evidence?'

'I hope so. It ought to send them to jail, don't you think?'

'Words and diagrams on a computer screen don't send anyone to jail unless there is an illegal act linked to it,' he said, pressing something that made the screen go blank.

'You mean I've got to catch them at it before you'll print something?'

He probably noticed I was getting agitated because he asked me if I wanted a cup of tea.

'No, I can see I have been wasting my time,' I said, struggling to get myself up from the chair.

'Here let me give you a hand,' he said, helping me up. 'Of course, if you had evidence from someone who had money accepted as an investment in a business that used trafficked girls, that would be different.' He gave me a knowing sort of look with his eyebrows raised.

~

At the time I didn't understand his meaning but it came to me later, after I had left him. Travelling home in the taxi, I tried to get my disappointment off my chest by telling Betty about it all. As I expected she wasn't too sympathetic about my public exposure and she snorted when I mentioned Ted's suggestion.

'Typical of that newspaper's underhand ways,' she said. 'They didn't hold back from putting me in print when I was accused of shoplifting even though I'd just had a baby. Now they want you to organise some sort of trick like in that film we watched,' she said.

'What film was that?' I asked.

'You know. The one with those two lovely Americans in it, one with red hair and the other with those deep blue eyes.'

I didn't know any lovely Americans and the taxi was just turning into my road. I needed to get ready to get out, but she went on.

'The Sting. That's what the film was called. It was about how they tricked some gangster out of his money by pretending to be something they really weren't. That's what he was suggesting you do. Set up a trap for your gangsters so you get some evidence about what they are really up to.'

Betty always was cleverer than me. She had won a scholarship when she was fourteen to pay for her to stay at school, but her mother needed her at home to help her bring up a load of younger brothers and sisters. If she said that is what the journalist Ted meant then that is almost certainly what he meant.

I put it to the back of my mind whilst I paid the taxi and went into my bungalow. The newspaper was where I had thrown it on the table, that terrible headline staring back up at me. If only they knew the truth. How could I trap the Sharmas into talking about their evil plans so they would be in large letters on the front page, instead of me? I didn't have a clue about how the underworld worked, so how could I outsmart people who were involved in it? There was only one person I knew with connections to criminals: Billy's elder brother, Bobby. That family are all involved in the law and Bobby was the one on the wrong side of it. Protection rackets were his main line of business; he'd always been a strong lad. The trouble was he was serving time in Wormwood Scrubs.

It's not exactly easy to phone someone in prison because the inmates are not allowed to take calls. But they can phone out using a prison phone once they know someone wants to talk to them. It took me the rest of the day to find the number of the Scrubs and then get through to someone to ask Bobby to call me. I gave them a good reason why he should call and he did, that very evening.

'What's all this about, you dying?' Bobby said, when he got through. He never had much subtlety about him.

'I'm not exactly dying but I am getting old. How many years have you got left in there?'

'Six years and 254 days,' he said, quick as a flash.

'That means I will be 103 when you get out and I'm unlikely to live that long.'

'So you thought you'd better phone me?'

'Actually I need some advice.'

'From me? You're asking me for advice! That's a new one.' His voice broke into a deep growl of a laugh. 'Pay up or else. That's the only advice I normally give anyone.'

'Have you ever had anything to do with the modern slave trade, trafficked girls, that sort of thing?' I wanted to get to the point in case we were cut off.

'You know they can listen in on these calls, don't you?' He was almost whispering now.

'Well if they are, I'd like them to know I am on the side

of the law. I am trying to set a trap for someone who is setting up massage parlours using slave girls.'

'Have you been drinking, Uncle Harry?'

'Haven't touched a drop for over ten years now. Not since your Great-aunt Betty took ill and I had to look after her. Why do you ask?'

'It's not the sort of question I would expect from a 97 year old, that's all.'

'I'm deadly serious. Do you know anything about women of the night?'

He broke into his deep laugh again. 'If you're talking prostitutes, I don't use them. You should ask Aunt Lilly about them. She's in the trade.'

We were not such a big family that the name of a relative would escape me, so he caught me by surprise.

'Who's Aunt Lilly?'

He went quiet for a bit, 'No-one you'd want to know.'

Naturally, I did want to know. 'Is she a real aunt?'

'Sort of,' he paused, then sighed. 'Maybe it's time things came out into the open. Give her a ring and see if she wants to talk to you.'

'What things are you talking about?' I asked.

'Just give her a call. If she wants to tell you, she will. Make sure you mention my name or she might mistake you for a client.'

He gave me a telephone number and after a chat about what the food was like in jail and how comfortable his bed was, we said goodbye. He was a good boy really; must have got mixed up with the wrong crowd somewhere along the way.

I looked at the time. Nearly eight o'clock. It was rather

late to ring Aunt Lilly, whoever she was, but I knew I wouldn't sleep if I didn't.

Someone answered the phone straight away. 'Sunset Enterprises. How may I help?'

I nearly rang off. I wasn't expecting a business, especially one that was open at night.

'Can I speak to Lilly, please?' I didn't think I should call her aunt at the office.

'Who's calling please?'

'My name is Harry Pigeon.'

'Are you an existing client, Mr Pigeon?'

'No. Bobby told me to call. Bobby Pigeon.'

'Let me see if Miss Lilly is available, sir,' she said and the phone went quiet. Not even that soppy music they usually play. Miss Lilly. First she's an aunt now she's a miss.

'I'm sorry, sir. Miss Lilly is not available at present. Can she call you in the morning?'

I left her my number and sat in my chair wondering what else I had got myself into. Why couldn't I just sit back and let myself gently leave this life? People in a nursing home had none of these worries. Their only care was when their next meal was coming or what was on the TV. I was sitting there, full of concerns over what was happening to those girls and who this mysterious Lilly was.

~

My lunch was on the table when the phone rang the next day. I'd almost given up waiting for the call.

'Good morning, I mean afternoon,' I said, noticing it had gone midday.

258

'Is that Harry? Harry Pigeon?'

'Yes. Who's calling?'

'I never thought I would hear from you again." She had a slight accent that I vaguely recognised. There was a pause. You forget who I am, haven't you?'

'I'm afraid…'

'This is Lilly. All your family forget me, except Bobby. Are you sure you want to know me now? You may not like what you find. Billy didn't.'

The mention of Billy's name and her oriental voice brought it all back to me.

'Li Wan? You're Li Wan, Billy's mother?'

'I was. Now, I'm Lilly. Better name for business. I'm not Billy's mother either. He disown me.'

'That doesn't sound like Billy. He's a very respectful boy.'

'He never forgive me for my business.'

'It's your business I want to talk to you about,' I said.

She laughed. 'Maybe you a little old for that, Harry?'

I laughed too, and that was enough to break the ice between us. We got on like a house on fire after that and had a good chat about the old days.

'Why you call me? Something happen to Billy?' she said, suddenly.

'No, nothing's happened to Billy. Can I come and see you? It's difficult to explain on the phone.'

'Anytime. Always free to see gentlemen,' she chuckled.

~

The very next day I was on the first train to London that allows cheap tickets. Lilly worked in King's Cross, near the station, and it didn't take me long to find the tall, modern block she'd described to me as her office. When I was shown into her room, it seemed more like a lounge than an office, although there was a computer on a low table in front of the L-shaped sofa she was sitting on.

Time had not been kind to her. I remembered her as a beautiful, slim Chinese girl with shiny black hair to her shoulders and a delicate, wide nose. It was no wonder my nephew Ron had taken a shine to her and offered her a cheap deal in the bed and breakfast business he ran, so she could work on the land out of view of the immigration officials. It turned out to be more bed than breakfast and Billy was the result. Understandably, Ron's wife was none too pleased, so Ron found Li Wan somewhere to live in London and that was the last I'd heard of her. Until nearly forty years later, and I was standing in front of this plump, little lady with taught skin that stretched in lines around narrow eyes that were watching me carefully though rimless glasses perched on the end of her nose.

'Sit down, Harry. I won't bite,' she chuckled, but didn't get up. 'Hip not so good today so I'm resting. Operation soon.'

I sat on the low chair opposite her, taking in her simple t-shirt and trousers, the colourful cushions that propped her up and the sweet smell of incense that wafted round the room.

'How's my Billy?' she asked.

'Seemed well enough when I saw him recently. He's helping youngsters who get lost.'

'Billy likes helping people. Except his mother. You know he came here once?'

'No, he never mentioned that.'

'He just came one day. Said he wanted to find out how I was, make sure I was OK. Just finished training. Can you believe my son is lawyer?'

'He's a very clever boy.'

'Clever, but not very smart. He said I had to stop my work and live normal life.'

'What exactly is your work?'

'I'm the Madam of Sunset Enterprises.'

'Madam?'

'Yes, top Madam. I have twenty escorts working for me now, all very classy, expensive girls. Regular or referred customers only, no riff raff. Bobby and his friends make sure we have no trouble." She waved her hand at the window. 'Out there, everyone respect me for good, clean operation. Except Billy. He say that one whore just like any other. I might as well be on street corner. He doesn't come back.'

I decided at that moment not to mention the part that Billy was playing in the recent events in my life. It would seem like rubbing salt in her wounds to talk about how close we had become of late and all the help he had given me, so I left him out of my explanation of why I had come to see her. It seemed a small decision at the time but the way things turned out, it proved to be very important.

'Do you have any other children?' I asked.

'No. Children not good for business when I first came to London. I was not always at top end of the trade.' She suddenly chuckled again. 'Also no husband.'

Her laugh was infectious and I found myself joining in.

She stopped laughing as abruptly as she started. 'Is Edna still alive?'

Edna was Ron's wife and the look in Lilly's eyes told me that she still thought ill of her.

'As far as I know, yes, in a home somewhere. You know that Ron is—'

'Oh yes. I nearly come to funeral. In Chinese, we say "bad beginning makes bad ending". I want to make ending bad for him – and for her. Bobby tells me that in England you say "better let sleeping dogs lie" and that Billy will never forgive me if I disturb his father's final day. So I stay at home.'

Betty used to say "that time heals all wounds" but in her case it obviously hadn't. She still bore a grudge.

'Now what's this business you want to talk to me about?' She grimaced as she swung her legs into an upright position.

'I was hoping you might help me to expose a nasty business.'

'All business can be nasty, Harry.'

'Yes but it doesn't often involve slaves, does it? I've come across this gang that are enslaving women to do your sort of work. Watch this.' I handed her the memory stick and quick as a wink she had it on her computer screen, poking her chin forward as she peered at the words and pictures. She said nothing, but made sucking noises through her teeth as she flicked quickly through the pages of the presentation.

'Who give you this?' she asked.

'It's a long story,' I said.

'Then first I offer you some tea.' She clapped her hands and a young girl, who looked more like the Li Wan I used to know, glided in.

'You want your filthy English tea with milk, or some real Chinese tea?' Lilly asked.

I've never been a fan of the coloured hot water they drink so I said I would stick with the filthy tea, and I started to tell her the story. I hadn't really intended to go into so much detail but once I got started, I found it hard to stop. I used to joke and say that I was a man of few words and Betty would say, yes but you repeat them over and over again for hours on end. That's probably a fair description of how I was that day. I wanted to get it off my chest, I suppose. From the moment Bituin crashed into my gates to when she and Nadia were recaptured, I went through it all. As I said, the only bit I left out was the part Billy played as I didn't want to provoke the jealous mother in her. She listened to my story carefully, her little eyes watching me intently, only looking down now and again to tap something into her machine.

I never for one moment thought that I shouldn't be giving her this information, that she might use it in the way she did.

'Now they're thinking of charging me with kidnapping. For some reason, the girls have changed their story and claimed that I forced them to come with me. As if I would do such a thing,' I said, finally.

Lilly looked at me as if she was assessing me as a potential kidnapper. 'Where are the girls now?'

'I don't rightly know but I'm sure that the Sharmas have forced them to tell lies about me by using threats against their families. That's why we've sent someone to warn them.'

Her narrow eyes got a lot wider. 'We? Who else is involved?'

'Why, the police of course. They're still not sure who is telling the truth so they've gone along with our plan.'

'Plan? What plan?' She shuffled along the sofa to get nearer to me.

'We've sent someone out to protect the girls' families so that the police can re-interview them once they know they're safe and to see if they change their stories.'

'Why you tell me all this?' she, finally, asked.

'I want you to arrange a meeting with Mr Sharma, pretending that you want to invest in his business. As you are already in the trade, he'll think you are genuine and tell you all about it in person. That way, we will have evidence to link him to this presentation. Then the newspapers can expose it all.'

She was staring at me, her eyes bulging. 'You want to use me as bait to catch them? You're fishing in sea full of sharks and you want to dangle me in water?' She shook her head in disbelief. 'You're a foolish man, Harry Pigeon. Your rod is too small for these fish.'

She must have forgotten about her bad hip because the next I knew she jumped to her feet and was clapping her hands. A young man shot into the room bowing and scraping as she shouted at him in short, sharp words I didn't understand, but they got him going. Just as he turned and fled an older woman came in who received the same treatment.

'I must go out now,' Lilly said in a calmer voice once we were alone again.

I glanced at my watch, 'I had better be getting the train home too. But first tell me what—'

'You must stay here till I get back,' she snapped.

'I don't like getting back after dark—'

'You stay here. Don't go out. Don't go home until I say. OK?'

I wanted to stand up. I didn't like this turn of events. Who was she to tell me what to do?

'Now look here,' I said, rocking forward to stand up. It didn't work; my body wasn't up to it. Whoever designed that chair must have had very short legs because I was nearly sitting on the floor with no armrest to lever myself up on. I sat back down, frustrated without the breath to finish my sentence.

She clapped her hands again. A huge man with a belly on him as big as those oriental wrestlers waddled in and looked down at me, then at Lilly. She made a small upward motion with her hand and before I knew it, he had picked me up as if he was lifting a feather and set me on my feet.

'He take you to a room where you can eat and rest,' she said.

He did, and he locked the door when he left.

CHAPTER 21
The Betrayal

If it hadn't been for Betty I don't know what I would have done, locked in that room. My mind was full of why Lilly had made me a prisoner and what she might be up to. I was working myself up into a right old state, and that's putting it mildly. I could feel my heart pounding in my chest as I cursed my stupidity for telling Lilly everything without really knowing anything about her since she was a teenage girl. After an hour or so, I nearly attacked the lady who came in and offered me some more tea, but the man with the oversized stomach was lurking near the door and I knew I would never get past him. I even checked the window to see if I could get out that way before I remembered I'd pressed the lift button for the 15th floor.

'Just sit there quietly and enjoy the food on your plate,' Betty said.

'It's alright for you. You've got nothing to worry about now have you?'

'Nor have you, yet.'

'What do you mean? Can't you see the mess I'm in? Everything was getting better until that disgusting newspaper article ruined everything and made me come here,' I said.

'Has anything bad happened yet?'

'I can't get out of this room for a start.'

She was really irritating me now with her calm voice. I knew what was coming; it was something she'd learned on a course she'd been on to help manage her pain. She was going to tell me to sit still and think about my breath and nothing else for a while. It did seem to help her, though, so I decided to give it a try. I closed my eyes and tried to make my mind go blank. It worked for a moment or two and I felt calmer. Then my brain got busy thinking about what Lilly was up to. What did she mean about my rod being too small?

'I'm sorry Betty, but it isn't working. I can't think about anything else but why I'm locked in here.'

'Don't blame yourself,' she said. 'You did your best. Try some of that food.'

'You know I don't like that Chinese muck.'

'Have one of those little dumplings. You know how much you like a dumpling.'

It was very small for a dumpling, but to my surprise it did taste nice and there were plenty of them.

'What are they like?' asked Betty when I tried a second.

'The first one had something like chicken inside it and this one tastes of pork. Nothing like your dumplings, that's for sure, but nothing could match your dumplings. Not with that lovely thick gravy you used to make.'

'I thought my Yorkshire pudding was your favourite,' she said. That got us talking about what she used to cook after the war when there was rationing and we had very little money to spend on food. I really got into gardening at that time. Potatoes, runner beans, sprouts, carrots; if it was good to eat, I'd have a go at growing it. Ever since then, I'd always thought of flowers as a bit of a luxury. It was only later when Betty was ill, that I turned my hand to plants to look at rather than to eat.

'What did you think about when you were gardening?' Betty asked me.

'Nothing much that I can remember. Except how to get rid of the slugs.'

She laughed at that. 'You always came back calm and cheerful from the allotment. I never knew what you did there, but I know it did you good. You got to be quite good at it in the end.'

'Quite good!' That did it. I had to remind her of all the wonderful crops I'd grown and all the prizes I'd won for my marrows and turnips.

~

Before I knew it, it was dark outside and I heard Lilly's voice beyond my room. She didn't come in at first so I banged my fist on the wooden door panel.

'Come in here and explain yourself, Lilly,' I shouted. 'What do you think you are doing keeping me locked up like this? Let me out before I—'

The door swung open and there was Lilly, hands on hips.

'Before you what, Harry Pigeon? Beat me with belt, like Ron did? Curse me and throw plates and pans at me like Edna did? Look past me with nose in the air, as if I not there, like the rest of your family when they saw bump instead of flat belly? Too late for that Harry, that's thing of the past. You and your family have no control over me now. I won freedom the hard way and no-one, especially anyone called Pigeon, is ever going to take it away from me again.'

That took the wind out of my sails. I remembered that Ron used to say she was not like us: one moment, all polite and inscrutable, the next shouting her head off for no apparent reason.

'My family never meant you any harm.'

She laughed, and shut the door loudly behind her as she waddled in. 'No, you didn't mean harm. But you did it, just the same. Do you know why I came to this country?'

'Didn't a typhoon knock down your village?' I said, in a quiet voice, trying to turn down the volume on our conversation.

'Yes, Harry, but typhoon didn't make me leave. The firemen sent to save us, they make me leave. They ask for money before they rescue people from the rubble. Everyone ask for bribes in Hong Kong then. No good asking for help or telling anything to police unless you took fat bribe with you. So when my mother was left buried under our house because we have no money to pay firemen to dig her out, I decide to come to England. "Home of democracy, no need for bribes," they said, "Everything's fair."' She made a mocking chuckle, 'What do you think I found, Harry?'

'As I recall, you came over in the 1970s when—'

She didn't wait for my version of events. 'Yes, corrupt men also on top in your society. Men doing same work as me paid three times as much. Only way I could pay my rent to Ron was with my body. That's what I found.' She came up really close to me staring me in the eyes. 'So when

I come to London with baby on my own, I decide to even things up. Do you know how I did that, Harry?'

She was going to tell me anyway, so I just shook my head and took a step back.

'I decide to use the one thing that women have that men don't have.' She moved nearer. 'You know what that is, Harry?'

I looked at her small breasts wondering if that's what she meant, but she put her hand on her trousers.

'We keep it between our legs.'

I felt a tiny spray of spittle on my cheek as she spoke and I took another step back, stumbling into a chair. I sat down abruptly giving her the advantage of height over me. She glowered down at me, breathing heavily, hands clenched as though she was about to hit me. To my relief, she sighed loudly, turned round and settled on a sofa, one leg up, the other down. Betty used to do that when her arthritis came on.

'Englishmen grumble when they pay through nose for something. They complain less when they pay through dick.' She laughed at her little joke but stopped abruptly to wag her finger at me. 'Don't tell me you never mean me any harm. Your family drive me to this work and take son away because of it. Even he disown me. You talk about stopping slaving yet your family make slave out of me. So I say you are phoney.'

'Just tell me what's going on, that's all,' I said, trying to stop myself from shaking.

'I've been to see Mr Sharma, as you ask.'

Hope rose in me for an instant that she had done what I wanted, that she was going to give me the evidence I needed.

'I tell him your story. All of it.'

I felt like a punctured balloon with the air hissing out. 'What do you mean, all of it? I didn't ask you to tell him all my plans, did I?' I could hear the tremor in my own voice.

'Oh, sorry, Harry, my mistake. I didn't think you would mind if I tell him how you were going to ruin my investment in his business.'

My head was spinning. 'I didn't ask you to actually invest, just pretend you wanted to.'

She made the chuckle she seemed to specialise in. 'Oh sorry, Harry, next time I listen to your instructions more carefully.'

I shook my head, trying to grasp exactly what game she was up to. 'What have you done, you silly woman?'

'I think you'll see it's you that's been silly and those two girls who have been clever. As your dick is too old, they make you pay through nose. How much money did they take from you, Harry?'

'That's none of your business.'

'Oh but it is my business. It's the business of Mr Sharma and I am a partner in his business.'

'Partner? You mean...' I was beginning to realise she was right: I had been silly.

'You men always think you are the clever ones, always a step ahead. Believe me, Harry, you are so far behind you are like spec of dust on the horizon. I have learned in my business to keep up with the leaders, people with vision.' She took off her round spectacles and wiped them with a cloth.

'Even if they're crooks?' I asked.

'Who isn't some sort of crook in this trade? But Mr

Sharma is different. He sees what's coming next. When I first meet him, he told me my business was doomed. At first I didn't believe him. It wasn't until I started losing clients and a few of my girls, that I realise he was right, that I had to join him or be ruined.'

'The recession ruined a lot of people,' I said.

'No, our problem isn't recession. It's internet.'

'Internet? I thought that was supposed to be helping business.'

'Not this one it isn't. Biggest business on the internet is porn, Harry, and internet porn is no good for my business. Men used to pay for sex. Now they expect to get it for nothing though computer.'

'You mean they have sex on their computer?'

She looked at me as though I was stupid. 'On internet, Harry. They watch it, they chat to sluts, they find dates. Mr Sharma wants to use this power of internet but direct business back to girls like mine.'

'You mean by forcing women into the sex trade against their will?'

'No, Harry. That's just a story your girls told you to get money from you.'

'That's rubbish and you know it.'

'I'm afraid they took advantage of you. They told Mr Sharma everything when he took them back and offered to help them. It seems your Filipino is a compulsive thief and the Romanian is a con artist. They've both done it before.'

'Done what?'

'Trick old men like you with tales of a slave ring to get money for their poor family back home, who of course are all part of plot. I hope you stopped the payments you're sending them.'

Bituin couldn't have made everything up, could she? I was having doubts about her for the first time. She did seem to have her bank details very handy and she did insist on having three months money in one go.

'You make it easy for them, didn't you? Hiding them away, taking them in your van, lying to the police, promising them things. Oh yes, they had you right where they wanted. Until Mr Sharma found them and took them back to where they belong. He wanted to make them apologise for their bad behaviour and give you your money back. But you not only fell for their lies but you started a crusade about them, didn't you? You told the police their crazy story about Mr Sharma's business. That forced him to tell the truth, to protect himself.' She was looking at me calmly, with what could have been pity in her eyes.

'I... I'm not...'

'Not sure I tell truth? We call them if you like. They'll tell you I'm right.'

'You've met them?'

'Only the Filipino. She is working for Mr Sharma in London again.' Lilly looked at her watch. 'Too late now. We call in morning. Time for bed.'

She had a certainty about her that spooked me. Had they really been telling me a pack of lies? Had I been charging around trying to solve a problem that didn't exist? Like the time I ranted at the doctor because Betty's medicine wasn't working, only to find that she'd been secretly pouring it down the toilet because it didn't agree with her. I felt a right fool when she had to confess in

273

order to stop me shouting down the telephone at the doctor. Now I'd fallen for a cock-and-bull story to open my wallet. Maybe I was ill, some form of dementia that twisted everything so I didn't know right from wrong.

'What about that presentation I showed you?' I asked.

She laughed. 'Mr Sharma was cross you still had that. It was done by his son, Vishal, when he was at university as a kind of joke, probably when he was a bit drunk, showing off to his mates. Mr Sharma only kept it because he said it was quite a clever send-up of proper business plans and showed how smart his son was. He said that you offered to send it back to him but your lawyer just sent him some sort of contract he couldn't understand. You really should delete it.'

My world was slipping away, piece by piece.

'I need to talk to my lawyer,' I stammered.

There was that dismissive laugh again. 'The one in Romania? Mr Sharma is sending Vishal to meet him, tell him what is going on before he gets you in more trouble.'

Maybe that would sort it out. Billy would know if Vishal was telling the truth. There were still a few things nagging at me that didn't quite add up.

'You said you are some sort of business partner with Mr Sharma. If the presentation is a load of rubbish, what sort of business is it?'

'What you show me did have some truth to it. That's what makes it clever. It's a spoof on what we are really doing.'

'Which is what exactly?'

'Turning a sleazy trade into respectable, organised business. I always try to keep Sunset Enterprise out of gutter and make it decent, something you not ashamed of. Mr Sharma says internet can be used to make the whole business like that.'

'By making it free?' I asked.

'Only the entry point is free. We are launching new website that has free content to whet the appetite, but only give you appetiser, not the main course. For that you must visit one of his new chain of health spas.'

'For a happy ending?'

'For relaxing, professional massage with special features to satisfy need.'

'Given by women slaves?' I hadn't given up.

She shook her head. 'Trust me, that was just a story to trick you into giving them money. Ask the Filipino tomorrow. She will tell you. Mr Sharma is offering employment to girls from many countries but they will be employed fairly.'

'So how does this business work?'

'Mr Sharma describes our trade as a pyramid.' She made the shape of a triangle with her hands and pointed at the imaginary base. 'The bottom step is easy to climb onto, so that many people can experience it. This is the internet part of our business today. Many more people are now involved with our trade because internet is everywhere and porn is everywhere on the internet. So this means we now have potential to build really big, tall pyramid because base is so broad. But all depends on someone's experience on first steps of the pyramid. If it's good, they will want to climb higher to find what is there. If not, they get off or stay where they are. Unfortunately most of porn on internet is bad, very bad. Have you seen it, Harry?'

'Can't say I have.'

'One thing I have learned in this trade is that you do not give it all away as soon as a man walks in. How would you feel if a woman just jumps naked on your bed and opens her legs?'

I had to admit it didn't sound very attractive but then I'm past that sort of thing.

'This is what they do on the internet. Mr Sharma says they go straight to main event without any warm-up. He says it's like going to restaurant and the waiter puts raw steak on your plate and expects you to eat it. His new website will provide the appetiser to tempt people higher up the pyramid. Flashes of flesh rather than raw meat.'

I was beginning to get the picture. 'What's higher up this pyramid?'

'Each level engages a different sense, one by one, so it can be savoured, not devoured.' I could almost hear Mr Sharma speaking as she described his vision. 'After glimpsing pleasures, they next hear tempting sounds. They speak to our trained girls who talk to them about the pleasures they can offer so that they are ready for next step, the one you came into at the Bollywood. He uses that place as a test bed for some of his ideas.' She rubbed the leg she had put up on the sofa.

'I didn't realise I was being used as a guinea pig.'

'Nor did we until you blundered in. He was using it to test first personal contact point up the pyramid – the special massage.'

'With happy ending,' I reminded her.

'We are thinking of using that as brand name for our business. What do you think?'

'Brand name?'

'You know, the name everyone will recognise us by. Like Marks and Spencer or Amazon. Everything we do will have the "happyending.com" logo with smiling, satisfied face.'

This was all a bit beyond me; I was tired and confused and needed to recharge my batteries but she was into her stride.

'My business will be the top, the peak that only few will reach, "happyending.com escorts". Best there is. My clients tell others who will want to climb up too. Although only a small percentage make it to the top, every time the base gets bigger, my business expand. We all win.'

'Except the girls who have been forced into this system of yours. I seem to remember the Egyptians used slaves to build their pyramids.'

She shrugged. 'Girls queuing up for job with us. Tomorrow we call the Filipino. You can ask her. Now I think you're tired. You sleep here, if you don't mind staying in brothel, that is.' She chuckled and led me out of the room.

~

I hardly slept that night although there was no sign of it being a brothel. Early next day, I was itching to make that phone call by the time Lilly came back into the room. She insisted I had a cup of my filthy English tea before she called Mr Sharma. She garbled into her mobile out of my earshot for a while and then handed me the phone.

It was Bituin.

'Sorry, Mr Harry. It is all true. I trick you.'

That was all she said, but it was enough.

CHAPTER 22

The Sting

Funnily enough, things almost went back to normal when I got back home to my bungalow. Doris shot round as soon as she read about it in the newspaper. She claimed she suspected something funny was going on from the very beginning.

'I knew a frail old man like you couldn't have kidnapped two healthy women, especially the one from eastern Europe. Women dig up the roads over there, you know,' she said.

Frail old man indeed, and there was me walking about my garden and she was sitting on her mobility scooter.

Mr Sharma arranged it all very cleverly as you would expect. Lilly was the intermediary between him and me and we came to an agreement. Bituin and Nadia would modify their stories to the police to make sure I wasn't charged with kidnapping and in return I acknowledged I had been misled about his business. We didn't go too far in accusing the girls of financial jiggery-pokery or they would have been in trouble and I didn't want that. No, I just insisted they left the country; I didn't want them in the UK any longer than they had to be. I wanted them sent home to their families.

When the editor of the newspaper rang to find out how I was getting on with exposing human trafficking, I had to tell him that it was all a misunderstanding and not quite as I had originally claimed. I tried not to read the paper when it arrived the next day, but I couldn't avoid seeing the headline:

Pensioner tricked out of savings by 'sex slave' girls

That's when Doris came nosing round, asking all sorts of questions I didn't really want to answer.

When I told Betty, I could almost see her smiling when she found out that the girls had been extracting money from me.

'Led up the garden path by a pretty face, were you Harry? I'd have thought you'd have learned that lesson a long time ago.'

Betty had all my past misdemeanours and mistakes stored carefully in her memory so that she could produce a suitable one to wave under my nose for almost every new situation that arose. As I expected, it was the calor-gas incident she used this time. She always said I lost my job because of my female customers. For some reason one or two of them took a particular shine to me, always asking for me when they came into the shop. That was good for business so I suppose I did milk it a bit, dropping in the odd word here and there about how smart their dress or hair looked and was that a new pair of shoes they were wearing. When electricity finally came to their villages and they started ordering electric cookers and appliances instead of calor-gas, they still asked after me. I didn't see any harm in taking down their orders myself and passing them through to the electrical department. But that was my downfall, as Betty was always reminding me. When the manager added up all the orders everyone had taken, he found that I was not only the top gas salesman, I was also the top electrical salesman too – I didn't even work for that department! Well that got right up the nose of young Freddie Fickling, the electrical manager. Unfortunately he was the nephew of the owner and I was made redundant. Yes, Betty loved to trot out how I'd lost my job by pandering too much to the ladies.

This time I was ready for her. 'Before you get carried away, I should let you into a little secret,' I said, as though it wasn't anything of consequence.

'What secret?' Betty asked.

'She's innocent. Bituin didn't hoodwink me or anyone else. She didn't make it all up for the money.'

'I thought you said you believed Mr Sharma's account of things,' she said.

'I had to, didn't I? To make sure that both girls were sent home, out of harm's way. I insisted on that.'

'How do you know she didn't trick you?'

'It was what she said on the phone, "Sorry Mr Harry, it's all true"'

'Surely that was admitting it.'

'Yes but, although she confessed, she called me Mr Harry.'

'She always called you that.'

'At the beginning she did and I had to tell her not to. One day, when I'd corrected her for the umpteenth time, she asked me why I objected to being called Mr Harry.

I said it was too dutiful, something we reserved for rich or powerful people when we had to bow and scrape to get something out of them. She thought about that and said, "Alright, I won't call you Mr Harry unless I need something from you. It can be like a code between us, and that way, I won't forget."'

'Maybe she was saying sorry for the terrible way she treated you,' Betty said.

'No, she laid particular stress on the Mr part to tell me she needed help, that she was being made to admit to things she had never done.'

'How can you be sure? Perhaps she just forgot about your little code.'

'I could tell by her voice that she wasn't quite normal. They'd forced her and Nadia into making false statements. I'm certain of it. If Billy can arrange protection for their families, I am sure they will change their evidence and I can persuade the police I was telling the truth.'

Betty went quiet after that. Not that her criticisms of me were always unfounded, not by any means. She knew all my faults and she made it her job to rid me of them, as if she was clearing a garden of weeds. Whenever I chided her for it, she said she did it out of love. She couldn't bear to see the man she thought so highly of, being less than perfect in some way or making a fool of himself. That made me feel a lot better.

~

It's a pity Mr Sharma didn't take the same approach. He was the opposite: his love for Vishal, led him to be blind to his faults. He didn't see him for the cruel, sadistic person he really was and as a result, he trusted him more than he should have. When he heard from Lilly that I had sent my lawyer to protect the girl's families, he sent Vishal after him. He didn't know that my lawyer was Billy, Lilly's son, nor did Lilly of course. He probably expected Vishal to come to some arrangement with my lawyer, just like he had with me, something that allowed everyone a way out without pain or loss of too much face.

But Vishal liked to talk with his fists. When he found out that Billy had visited Nadia's mother in Romania offering her a safe house in England so that her daughter could speak freely, he was not content to put a stop to that. No, he went after Billy, no doubt to rough him up a bit and frighten him off for good. Fortunately, Billy gave his gang the slip and he managed to get on a plane to the Philippines before they could catch up with him.

That just made Vishal even madder. He obviously had some good contacts amongst the Philippines' customs officers because they pulled Billy over when he landed and – guess what – they found a mysterious package in his suitcase. It turned out to be full of heroin. Billy swore he hadn't seen it before but it did him no good; he was marched straight to prison. When Mr Sharma found out, he told Lilly.

'Tell Harry, or Norman as he likes to call himself, that his lawyer's been arrested for drug smuggling so he probably won't be coming home for a while,' he'd said.

Lilly sounded smug when she phoned to tell me. 'You more phoney by the day, Harry. You complain enough about human trafficking, but now your lawyer's been arrested for drug trafficking. Which side you on?'

I decided it was time to let her in on my secret. 'I'm on Billy's side.'

'What's Billy got to do with this?' she asked. I could imagine her little eyes suddenly getting bigger.

'Oh didn't I tell you? He's my lawyer. The one who the Sharmas have had locked up.'

She went so quiet that I thought the phone had gone dead. 'Why you not tell me this before?'

'You didn't ask,' I said.

I wondered how Lilly would react; after all, Billy had actually rejected her as his mother. But love, as we've said, is a funny thing. Betty's love for me led her to try and straighten out my imperfections. It made Mr Sharma blind to his son's obvious faults. It turned Lilly into a mother again, and a crusading one at that.

'Don't tell anyone about this, not yet,' she said. 'Must go to him. Death penalty for drug smuggling in Philippines.'

'What! You mean…'

She'd gone. To my relief, she got on her charger and rode to her son's rescue.

It wasn't done rashly without thought for the consequences; that wasn't her way. She went back to see Mr Sharma and, without mentioning her connection to Billy, she quietly reminded him of the harsh penalties, including execution, for smuggling drugs into the Philippines. People might get the wrong idea of the happyending.com brand if it came out that they'd set someone up for the firing squad.

'They'll joke it should be stickyending.com,' she told him. 'Maybe I go to Philippines to help Vishal get out of mess he has got himself in. I have connections there from my time in Hong Kong.'

Mr Sharma had realised that the story could generate very bad publicity so he gladly accepted her offer of help.

I mentally sent a message to Billy to sit tight. The cavalry was coming.

~

What happened next made me cry, when Lilly told me about it later. She contacted Vishal when she arrived in Manila and, naturally, he believed she was still a partner in their business, which technically she still was. He made no secret of how much he disagreed with his father's gentler methods and cited his handling of my case as a sign of weakness.

'If he had listened to me, that fool would have died in his bed,' he told Lilly. 'Fires in the house kill old people all the time, and I would have made sure he felt the heat of one. Instead we've had to chase around the world sorting out the problems he's made for us.'

That wasn't the part that made me cry. When Lilly secretly went to see Bituin's mother and sister, she found them battered and bruised and the contents of their house smashed up. They wouldn't talk about it but Lilly only had to look at the mess someone had made of their bodies and possessions to guess who was responsible. It particularly upset me because I was the one who had got them into this pickle and there was nothing I could do to help them.

Fortunately, Lilly could. Once she got her teeth into Vishal Sharma she didn't let go, making it her business to find out exactly what he was up to.

~

Several days later, I was sitting in my comfortable chair watching a squirrel try to get the seeds out of the bird feeder. He had just managed to wriggle his body in through the wire mesh when the phone rang. There was some strange clicking on the line but there was no mistaking that voice. It was Lilly and she sounded quite agitated.

'Harry, Harry, can you hear me?'

'Just about, yes. How's the weather over there in the Philippines?'

'Hot. Harry, I make terrible mistake. What you say is true. Hard to believe. Vishal is tricking girls by making offer of work then turning them into prostitutes. Just like I was…'

I heard a snuffling on the line. 'Hello, are you still there?'

She sniffed and coughed. 'Still here, Harry,' she mumbled. 'I was once cheated into sex trade like these women. But I don't trick girls that work for me.' Her voice became louder and louder. 'I am honest madam, never make girls do cheap sex work for no pay. My girls high-class professionals. If do a good job and please customer, you get well paid. Do a bad job, then you get warning. Do bad job twice, then no job. This Vishal not like this. He is making them slaves who work all the time for no pay. He put my Billy in jail and now he is recruiting Filipino girls to become what he call nannies and receptionists. He even ask me to do interviews for him.'

'I expect you gave him a few harsh words about that,' I

said, relieved that she had finally realised what was really going on.

She laughed. 'Oh no Harry, I accept. I make record of everything. We have to stop him.'

'God bless you Lilly.'

I couldn't believe it. The poacher had turned gamekeeper.

'First I have to get Billy out of jail,' she said.

'How can you do that? I thought Vishal filled the wallets of the local police with enough cash to keep them on his side?'

'Yes, so I contact Billy's brother, Brian, to use his international contacts in Philippines to override local police here. I go see Billy now and find out.'

'Tell him I'm sorry I got him into all this, would you? We'll get him out somehow.'

It turned out to be not quite that easy. Lilly called me the next day to say that they would not release Billy until there had been a trial but they had not set a date for it.

'Sometimes it takes years before trial,' she said. 'I have to use my connections now.'

'Oh and what are those?' I asked, surprised she had any links in the Philippines.

'Chinese have connections everywhere. Go to library. Look up Triads.' With that she hung up.

~

I had nothing else to do and the library was only a short bus ride away, so I took up Lilly's suggestion and went that same day. What I found out, opened my eyes to a world I never realised existed. The lady behind the desk looked a little surprised and asked me how to spell the word when I asked for information on Triads. As I didn't know, she did some searching on her computer.

'Is it a method of charging for electricity?' she asked.

'No, I don't think so.'

'Designer clothes?'

'No.'

'Chinese organised crime association?'

'That'll be it,' I said eagerly.

She looked over her glasses at me. 'Try the encyclopaedias in aisle 2.'

I became so engrossed reading that the next thing I knew she was coughing behind me. 'We are closing in five minutes,' she said, peering at the book in front of me.

Sitting on the bus on the way home, I marvelled at what I had found out. Apparently, there are as many Chinese living outside of China as there are British people living in Great Britain. That's quite a few, and when they first started working abroad they weren't always treated very well – just as Lilly wasn't when she came to England. But the Chinese are clever people so they set up these societies centuries ago to protect themselves when they were overseas. The Triads, they were called and they were particularly strong in Hong Kong where Lilly came from. When she first went to work on the streets of London, she must have turned to them for protection. From what I read, she would have had to give them a large part of her profits to keep herself and her girls protected from trouble. Must have been worth it, though, to keep the London gangs – not to mention the police – from her door. I found the really interesting bit in a section on the Triad code. That said they had to protect not just their own members but their families as well. That meant Billy.

Several days later, Lilly phoned me again.

'Please give important message to Brian,' she said in a quiet voice. 'Expect first consignment in one week. He will get more details soon.' She didn't say any more than that.

When I called Brian, he listened carefully. 'Harry, I want you to stay at home for the next few days. You may also notice a police car keeping an eye on you. It's just a precaution. Things are hotting up,' he said.

~

That was all the information I had. So I got on with my life, chatted with Betty, did a bit of gardening and watched bad TV programmes to take my mind off what was happening. About a week later, Brian knocked on my door.

'Afternoon Uncle Harry,' he said coming straight into the house. 'I'll put the kettle on, shall I?' He looked very pleased with himself as he made tea in the kitchen and asked me about the garden.

I couldn't bear it for long. 'Now young man, are you going to tell me what's going on over there in the Philippines?'

'I was coming to that,' he chuckled. 'But the main action has not been in the Philippines. It's been right here. We've arrested Vishal Sharma.'

I put my cup down so sharply that tea slopped into the saucer. 'What! How? What for?'

'We had a tip off from some Chinese gentlemen who claimed that Filipino girls were being recruited for bogus jobs in England and then forced to work in the sex trade. They gave us the details of a flight carrying some of these girls and asked us to follow them when they arrived at Stansted airport. Sure enough, a group of men did meet young women from the flight and took them to a big country house. We managed to interrupt their so-called interviews and arrested the gang including Vishal Sharma. This is of course confidential, but the story we got from these women fits your version of events.'

'You mean the one Nadia told me about?' I asked.

'Yes, their so-called jobs turned out to be giving erotic massages in health clubs. And if they didn't agree they were threatened with violence and sexual assault.'

I was speechless, absorbing the news that I couldn't yet believe.

Brian sat down next to me. 'Are you alright, Uncle Harry? I thought you'd be pleased.'

'Pleased? 'Course I'm pleased. But you've reminded me just how wicked these people are. What's happened to Billy and my two girls?'

'Your two girls have returned to their homes and we have applied to re-interview them in the light of these arrests. Unfortunately, Billy is still in jail.'

'He played a big part in exposing this gang. I wouldn't want to see him harmed.'

'Nor would I. He is my brother, you know. We're doing everything we can.'

He stood, drawing himself up to his full height so that he looked down on me as if I were a child.

'In the meantime, you have to sit tight and stay here, Uncle Harry. No more expeditions in that van of yours, do you hear?' He waved towards the police car outside the window. 'We will continue our surveillance operation for your own security – and to make sure you do what you're told. Alright?'

'Alright,' I said. 'I'll be a good boy.'

I couldn't wait to tell Betty once Brian had gone. She didn't have much to say except to tell me it was Monday and I hadn't done the washing.

~

That week was one of the longest in my life. I tried to keep busy so I didn't have to think about what could be happening to Billy. I cut the lawn twice and I must have cleaned the house a dozen times from one end to the other.

I was dusting the ornaments on the mantelpiece when I saw a taxi pull up outside. When the rear door opened and I saw who stepped out, bold as you like, I dropped the brass candlestick I was holding into the hearth.

It was Billy.

It was worth the cracked tile just to see his round, smiling face. I was glad I wasn't holding anything in the other hand because when I saw who got out of the other side of the taxi, I would have dropped that too. Yes, you've guessed it: it was Lilly. And the best thing of all was that she slipped her arm into Billy's as she came through my gateway. I couldn't get to the front door quick enough to let them in, although I could hardly see for the tears that blurred my eyes. I stood there speechless so Billy stepped in and gave me a hug so tight I could hardly breathe. I glanced up over his shoulder and saw Lilly demurely waiting to be invited through the door.

'Come in Lilly, come in. Would you like a cup of disgusting English tea?' I managed to say. 'Why didn't you phone to say you were coming? I would have bought some of your thin, weak tea.'

'That's probably why we didn't phone,' chuckled Billy.

Lilly was staring at Betty's picture on the wall. 'Your wife so kind to me. Even sent me food parcels.'

'She what?' I knew Betty was fond of Lilly, or Li Wan as she would have known her, but I had never heard of any food parcels.

'When I first went to London – or I should say – when I was sent to London by his so-called father,' Lilly said giving Billy a shove on the shoulder, 'the only one who tried to help me was Betty. She send food in little parcels. Mainly cake and biscuits. But made me feel good every time one came.'

'Well I never. I didn't know anything about that. How did she know your address?'

'I think Ron tell her. He did at least find me somewhere to live with my little baby boy. Do you remember our flat, Billy?'

'No, but you've told me about the cold and the leaks. Oh and the mice,' he said.

'Rats, Billy. Big rats. When you saw one, you'd crawl towards it and try stroke it like a cat. That was before they took you away because of my... the only work I find to feed us.'

I coughed. I was dying to hear about how Billy had got out of jail.

'And now you've got your big boy back home. You pulled it off, Lilly.'

Lilly was still admiring the pictures of Betty so Billy answered for her. 'Yes, she got me out alright. She used what you might call her local connections to persuade the police that I had been framed. The fact that payments to the police must have dried up once Vishal was arrested probably helped too. I was released a couple of days ago and we flew home together.'

'Sugar with your tea?' I asked pouring him a cup in the kitchen. 'What will you do now?'

'No sugar or milk,' he said, holding his hand over the cup. 'I like it neat. So does Lilly.'

'Like mother, like son eh?'

'In more ways than one,' Billy said beaming towards Lilly who was still studying pictures of old aeroplanes on the wall. 'We're going into business together, aren't we mother?' I hadn't heard him call her 'mother' before.

What he'd said shook me. 'You mean you're going into the... er, what do you call it... escort business?' I looked towards Lilly.

Billy laughed. 'No of course not. That's in the past. We talked things over on the long flight home and we're now partners in my business, helping find missing people. She has very good connections for that and I'm sure we will be particularly successful in finding missing women, especially trafficked girls.'

'Like Bituin and Nadia. That's wonderful. Are they back home, by the way?' I asked.

292

I didn't realise that Lilly had been listening but she came through the kitchen door to answer my question. 'They safe, don't worry. Change their story now. They agree with you. Sorry I doubt you.'

They sounded very matter-of-fact but those words meant everything to me. I hadn't been wasting my time. My life did have a meaning.

Lilly had a sad, serious look about her. It reminded me of the only time I had seen her with Billy as a baby. Betty had insisted that we visit her in hospital a few days after he was born. We were her first visitors. Life must have been a real struggle for her back then, as Betty had realised and, I have to confess, I had not.

'And I am sorry for the way you were treated all those years ago. I should have done more to help,' I blurted out, finding it difficult to meet her eyes which were scrutinising me carefully.

'Water under bridge. Now I find new life, helping women thrown into garbage like I was. What will *you* do now, Harry?'

That was a good question. Life had gone a little quiet since I had come back to my bungalow and I didn't want to go back to where I was before that car had bumped into my gates. There was one particular thing that I wanted to do before my innings was finally declared over, but first we had to get through the trial.

That was more difficult than I expected.

CHAPTER 23
The Happy Ending

Justice was done in the case of Vishal and his cronies who were all found guilty and given the long sentences that they thoroughly deserved. Mr Sharma was never arrested as there wasn't enough evidence against him and he quietly disappeared. The problem is, of course, he may be putting his business plan into action somewhere else. Billy tells me the government has begun to recognise the scale of the problem and has introduced new anti-slavery laws, and about time too. But, as I said to Billy, it's no use having new laws if people still use women who are turned into prostitutes against their will. So remember that next time you go for a massage and get asked if you want a happy ending. You can't be too careful.

What happened to my two girls is still happening to others. The newspaper summed it all up:

Sex traffickers jailed after forcing women into brothels

Criminals who enticed women to travel to the UK to work as nannies or receptionists before they were forced into a form of prostitution were jailed today. The gang led by Vishal Sharma trafficked young women aged 18 to 30 into so-called health clubs across the UK where they were forced to perform up to 25 sex acts per day on male clients. The gang made huge profits by controlling the women with threats of violence and extortionate loans to cover the costs of their travel to the UK and board and lodgings. Sharma who lived in a luxury apartment in Kensington, London from where he ran the operation was jailed for 12 years. He and four others were found guilty of conspiracy to traffic women for sexual exploitation. A prosecution spokesperson said: "The victims have been deeply traumatised by their treatment. They came to the UK for regular employment, to make a better life. Instead they found themselves trapped and at the mercy of this abusive group.

Although I was pleased with the verdict, the court hearing was a bit harrowing, I can tell you. When I gave my evidence, I could feel Vishal's eyes boring into me when I spoke. I'll be long gone before he gets out so I'm not too worried about him. Nadia stood up well when it was her turn to give evidence in the dock. Thankfully, she was wearing more clothes than when I had last seen her and she looked all the better for that: tall, elegant and confident. She was back in Britain, living her dream of studying to be a teacher and running in all sorts of athletics competitions; winning most of them too from what she told me.

When I saw Bituin, it was a different story. She looked drawn and nervous and hardly took her eyes from the floor. I didn't hear her evidence as she chose to give it in private, but I guessed that what Vishal had done to her and her mother had really got to her. As soon as the judge read the verdicts and the trial finished, I tried to find her in the crowd to at least say hello, but she kept her head down and hurried away. I'm even slower with my walking frame these days and she disappeared before I could catch her. I sat down, holding my head in my hands. I'd thought the day would have a happy ending but I was wrong.

~

'Remind you of the end of the war, does it?' It was Betty. 'I thought you would be happy then, but you weren't. You just said something about losing your purpose in life when you came home.'

She had a point. After the war, I think we all felt a sense of loss after the celebrations had died down. For six years or so we had a common purpose: to defeat the enemy and everyone – well nearly everyone; there's always a few shirkers whatever you do – worked day and night for that. When we achieved that aim, it took a while to figure out what to do next. I was demobbed and I had to go up north to find work, leaving Betty behind. So yes, I did feel out of sorts after the war.

'You could have talked about it more,' Betty said.

'I suppose I could. You didn't say much about what had happened to you during the war either. Especially the…' I stopped not wanting to go on.

'Especially the what? The baby? Is that what you were going to say?'

'It's alright. We don't have to talk about that now. I know it's too painful for you.'

'For me? You're the one who found it painful and just shot off to the chicken shed or the allotment whenever the subject looked like coming up. It wasn't me that avoided the subject. I wanted you to find out where she was buried but you didn't want to hear about that did you? Just like now.'

'What do you mean?'

'You've lost your new daughter and you're just sitting there, doing nothing about it.'

I hadn't heard Betty so agitated for a long while and she was right as usual. That was the one thing I did want to do. Find my new daughter, as Betty had called her. And here I was, sitting around, feeling sorry for myself instead of doing something about it.

~

Nadia came over and crouched beside me, as low as her tight, grey skirt would allow, and looked me in the eye. She had let her short blonde hair grow a little which gave her even more of a pixie look.

'Anything wrong, Harry?' she asked.

'I'll be alright. Don't worry about me,' I said wiping at my eyes.

'I'm so grateful for what you done for me, Harry. How can I ever thank you?'

'Well, you could start by catching up with Bituin for me. Tell her that I would like a word with her before she goes.'

I couldn't have asked a better person, certainly not a quicker one. She was off like a flash, head turning everywhere, looking for Bituin. After a few minutes, she returned, alone.

'I found her but she has to go to her hotel and then airport for flight home this evening. She says goodbye and hope you can forgive her.'

'Forgive her? For what?'

Nadia sighed. 'I should ask you too. We caused you lot of problems.'

So that was it. She couldn't face me because of the shame of lying about what had happened. It had come out in court how I had been held under suspicion of kidnapping, and the prosecution had made what I'd been through sound quite tough to make sure the judge knew what sort of rotten people Vishal and his gang really were. She must have felt guilty about that and now she was rushing home, to disappear out of my life forever.

Just like my little baby daughter had done. Betty was right. This time I had to do something about it.

'Can you catch her, quick, before she goes? This time tell her Mr Harry must speak to her.' I put the emphasis on Mr

Off she flew a second time and I had to sit waiting and hoping.

'At least I'm trying this time,' I said to Betty.

~

I later heard that Bituin had got into a taxi which drove off just as Nadia caught up with her. You won't believe what that girl did next. She ran after the taxi for a few hundred yards until it stopped at some traffic lights where she caught up with it and waved frantically at the driver. How she managed to run in that skirt I'll never know. Must have been a surprise for the taxi driver but apparently he pulled over and Nadia persuaded Bituin to come back to see me.

When I caught sight of them walking slowly towards me, Bituin still had her face down and she stopped some distance away.

'Come here, young lady,' I said. 'It's time you gave me a big hug.' I stood with my arms outstretched, trying to stay calm.

She looked at me carefully for a few moments but lowered her head again as she spoke. 'I'm so ashamed…'

I beckoned her forward. 'There's nothing to be ashamed about. Nothing at all as far as I'm concerned. Let's find a quiet corner where we can chat, shall we?'

She hesitated, looking at her watch.

'If you dash off now without telling me all about it, then you would have something to be ashamed about.' I had to lay it on a little thick to make sure she didn't disappear again.

We found a café that wasn't busy and the three of us snuggled into an empty corner. Once she started, it all came out. It took a while and Nadia was out of tissues by the time she had finished. What they'd put her through was terrible. Nothing too physical this time. They'd tortured her mentally, telling her what they were going to do to her mother, sister, even to me if she didn't do and say exactly what they told her. Even after Vishal was arrested, she hadn't felt completely safe. Nadia had been given the same treatment but seemed more able to cope with it.

'So, what are you going to do next?' I asked when she had finished.

'I go home, work there. Like to stay but no job here,' she said as Nadia tried to wipe some of the dark smudges from her cheeks.

That's when I remembered what Betty had said: "You've lost your new daughter and you're doing nothing about it." I wasn't going to lose this one, not if I could help it.

'If you want to live here, you can work for me. I need a housekeeper,' I said, surprising even myself. My father had had a housekeeper when he lived alone so why shouldn't I?

'You serious, Harry? We'll need visa,' she said, her face lighting up.

'After all you've done to bring criminals to justice, surely we can fix that. Billy can get you a visa, I'm sure.'

'What does housekeeper do, Harry?'

'Nothing exceptional. Some cooking, a bit of washing, gardening if you like. Oh, and working the satnav when we take the van out.'

She clapped her hands and made her little giggle at that, and we all parted in high spirits. Even Betty didn't seem to mind.

~

The devil is in the detail, they say, and it certainly was over this arrangement. Billy set about applying for the visa although he wasn't as optimistic about it as I had been.

300

The Home Office follow their rules, no matter who you are or what you've done, he explained. One of the rules was that Bituin couldn't apply for a visa unless she was out of the country so she did have to go back home to the Philippines with her mother.

Basking in the glory of the court case when the news went round our small town, I was even more popular with the likes of Doris, so I wasn't wanting for tea parties and that sort of thing. I did notice that the daily chores were getting more difficult and I started sending my clothes to the laundry. I was right about needing a housekeeper.

Billy phoned several weeks later to tell me that Bituin's visa application had been turned down. The job we were offering her could be done by a British citizen and there were plenty of those out of work who took priority.

'Yes but none I know who I would trust in my house,' I told him.

'Perhaps the best we can do is to invite her over as a tourist for a few weeks,' Billy suggested.

~

It all went round and round in my brain as I sat in my chair with a cup of hot chocolate that afternoon. Think how much nicer this would taste if I had a housekeeper to share it with, I thought to myself.

'Like your father and Aunt Daisy,' Betty said.

'Yes, just like them,' I said, picturing the pair of them in the kitchen by the stove waiting for the kettle to boil, while he smoked his pipe and she busied about with the ironing or some knitting.

'He nearly lost her during the war, didn't he?' Betty reminded me.

I sat up straight in my chair. Betty you're not suggesting... you don't mean that I should do what my father did, do you?'

My father had taken on a housekeeper when my mother died to look after him as he worked long shifts on the railways. He employed Daisy, a humble spinster with so much rouge on her cheeks that she looked a bit like a circus clown, but she baked a very nice apple pie and my Dad was more than happy with her. When the war broke out, he was classed as an essential worker and continued driving steam trains around the country while Daisy baked and washed at home.

Until one day, Daisy received a bombshell that upset them almost more than if it had been live ammunition. It was a letter from the Ministry of Works informing Daisy that the regulations for the conscription of women to work on a farm, or in a factory, had changed and was now extended to those up to forty-three years old, instead of thirty as previously. She was to report to the engineering firm up the road to start work on the production line the very next week. My father was incensed that they wanted to take his housekeeper away and he rang a solicitor to ask if there was anything he could do about it. He was told that the only exemptions applied to married women and those in ill health. It happened that Daisy was in particularly rude health, although she was a little simple in the head.

He had no alternative. He married her.

It was a simple registry office affair but it did the trick

and Daisy continued as his housekeeper until the day he died. She had to live–in of course, to make it look realistic, but they always had separate bedrooms, he in his big four-poster wearing his long night-shirt down below his knees, and Daisy in a special strong bed he bought for her. I never did see what she wore in bed. She insisted on no hanky-panky and looking at her I should think my father was only too happy to stick to that arrangement.

'You silly old fool. Of course I'm not suggesting you marry her. You're far too old for that kind of thing. But your father didn't give up, did he. He found a way and so should you. You need someone to look after you or you'll end up in a nursing home,' Betty said.

Nursing! Why hadn't I thought of that before? That was it! I got straight on the phone to Billy and a few other people.

~

The next day, I called the Philippines. It wasn't cheap but I was past caring.

'Still hot over there, is it?' I asked when I managed to get through after a couple of tries.

'Yes even hotter than normal. Some tourists taken to hospital with heat-stroke,' she said.

'Hospital – that's just what I wanted to talk to you about. You never did finish your nurse's training did you?'

'No, Harry. I was in final year but had to go to work when my father died.'

'Just as I thought. How would you like to finish your training over here?'

'That would be dream come true, Harry. But students like me have to pay and we don't have the money.'

'Don't you worry about that, young lady. You'll have to go to university for a while and then you can train at the hospital up the road from me. You can live here, free of charge in return for a little housework.'

She sighed. 'You very kind but I can't take more money from you, Harry. Bad things happened last time.'

'That's because bad people got involved. They're in prison now. This is just between you and me. Listen, I have a nice little house here that is worth quite a bit and when I die, it will be sold. Unless I spend some of it now, all the money will go to some charity I know next to nothing about. I would rather spend it while I'm alive on a good cause that gives me pleasure in return. So do me a favour, and say yes.'

'Alright, Mr Harry,' she giggled. 'This time I try not to drive into gates.'

~

That was a few months ago. Today, I'm standing on my doorstep, a coat over my pyjamas, while I make my daily report to Betty.

'Hello dear, I still love you.'

'I should hope so, although I don't hear from you as much since you've had a new woman under your roof.'

'Come on, Betty, we've been through this before. Remember that card I sent you all those years ago. You kept it, it's still in your drawer:

Loved you yesterday. Love you still. Always have. Always will.

'That's as true today as it was then,' I said.

'Thank you, dear. Did you manage to find her a thick sweater? Poor thing must be freezing in this cold weather.'

'No, I'm going to catch the bus into town today to buy one. None of yours would fit her.'

'Try the Co-op. They have some nice things for women.'

'They only sell food now, Betty. I'll try Marks and Sparks.'

'Make sure it's a plain one. She won't want one of your multi-coloured Christmas specials.'

'Yes, dear.'

'And get a close fit, not one of those baggy things you men seem to like.'

'Yes, dear.'

'A V-neck, but not too low. She'll need a nice blouse to go under it.'

'Yes, dear.'

'Has she got any good walking shoes? They walk miles up and down the wards.'

At that moment I caught sight of a cyclist turning into our road. I waved and immediately wished I hadn't in case she took a hand off the handlebar to wave back. She hadn't been cycling long and I didn't want her crashing into my gates again.

'You can ask her for yourself. She's just got back from night-shift,' I said.

Bituin wheeled her bike up the path looking tired but happy. 'Morning, Harry.' She glanced in the direction I was facing, across the field towards the cemetery. 'Morning, Betty,' she called.

'Betty was just asking if you had some good shoes for the ward,' I said.

'Oh yes thanks, Betty. Very strong shoes. Give me blisters first week, but I'm used to them now.'

She gave me a peck on the cheek and brushed past into the kitchen. 'Tea in pot?'

'Yes it should still be warm enough. Shall I make you some toast?'

'I'll have shower, so no hurry, Harry.' She gave her little giggle and disappeared into the kitchen.

'She's a lovely girl, isn't she?' I said to Betty.

'We really did find a daughter again after all these years, didn't we, Harry?'

'We did, Betty. That's what I call a happy ending.'

About the Author

David Stokes is an Emeritus Professor and a Company Director. He has published widely in non-fiction during his career as an academic, including one business title which has been available for 25 years and is in its 7th edition. This novel was inspired by the life of David's father, an RAF war veteran who died aged 102, although, he is keen point out, this story is entirely fictional. David lives in Guildford, Surrey.